The Silence of the Vessel

Brenda MacLennan-Dunphy

Pottersfield Press,
Lawrencetown Beach, Nova Scotia, Canada

Library and Archives Canada Cataloguing in Publication

Title: The silence of the vessel / Brenda MacLennan-Dunphy.
Names: MacLennan-Dunphy, Brenda, author.
Identifiers: Canadiana (print) 20200278754 | Canadiana (ebook) 20200278762 |
ISBN 9781989725191 (softcover) | ISBN 9781989725207 (EPUB)
Classification: LCC PS8625.L4535 S55 2020 | DDC C813/.6—dc23

Cover image by Maria Cosme

Cover design Gail LeBlanc

Pottersfield Press gratefully acknowledges the financial support of the Government of Canada for our publishing activities. We also acknowledge the support of the Canada Council for the Arts and the Province of Nova Scotia which has assisted us to develop and promote our creative industries for the benefit of all Nova Scotians.

Pottersfield Press
248 Leslie Road
East Lawrencetown, Nova Scotia, Canada, B2Z 1T4
Website: www.PottersfieldPress.com
To order, phone 1-800-NIMBUS9 (1-800-646-2879) www.nimbus.ns.ca

Printed in Canada FOREST STEWARDSHIP FSC COUNCIL

Pottersfield Press is committed to protecting our natural environment. As part of our efforts, this book is made of material from well-managed FSC®-certified forests and other controlled sources.

Dedication

To my father, Neil MacLennan, who could never rest his faith in anything or anyone, and my mother, Bunny (Gillis) MacLennan, who kept her faith in family and religion against all odds, and was an inspiration of calmness and serenity to all who knew her.

Contents

Chapter 1

Awakening

Who looks inside dreams. Who looks outside awakens.

– Carl Jung

She sometimes wondered if she was autistic. The way she liked to wear headphones and not play any music, so she could listen to her own thoughts for a while without looking stupid. How she had a hard time connecting with people, and liked older people better than her peers. How she hated the chaos of the third figure of a square set when everyone was trying to find their way, even when everyone else was laughing and enjoying the panicked look of tourists being pushed around as if they were soft and pliable toys. Her parents could never make any sense of her, with her discomforts and her need to be quiet, and they'd given up trying to make her learn the Gaelic after her tirades about the spelling of the words when she was old enough to articulate her opinion.

Since they'd moved to Mabou last year, the most peace she felt was when she'd sit in church, like today. Good Friday mass, something most people dreaded. But not her. Everyone going through the motions, up and down, the murmur of call and response speaking to something deep in her soul. She could feel herself rise above the congregation, float up to the ceiling with the words of the mass lifting her, freeing her. From up there, she could see her churchgoing classmates, the illustrious upcoming graduates of 2017. Some would be sneaking their phones out, some counting the minutes until it was over, pretending to read the hymns or battling a hangover from last night. She could feel the old people's emotions, sense the vibrations of their mouths moving, their hands clasped, desperately seeking strength and redemption. She didn't want it to end, this feeling of tranquility, of belonging, being a part of a greater community. She wanted to melt into the moment and not be tossed and turned by the decisions that graduation was forcing on her. She just wanted to be a good person, a better person, in a world that didn't seem to value that. Where could she get what she needed? How could she figure out what to do in life, to make it all worth it? Being a teenager sucked. She couldn't wait until she was old.

* * * * *

"I want to be a nun."

Elspeth leaned back on her knees, pulling her head out of the fridge, which she'd been cleaning. It was a new fridge and she wanted to keep that clean, unsoiled smell for as long as possible. Actually, she was compulsively cleaning the whole house, since it was all new, and since she had retired, it had become her new obsession. She looked up at her teenage daughter whose auburn hair framed her serious green eyes and round face. She had a nagging thought that she was too old for all of this.

"Dé? Did I hear you right? You want to be a nun?" She put the dishcloth in the warm, clean water of the sink and looked out the window at the Mull River slowly drifting by. She did a quick scan to see if there was any eagle action. She knew not to overreact to her sensitive daughter. If she had brought this up, it was because it meant a lot to her. If she made a quick, what she thought was funny, comment, Cecelia could snap at her and close up and she would never know what she was thinking.

Cecelia swept her hair up into an untidy bun, a motion she would repeat constantly through the day since it was so thick that it worked its way out of any attempts to tame it. She sat on the stool closest to the sink on the other side of the kitchen island.

"Bridget's cousin Diane is going to be a nun. They're called Mary's Maidens and they're a regular order of nuns, just like the ones up at the Convent, though they are old and this is about getting young people into the church. Down in Brazil. Bridget said it sounds cool and they're going to work with the poor and do good things in life. At least until the planet collapses."

Elspeth sighed. "*Ìos*. The planet is not going to collapse, Cecelia."

"Oh, look, Mom, you are deluding yourself. Just like the rest of the world. Your generation and the ones before it have made a mess, raping and pillaging the world, and we are going to have to deal with things in a different way. People are going to need help. I think being a nun would be a good thing for me to do. I have no desire to go to St. F.X. and spend a shitload of money on some kinesiology degree that will get me a job as a personal trainer at Good Life. I need to do something real."

There was a moment of silence while Elspeth thought about her options on how to deal with this. Cecelia had not settled in well in Mabou, though she had never been the life of the party in Sydney either. She had blamed herself and Andrew for being old, with their heads stuck in history books and genealogy, spouting Gaelic at her all the time, for her inability to mix in with the Sydney crowd. She had hoped with her retirement and the move to the western side of Cape Breton, where those habits were more the norm, that she would find her place, but she hadn't. She was still an outsider, with only one friend close enough to come and stay over once or twice.

"You won't be using that sort of language if you are heading to the Convent." She leaned across the counter towards Cecelia. "No one joins the convent anymore, not really. Even the convent up on the hill isn't a convent anymore. It's a renewal centre, trying to bring in some cash to survive and keep the lights on in that huge building. I think there's only five nuns left there." She told herself to slow down. She'd only get snapped at for controlling her. "Bridget's cousin? You want to follow her? You don't even like Bridget that much. It sounds like a fad thing to me, or a cult. God only knows! Don't start thinking about that, Cecelia. *Gu h-onarch.* I talked to Bridget's aunt at church the other day and they are all kind of upset about it. Well, except for Bridget's mother, but that poor woman hasn't been the same since she lost her husband and her son within a year. *Ìos.* Who do they think they are fooling? Mary's Maidens, imagine." Elspeth wrung the dishcloth out with all her strength. There was nothing that got on her nerves more than women being stupid and thinking that somewhere or other there wasn't a man pulling the strings.

"I'm serious, Mom. I graduate next month and I don't want to go to university. I'll take a gap year and explore the idea. Brazil. The nun thing. You suggested a year off yourself. You always said never to close your mind about something." Cecelia looked at her mother, knowing that throwing her own words back at her would make her pause.

"Ah, Cecelia. I meant go backpacking through Europe or spend some time with your dad's people in Scotland, not sign your life away." Elspeth could feel her voice rising, frustration taking over. She tried to cool herself down and took a breath, looking at her daughter whose implacable face stared back. Cecelia had always been an odd child, calm and almost cold. Elspeth didn't know how to reach her sometimes.

"Mom. That was you, back in the day. I'm not the backpacking free spirit you were." She kept her eyes on her mother. "And I'm not going to university."

"You're going to break your father's heart, you know that." She knew that Andrew was so old-fashioned, and had spent so many years within academia, he couldn't understand anyone not wanting to breathe in that experience.

"Don't bring him into this. You both love that world, the books, the papers, and all the power to you, but that's not me. Sitting in classes about bullshit." Cecelia sounded hot and angry, her eyes brilliantly shining, unlike her usually controlled self.

"Cecelia!"

"Okay. Well, maybe not bullshit. But history, Celtic stuff. I need to do something real. I want to help the world, help people." She calmed down and took a breath. "Sorry, Mom. I hate to disappoint you, but this really means a lot to me. It's the first time I've felt really excited about something in a long time."

"That's admirable, it is. But there's no need to get sucked into something that you don't know anything about. That *I* don't know anything about. Let's just slow down a bit here."

"Mary's Maidens, they've been sanctioned by the Vatican. They can't be that bad." Cecelia had been doing some research, knowing how her mother would react. "And they have events all over Canada now. You can see it on their Facebook page. They're run by women. You've got to like that, Mom."

"I don't trust anything in the Catholic Church to be truly run by women, Cecelia, no matter what you read on the Internet." Elspeth felt the ground slipping out from under her, as had often happened in the past dealing with her daughter. She felt the age gap between them, two generations removed from her in so many ways, making it so difficult to connect.

"I'm going to meet Bridget's cousin. See what she says," Cecelia said. "You can come with me, if it will make you feel better. Diane's been down in Brazil for two years now. She's come home for a bit, to work on extending her visa. She's doing some missionary work."

"You've set this up?"

"Yes, for after church on Sunday. We are going to the Mull restaurant for lunch."

Elspeth took a deep breath. "I wish your father was home. You'd listen to him. Maybe." Missionary work. Cult recruitment more like it, she thought.

"It's going to be okay, Mom. I feel that I've been searching for something my whole life, and maybe this is going to be it. You should be happy for me." Cecelia now sat looking calmly at her mother, immovable and serious.

Elspeth looked in the mirror across the open-concept living room. She knew this moment would be seared into her brain. Cecelia looked about ten years old to her mother with her freckled face and clear green eyes, while her own unruly head of gray hair seemed ghostlike to her, as if she had already blended into the background of her daughter's life. She badly needed a haircut. Before graduation for sure. She knew that the girl was eighteen now and had never been willing to accept her advice without good reason. "I do want you to be happy, *m'eudail*. I do."

The grandfather clock Elspeth had salvaged from the old house in Glencoe before it was torn down ticked loudly in the foyer. She sighed, which released a bit of her pent-up stress and said, "Your grandmother would have been pleased. She always wanted me to be a nun."

She laughed, thinking back to the old Glencoe farmhouse, with its little cup of holy water affixed on the doorframe inside the kitchen. She remembered instinctively dipping her fingers in every time she entered the house, even long after she had gone to university and had lapsed into being a sporadic holidays and funerals Catholic. Her mom had been disappointed with her, always asking if she was going to mass down in Sydney, having her do the rosary in the kitchen when she was home. She'd been a bit more of a frequent visitor to mass since she had moved to Mabou, just to feel part of the community more than out of any spiritual fervour.

"I don't think you would have made a very good nun, Mom." Cecelia smiled at the thought of her wine-loving, square-dancing mother in a habit.

"Me neither, Cecelia. Me neither." Elspeth took another breath. "Okay. Sunday, after church, we'll see what this girl says. But be smart about this, Cece. Don't let yourself get pulled into something that could ruin your life."

"Ah, Mom. Don't be so melodramatic. You always overreact." Cecelia smiled at her mother and jumped off the stool. "I'll call Bridget and tell her you'll be there too."

* * * * *

"Anndra, tha mi trom! Thuirt i gu bheil i airson a bhith na cailleachan-dubha!" Elspeth hadn't taken long to call her husband Andrew, who was over visiting his ninety-five-year-old mother in Scotland. She switched to English just to show how serious this was. "She says she wants to be a nun. It's no laughing matter!" she said as she heard his deep chortle that sounded like a short, sudden rumble of thunder.

Andrew's mother had taken a fall on the ice in February and so Andrew and his siblings were taking turns helping her at home. She was adamant that she was staying in her own bed and not going to the home with the old people. Andrew had committed to May and June and didn't plan on being home until the day of graduation since his mother's birthday was the day before it. He didn't want to miss the summer season, which was always the busiest and best time to be home in Cape Breton. He was not only an expert on the Scottish Highlands Clearances but could still keep up with the young pipers, though now, at seventy-eight, he had cut down on the whisky before performances.

"Dhia fhéin, Elsie." There was a moment of silence on the phone and Elspeth wished she could watch his face as he tried to come up with some way to reassure her. She missed him being there, being a soft and safe rock for both of them in the house. "I'm sure it won't amount to anything. Last year she wanted to be a writer and live back up in the old house for a year with no running water or electricity. In grade ten, it was that she wanted to work

with the blind so she went around with a blindfold on her eyes for a week so she could see what it felt like. She's searching, looking for what she wants to do. That's what people her age do. There's so many choices these days. *Na gabh dragh.*" Andrew's Scottish brogue sounded stronger over the phone, probably from being home with his family, the Portree brogue becoming more ingrained every day.

Elspeth tried not to let herself get too riled up, which she seemed to do whenever Andrew told her not to panic. "She's done some research on it, this Mary's Maidens. I haven't gone online yet, but she's said that they are Vatican sanctioned and doing good work. I don't know. Maybe it would be a good experience. She could travel, meet some kind people. There are worse things she could be getting into, I suppose." She took a deep breath. "I just don't feel right about it. They aren't allowed to come home once they join except on 'missionary work.' What does that sound like to you?" Elspeth's voice was rising with alarm, but she tried to keep it low so that Cecelia wouldn't hear her from her bedroom down the hall.

A blare of another burst of laughter made Elspeth pull the phone away from her ear. She didn't know whether to feel angry or smile at his reaction. She felt a twinge of heartbreak and shook her head waiting for him to speak. "There's no way in this day and age that they could keep someone from coming home. There's just no way that would happen. She'd be able to come home. Isn't this Diane one home again? Down deep, you simply don't like the church, Elsie. You don't trust anything about it. I don't know why you keep going."

"Ach, it's easier for men to walk away from the traditions and community of it all. What will we have if we don't have those ceremonies for weddings, deaths? Maybe I just lack imagination, or courage. I don't know. Anyway, this isn't about me, it's about Cecelia." Elspeth pulled her feet up on the bed, surrounded by the six pillows that seemed to be the minimum needed in Pinterest bedroom arrangements, and she looked out the glass doors leading to the balcony where she and Andrew often sat and had their morning tea. This house had been her dream for so long that now it felt almost unreal to be sitting in the room she had so long imagined.

"It won't hurt to meet with the girl. See what's up. Get on the Net too and try and get some background so you go into the Sunday meeting with questions. You know what to do, *nighean*. You know what to do. Think of it as a project from work. You can sink your teeth into anything. I've seen you. You don't give up."

"We'd have to go and check it out, Andrew. See these Maidens in action. We'd have to."

"Look, nothing is going to be decided that fast. Let me get home and we'll talk about this. Let's not pack our bags for Brazil just yet."

"Ah, you're right. I'll just try to stay cool, calm, and collected. At least until you get home from Skye." Elspeth sat back on the bed, making sure the red wine didn't spill on the white duvet. "How are the plans for your mother's big day coming?"

* * * * *

Cecelia yanked the cord on her blind to pull it up. Her room looked out towards the street aptly named the Back Road and looked over toward the church. She could see the top of it against the evening sky, an artist's palette of colours highlighting the white spire. She felt comforted by the sight of it, as she had every day since arriving in Mabou. She wondered if that was why she felt so drawn to the idea of joining the church.

Her hands were shaking she was surprised to notice. Nerves. She had known it was going to be hard to say those words to her mom, to tell her what she wanted to do, and now that it was done, it was both a weight lifted from her mind and a feeling of responsibility placed on her shoulders. Now, she knew she would have to follow through on the meeting with Diane, and possibly change her life forever, but it felt good to get the process started.

She picked up her phone and checked for messages. She scanned her Facebook page and checked out some of her classmates' prom dresses. It had been a constant red carpet parade for months now. The money people were spending! If they would donate some of that to help the poor or the environment, the world wouldn't be in the mess it's in. It wasn't only the dress though. The girls were already getting appointments set for their pedicures and their manicures, their hair and makeup. Cecelia pressed the button to turn off the screen and threw the phone with a bit of force against the pillows on her bed. "Bullshit. It's just a bunch of bullshit." She really would have to clean up her language if she was going to be a nun.

* * * * *

"You can see, Cecelia, that the accommodations are lovely, and the house in São Paulo is super clean, and close to the beach." Diane's dark brown hair was pulled back into a conservative ponytail, and she was wearing a plain, gray jumper over a white blouse, a gold cross necklace her only jewellery. She was sitting at the table while Bridget and Cecelia were both looking at the pamphlets she had given them. Elspeth was uncomfortably sitting on the sidelines, waiting to get her hands on the brochures.

"We spend most of our morning, the early morning, in prayer and reflection. Then we have a mass in the sweetest chapel in the garden, and sit around in a circle under the jacaranda trees and set our goals for the day. You know, our personal things that we want to work on and to set the focus on helping others as well. It's all very self-affirming. After lunch, we usually have a different task. You know, you might end up going into the favelas to do some missionary work, or teaching English in the pre-school, or maybe you might end up on house duty, but that's usually only one day of the week. In the evening, you have some personal time, so there's the beach or you can read or something. Then we usually have prayers again before we head to bed." There was an energy that drew you to her face as Diane talked, her voice rising and settling through the sentence with her excitement of sharing her experience with someone who was interested.

"And there's only women?" Cecelia asked. "It's not that I hate men or anything, but I like the idea of women being in charge."

"Yes, we are all women in the house. In our house, there are three floors of girls, but they are talking about building on since so many girls are coming. There's an order for boys too. Gideon's Guardians. It's the same kind of set-up, but for guys. We don't see them often, but they are in the city as well. They are studying for the priesthood, so they spend a lot of time in the books. The good books, of course." She smiled at the girls.

"The Bible, studying passages, that sort of thing. We usually only see them at one mass a month. We're all pretty young, and I know here it would mean romance and drama, but that's just not part of the picture there. We all want to focus on being good people, doing things for others. The founders of the orders really want to ensure that the youth of today don't get lost. So many young people can't find their way, there's so much distraction out there. And the way the media betrays girls. Let's be honest." She looked around as they all nodded their heads in agreement. Even Elspeth. "This commitment to simplicity and helping others should be what everyone is aiming for, especially with the world destroying itself in so many ways." Diane folded her hands on her lap, seeming to almost restrain herself from getting too excited. "We are all strongly committed to our vows of chastity, you'll be glad to know." Diane nodded and smiled at Elspeth while saying this.

Elspeth wanted to roll her eyes at that comment, but asked instead, "When did you go to Brazil, Diane?" hoping that her voice didn't sound aggressive. "And I guess an even bigger question would be why did you join Mary's Maidens?"

"Mom!" Cecelia sounded like every other teenager whose parent is embarrassing her in front of her friends.

Elspeth replied quickly, "I'm curious. You have to ask questions, Cecelia. It's a big decision."

"I don't mind, Cecelia. Your mother is right. It is a big decision, and one that I didn't take lightly. I had gone to university in Quebec, to McGill, and my first year there, well, I went a little wild, to be truthful, got in over my head, you know? I drank too much. Found myself embarrassed about what I did and didn't remember doing, and I wasn't interested in the program I was taking. I felt like I was merely going through the motions, and I started thinking, Is this all that life is? Going through the motions? Anyway, I started going into all the old churches around Montreal, and every time I went through the door, I would feel my shoulders relax and my head lift."

Cecelia's eyes didn't leave Diane's face as she talked. Elspeth could see that her daughter was hearing someone express exactly what she had been feeling. That knowledge did not make her feel more at ease.

"But don't you miss boys. Dating?" Elspeth asked, grasping at this point, she knew. "Having a family, eventually?"

"Oh, I have a family. A huge family, Ms. MacKay, but it's not the regular type of family because you get to choose to be a part of it. We discuss so many important things ... like sexuality, and the biological needs that might push against what our spiritual needs are. The Church has learned the hard way that we can't ignore that, but we build skills to make celibacy an experience in itself, without any of the shame or guilt that comes with promiscuity." Diane was speaking so clearly, she even had Elspeth partially convinced that it would work. "Besides, with the environmental crisis facing society today, there is a real need for people not to procreate and add to the demands on the planet. I think you will see many young people choosing not to have children, don't you think?"

Bridget and Cecelia nodded, solemnly, seriously as young people with the confidence of knowing exactly what the world needed them to do. Bridget said, "We had that discussion in Global Geography. We've got to diffuse the population bomb before it kills the planet. We're the generation of procreators who can change the cycle. We have to make the hard choices because that's what we're left with. We have to say no to having kids. It's that simple, and having the support of Mary's Maidens, well, that sounds good to me, and my mom."

"But there's got to be a bit of attraction, say to those ... What are they called? Gideon's Guardians? You can't fight biology." Elspeth couldn't believe she was the one pushing a discussion on sex, but they had to be realistic.

"Oh, now. People can control themselves. If they try." Diane looked over at Elspeth as if she had uttered a stream of curses, or explained some horrendous murder, or if she was plain stupid. "We use our spirituality, our goals for ourselves for the world, to replace those basic biological needs. People can be asexual beings, Ms. MacKay. They can, if they train their minds to overcome those body yearnings. Just like you have to train yourself to avoid sugar if you are a diabetic, or alcohol or drugs if you are an addict. We use those tools to help ourselves concentrate on what is important in the world, and not be selfish."

They've got her well trained, Elspeth thought. She really does believe in her spiel. She thought back to Cecelia's lack of romance, and realized that her daughter would definitely agree with Diane. Cecelia had only had one little love interest, back in grade nine with a short, spotty boy with a lisp and a bit of a saliva problem so he had to keep wiping his mouth at regular intervals. It hadn't gone much further than the Christmas semi-formal dance, a couple of movies, and a box of chocolates at Valentine's. It had faded into oblivion before March Break.

Diane took a sip of her tea, a slight blush on her cheeks showing her appreciation of her audience's rapt attention. "Then one day, there was someone outside Mary, Queen of the World Cathedral, with a pamphlet like the one you're looking at. Her name was Sophie and she was home from Brazil to get her visa, and as part of her trip home, she was spreading the word about the order. We talked and talked for hours and by the end of the week, when she was heading back, I was on the plane with her."

A terrible sense of dread crept up the back of Elspeth's neck.

* * * * *

"This makes so much sense to me, Mom. Listen ... 'pride and sensuality have been undermining humanity. Governments are swayed by greed to commit moral atrocities against the environment. Human beings have become narcissistic and only consider their own desires, not what is good for others or for the world.' Oh, yeah. Narcissistic. That's a good word for the world today. All the endless selfies and self-improvement, but it's all about the body, you know? Not about the inside of people. Does anyone think of helping out, really helping out, their fellow man or the world in general? Do they think about the big picture? The world, the environment, the poor? Nope." She leaned towards her mother, practically vibrating with energy, something her mother was not used to seeing.

Cecelia hadn't stopped talking since they had arrived back from lunch, and although Elspeth was glad to hear her enthusiasm, she hadn't lost that sense of dread she had listening to Diane. "Let's slow down a minute, Cece. Take a breath. There's no need to jump on the bandwagon right away."

"But, Mom. Diane's been there. She seemed nice, didn't you think? And normal."

"Yes. She seemed normal enough. Everyone can come off as normal for a little while."

"You just don't like the whole idea. I could see it on your face the whole time we were with her. You've already made your mind up. I can see." Cecelia jumped off the stool, retreating both in mind and body, ready to build her wall up again.

Elspeth didn't want the conversation to end this way, and she could hear her voice catch. She felt weak, inconsequential. She wondered quickly if all mothers felt this way when their children were plotting their departure from home. "It's such a long way away, Brazil. If there was something in Canada, you know, where you could check it out? You could be a nun in Canada, couldn't you?"

"But this is fresh, and new, and they are trying to do something special, can't you see that? The old Catholic regime is so tainted and sad. It's negative, but these groups, Mary's Maidens for sure, they're looking at the whole picture, even the environment, not only the religion stuff. I think it's pretty exciting! It's something

I'd like to be a part of." Cecelia's voice showed her frustration and she pounded her finger on the pamphlet as she made her points. She took a breath before continuing, "They focus on the things I'm interested in – quiet study and contemplation, simple living. I don't fit into this century, I don't think. I should have been born a hundred years ago when life was simpler!"

"I get that. I really do, Cecelia. I understand what you're saying, but everything was fresh and new once, even me, for God's sake." Elspeth felt like water was rushing through her fingers, and she was trying to capture it. "What about, say, after the summer, we all go down to Brazil? Your dad, you, and me? We could see for ourselves what it's all about."

"Oh, yeah. Right. That'd be sweet. Me starting to find something for myself with me old ma and pa along." Cecelia looked over at the crushed expression on her mother's face and felt immediate regret about the "old" comment.

Elspeth took a second, willing her eyes not to water from the sting. She picked up the church bulletin, the teenage Challenge retreat at the Renewal Centre circled in the corner. "Look, next week is that Challenge event. You stay up at the Convent for Friday night and Saturday night. I don't know what it's all about but it sounds like something you'll like. You don't have to do it, but it might give you some time to think about all of this. And look, until then, let's just let it sit. Let's not go over this again and again."

Cecelia came back and took the bulletin from her mother. She read again the piece about the Challenge weekend and how it was supposed to strengthen the faith of the teenagers and some reviews by past participants. It sounded kind of lame to her but since she had been pushing her mother so hard, and she did like the idea of staying up at the Convent and exploring around that old building, she nodded her assent. The kids at school all seemed excited about it and the girls had been asking her if she was going to go. She hadn't really thought of it as something she would like, but maybe it would be a good place to start. "Yes. I'll sleep on it for a while. I'll go to this Challenge thing too. Can't hurt." She put the bulletin back on the counter and went down the hall to her room.

Chapter 2

Challenge

"Life is either a daring adventure or nothing at all."
— Helen Keller

It was a Friday night, and the Convent, officially called The Renewal Centre but would always and forever be called the Convent for anyone in the county, was hosting the Teen Challenge weekend. The imposing brick building on the hill above the church, looking down over the village of Mabou and out towards the Gulf of St. Lawrence, was ablaze with lights in all of its windows. Three stories of illumination, counting the cafeteria and gym in the basement, shone with the excitement of the teenagers inside. The ghosts of its past lives had been awoken and there were slight echoes in the dark corridors leading to the basement gym of when the building had hosted students attending school in Mabou. Submerged secrets of girls from all over Inverness County and beyond, their huddled conversations in the bathrooms, talking about the boys at school, seeped out like sap in springtime. Hidden deeper, there was a hushed layer of young novices' voices whispered in prayer in their rooms, but now, that coating was buried deep, only stirred up once a year for the weekend retreat by the teenagers who came to Challenge.

Challenge was a special time for the mostly Catholic teens. A bit of peer pressure and the hype of the weekend allowed the numbers to rise over the years. Church leaders and dynamic twenty-somethings shared their weekends with the soon-to-be adults, giving talks about relationships and how the church could play a part in their lives once their parents stepped out of the picture, forcing them to mass on Sundays. There was "the secret" at the end too, everyone sharing in keeping it a surprise, hoping that the ones to come would want to keep the magic alive as well.

It was well set up with lots of food and breaks and enough creativity to keep the young people engaged. The nuns didn't seem to mind the Scavenger Hunts or the Amazing Races that the church leaders designed to have the teens run rampant all over the building. The old women, no longer habit garbed, crosses swinging from necklaces, would glide in and out of rooms, assisting here and there, shadows of a past life wafting through the event.

Cecelia didn't care to be a part of such a big crowd, but she was trying to get in the spirit of things. She had always been a shy person, pulling back and standing on the sidelines rather than jumping in the middle. She was okay during the prayer sections when the barrage of noise settled down and she could hear her own thoughts. The girls in her room were busy writing letters because everyone was supposed to write positive things to each other. Part of the process. Part of the weekend. She was fine with all that, but it felt kind of staged. She could hear in her head the usual prattle of positive words that got bantered around in self-esteem classes at school, but ended up being meaningless in reality. She hadn't received many notes and didn't feel much like sending any either, and she wasn't sure if that meant she wasn't a good person or what.

She looked out the window, hoping to appear as if she was comfortably lost in her own thoughts, but in reality she felt close to tears. Suddenly, she realized that she felt emotionally unsteady, ready to break, and she remembered that she sometimes felt that way when she was about to get her period. She felt an urgent need to go to the washroom and check, and sure enough, as she stood she felt that familiar gush of her period. She ran quickly out of the room trying not to panic, holding the pamphlet they had been working at behind her in case she was already showing. She didn't want to end up in a mess, the talk of the school for years to come. It had started, but it wasn't much, not yet, but of course she had not even considered bringing any supplies with her. She did the best she could with the toilet paper, and came out of the stall, again fighting the tears that were so close to the surface. She didn't know how she was going to make it to tomorrow morning. She wondered if she could just make an excuse and go home, not stay until the end.

As she walked out of the bathroom, one of the old nuns stopped her. "Are you all right, dear?" she asked, her brown age spots peppering the hand that now rested on Cecelia's arm. "You don't look well. Why don't you come in the rest area here with me and take a little break?"

It had been such a hectic day, full of noises and people and constant talking, talking, talking. Cecelia looked into the little nun's eyes, a faint reflection from the neon lights in the room in her glasses, and felt an instant sensation of calm come over her. "Yes, a little break would be really nice."

She followed the woman, her simple, blue skirt hanging loosely off her tiny hips. She looked fragile, but nimble, opening the door and switching on the light to a small reading area that looked down towards the harbour. The smell of old places and damp books filled her nose, but there was also a quiet that seemed to permeate the dark wood in the room that Cecelia found comforting, so different from the open-concept brightness that the new house was centred around. The nun closed the door and motioned for Cecelia to sit in an old wingback chair facing the window.

"Would you like a glass of water, dear?"

"No, thanks. I'm good," Cecelia said, then felt paranoid about using the word good. Maybe it should have been "fine." Maybe it sounded like she was a good girl. Which she was, but should she say that to a nun? She then realized the opportunity that was in front of her. Here she was, sitting close and personal with a real nun. Normally, she would have been happy to sit and have the usual conversation she would have with old folks, but not tonight. She realized the opportunity she had because all she had been thinking about all week was Brazil and being a nun. A real live nun, and here she was, alone with one. She hated it when people tried to get friendly, asking things they shouldn't. She felt like she was standing on a cliff, the water below. She could be frozen solid or dive right in. "Would you mind if I asked you a few questions? No problem if you don't want to."

The old lady looked at her, surprised. "Ask me some questions?"

"Yes, just a few. I'm, well, I'm curious about a few things and this Challenge stuff seems kind of packaged. I want to see how a person really fits into all of it, you know. God, living in a convent. Being a nun. A personal story. Would that be okay?" Cecelia looked at her closely and the old nun's face was hard to read. She didn't say anything until Cecelia said, "I mean, I totally understand if you don't want to talk about it. I hate it when people ask me questions."

The old lady looked over at her slowly, eyes widened. She nodded her head slightly, not saying no.

"So, why did you want to be a nun?" She tried to tame her thick fox tail head to look a little neater. She had lost her last elastic and her hair was too thick to sweep up into a nice bun without one.

"I never thought of doing anything else, I suppose," replied the elderly woman. "At least, I don't remember thinking of anything else. I have a hard time remembering my life before I joined the order. It's so fuzzy in my head that I don't really know if things were real or not. Age, I guess." She looked nervous all of a sudden.

"I'm Cecelia, by the way. We moved to Mabou last summer, when my mom retired. It's a bit much, you know, Challenge, at least for me. All of them all riled up about God and stuff, but it's only for the weekend. For show. I mean, we go to church, and we're not into too much God stuff at home, and the kids all rah-rah all of a sudden. It feels kind of fake to me. When it's just me, and church, it's different. I guess I want to know where I fit in, and thinking that maybe all the rest are simply going through the motions, you know, because I see them at school, and I'm sorry, but they aren't always that nice." Her eyes widened. "I don't usually talk that much. Sorry. I'm probably not making any sense. What's your name?"

"I go by Sister Mary Jerome." The nun smiled, pleased with the girl's honest candour.

"You go by? Is that not your real name?" Cecelia couldn't help but feel both scared to ask questions and afraid of letting the chance pass. She hadn't felt so eager about anything for ages, which made her realize how important this was to her.

"It's so long since I've used my real name that it seems funny to say." The old lady's hand, knuckles enlarged and crooked, came up to her face, a slight red blush filling areas that used to be all gray. All of a sudden, she seemed so much younger.

"You don't like it? Is that why you don't use it? I don't really like Cecelia either, but my mom really loved the Beatles song. I mean, Simon and Garfunkel. How could I forget that? The folks have basically worn out that *Bridge Over Troubled Water* album. Do you know it? You know the one," she started singing, her voice echoing in the room with its tall ceiling and old wood, "'Cecelia, you're breakin' my heart ... You're shakin' my confidence daily ... Oh, Cecelia, I'm down on my knees, I'm down on my knees for you, please...'"

"'I'm beggin' you please to come home,'" Sister Mary Jerome smiled. "Yes, I know the song."

She stopped, embarrassed. "Mom and Dad are always singing it to me. I can't seem to say the words of that song; I have to sing it. They've got me trained, brainwashed or something. I really am not like this normally. I'm pretty serious. Maybe it's my period putting me on edge."

"You are an interesting girl, my dear." She patted Cecelia's head, catching a stray piece of hair and tucking it behind her ear. "I had hair like that once, but it was thick and black, not like your beautiful colour. That was before I put on the habit. By the time I took it off, my hair was white." She looked out the window of the Convent, down past the church, to the harbour and the setting sun.

"So what is your real name, Sister Mary Jerome?"

"I guess there's no harm in it. My real name is Madonna," she replied, with an embarrassed smile.

"And you became a nun!" Cecelia felt a trickle of excitement. Madonna. Like Mary. The Virgin Mary. Mary's Maidens. Again, she had the feeling that she was in the right place, at the right time, with the right person. She felt so energetic, much more aware, engaged, than she had in a long time.

"That's why I kept the Mary Jerome name. I thought Sister Madonna was too presumptuous, I guess, well, just a bit too much." She laughed and shook her head. "Silly, I suppose."

"That makes perfect sense to me, Sister Madonna. Do you mind if I call you that? I think it sounds lovely, much more fitting than Sister Mary Jerome!"

"Why don't you call me Madonna, dear?"

"Okay, Madonna. I can see why you wouldn't want to get the other Sisters jealous with a name like Sister Madonna. You'd be every priest's favourite!" She wanted to keep asking questions, but was afraid that she would seem weird, freak the old lady out. "I feel better now, though I could use a few supplies. Feminine hygiene products, if you know what I mean."

"Oh, sure, dear. We keep a good supply of them under the sink in the basement bathroom. You go down to that level and you'll be fixed right up." Madonna felt so happy to be able to help.

"Perfect. I think I can go back in to Challenge. My friends will be wondering where I am, guessing the worst. You know how teenagers get. Everything is a drama, I'm afraid. I don't want to miss the big event that everyone keeps hyping up. The school crowd goes on and on about Challenge." Cecelia was afraid that she might have said something insulting.

"Oh, the teenagers always enjoy Challenge weekend, dear. They run around this convent like it was back in the day when the rooms were filled with girls. They'd stay here while they were getting their secretarial training down at the school. They'd come here from all over the island, I heard. They still drop in, now and then, to see their old rooms. I've heard the stories, glue on the toilet seat, that sort of thing. Now, it's only for the occasional weekend that we host people, but I like the noise and the commotion. It reminds me of my time with the youngsters in Honduras. Now, Sister Charlotte. She's another story. She hates it when there are too many cars in the parking lot and she gets blocked in, or God forbid, someone takes her parking spot. Oh, I shouldn't be talking like that. Forget I said that, Cecelia!"

"Now, don't be embarrassed with me, Madonna." She got up to leave. "Could I come back and visit you some time? I'd love to ask you some questions about what you did in Honduras. I'm trying to make a lot of decisions right now, and, well, it would be nice to have someone to talk to. Someone that might understand what I'm saying. Would that be okay?" Cecelia turned back from the door, as if her feet wanted to go and her head wanted to stay.

"That would be nice, Cecelia. I find the days long sometimes and a young friend like you visiting would be lovely."

"I'll call first. See if it's a good time."

"Any time's a good time for you, my dear."

Cecelia smiled at her and left the room, leaving the door open. Madonna looked down at her hands, and clasped them together as if in prayer to stop their trembling. She didn't know why she felt so sad, and did not believe that the young girl would ever remember to call or visit, but the gesture had been kind, and for a few minutes, she had not felt like a ghost of a person fading away as life swept by.

* * * * *

"Sister Mary Jerome! Sis ... ter Mary Jer ... ome? Sis ... ter? The phone is for you!" Sister Mary Augustine's voice bellowed, echoing through the corridor of the main floor of the Convent, the old carpet not dampening the harshness or the scratchiness of the old woman's voice in the least. It wasn't until the last bellow that Madonna realized the phone call was for her. She never had phone calls. Ever.

She quickly put her book face down on the table, cringing

while doing it, but feeling too rushed to find her bookmark, which must have fallen into the crevice of the wing chair again. She felt her heart palpitating while she rushed down the long corridor towards the phone. She could not imagine who would be calling her and a sense of dread came over her. It couldn't be family. She knew that.

"Hello," she said timidly, holding the cold, black receiver in her hand. The Convent had some new devices but they stuck with the old, heavy phones, themselves an echo to the past along with their rings in the corridors.

"Sister Madonna? It's me. Cecelia. Remember, the girl from Challenge?" Cecelia's bright, young voice sounded a bit uncertain, as if she wasn't sure the old lady would remember the event at all.

"Oh, yes. Cecelia. So nice to hear from you. Are you feeling well?"

"Fine. I'm fine. That was nothing, that night. Really. Anyway, I'm wondering, and it might sound crazy, but I was wondering if I could drop by and visit you. Have a cup of tea or something."

"You want to visit me?" Madonna looked at the phone as if it was alive, frightened slightly. "I don't have many visitors, myself."

"Well, I'd like to visit you … If that would be okay with you." There was a pause. "Maybe I could come tomorrow? The evenings are getting longer and I could walk over right after school and still be home for supper. I'd be there by 3:30. Would that be okay?"

Madonna didn't know what to say. How could she say no, but she felt nervous, not sure why this girl would want to visit an old lady like her. She could feel the seconds ticking by and didn't know how to say anything but yes. "That would be fine, dear. Both side doors are unlocked during the day, so if you come up behind the church or the driveway, you can find me in the meeting room. You know the one?"

"Yes, we had our wrap-up there, at the end of Challenge. I'll find you." The phone clicked and Madonna stood with the phone in her hand, looking at it.

* * * * *

Madonna was reading in the afternoon sun that warmed the large meeting room when she heard Cecelia enter the Convent along with the smell of fresh May air. She didn't get up to meet the girl. She knew she'd find her and she wanted to anticipate it, listening to her steps and quick conversations with a couple of the Sisters who came out to see who the visitor was. Madonna felt rather special, and she didn't get to enjoy that sensation very often.

"Gorgeous day out there, Madonna. I remembered to call you Sister Mary Jerome when I ran into Sister Charlotte." Cecelia smiled conspiratorially as she settled into the matching wing chair on the other side of the coffee table.

"Yes, I'm enjoying the sun, and watching the leaves peeking out on the trees. I always feel like they are old friends that I haven't seen for a while, back to visit." Madonna put her bookmark in her book and placed it on the side table. "How is school going?"

"Oh, the usual. Dull as dishwater, but you have to get through it. Not far from exams now, so it's beginning to speed up in some classes and slow down in others. I usually have a book hidden under my desk. Most of the students have cell phones under there now, but my mother won't let me take my cell phone to school, so I'm stuck with a book."

"I think your mother is a smart one."

"Oh, I know, I know. It's the bane of everyone's existence, it seems to me, the cell phone. But if it wasn't that, it would be something else, wouldn't it, Madonna? I'm sure your parents went off on you about something?"

"Not me, Cecelia. I didn't cause much fuss. Most of the time." Madonna suddenly felt haunted by memories that she had not thought about for years. "I was what you'd call a goody-two-shoes, as far as I can recall anyway."

"I suppose that's why you're a nun." Cecelia could feel her face betraying her curiosity. She was not used to forcing her way into people's lives.

"Maybe that was a part of it." Madonna looked out the window, her hands clasping a bit tighter.

"Why *did* you become a nun, Madonna?" She leaned a little

closer, wanting to be sure to catch the answer. She thought about recording some of the conversation on her phone which she had picked up at home, but she didn't want the old lady to get nervous, maybe not be as open and relaxed. She knew she'd be hyper worried about what she was saying if her voice was being recorded.

"That's a big question, my dear. Back then, there weren't too many options for girls. You got married, or you stayed single, or you were a nun. Married, single, or a nun. That was about it." She stopped talking and just sat there for a minute, a puzzled expression on her face. "I think I was well suited to be a nun."

Cecelia felt her heart speed up, wondering if she was ready for the answers she sought. She realized she didn't yet know the questions to ask. What was she really looking for from this old lady? Was it even fair to make Madonna dissect her life, when she didn't know if she was just going to come off as a flighty teenager, asking for a solution for her future from this woman's past? She could feel the words pressing to come out, but she swept them aside for another day when she had a clear vison of what she wanted, and said instead, "You are very interesting, Madonna."

"Me? Interesting?" Madonna looked down at her hands, rubbing her arthritic knuckles which were forcing her fingers to point in differing directions. "I'm only an old woman, I'm afraid, Cecelia. A nun at that. Who would be interested in me?"

Cecelia sat forward in her chair. "I am. I'm interested." She stopped talking, still afraid to say the words she wanted to say out loud. Being a nun. It sounded crazy, and she knew that. If she were to say it out loud to Madonna, well, that would make it a reality, and it was a reality that she wasn't sure she wanted to admit yet. She changed the subject.

"My parents are older and they always wanted to retire in Mabou as if it was some Shangri-La or something. Every summer we had to come over to this side of the island and we'd camp out in the old house, Mom's old family home, up in Glencoe, for a solid month. Finally, last summer when Mom retired from Cape Breton University, here we came, ready or not, to Mabou. The old place was such a mess by then. The flies would be two feet deep when we got there, and there was always the mice and the squirrel damage to deal with. It was always such a battle, taking back the space for ourselves every summer. But it was still sad, you know, seeing it come down." Part of Cecelia missed the old place, the quiet and solitude, the privacy of the woods around her, and she felt a twinge of getting old, realizing that she could never be in that house again.

"Why Mabou?"

"Ah, my folks are deep into the Celtic stuff. Mom taught in the Celtic Studies department all her life at CBU. Cape Breton University." Cecelia waited for Madonna to nod in recognition of what she was talking about. "It's her religion, if you ask me. Dad's pretty much the same, but he stayed tied, at least job wise, to the university he taught with in Scotland. Does occasional distance courses, writing, that kind of stuff. Anyway, here we are and I'm the new kid on the block, in grade twelve, which is good in some ways but tough in others."

"How so?" Madonna felt a comfort, a connection, with this girl that she had never experienced with a teenager before. She had worked with so many young people in Honduras, but there had always been such a communication gap with her halting Spanish. She decided to relax and enjoy the moment, warmed by the energy and spark coming from the girl.

Cecelia sat back, crossing her arms. "Well, everyone's got their friends, you know. Their secret jokes, stories of their teachers from way back. Gosh, graduation is next month and you'd think the end of the world is coming, the way they're all going on about it. I have to look interested but when they get all teary-eyed about a Mr. Davis story from grade ten math or a Christmas concert episode from elementary school, I roll my eyes. I know I do."

Madonna smiled at Cecelia, whose green eyes were wide open, her face flushed. "I can understand that. Are you nervous about it all? Graduating and going off into the big world?"

"I'm not sure where I fit into the big world. I feel fed up sometimes with what's happening out there between the environment and the politics of it all. I feel so young and yet I feel so old. That there's all the time in the world for me, and yet time is running out." Cecelia hesitated and realized she may have been insensitive. "Not that there's not lots of time ahead of you too, Madonna."

"Oh, that's okay, dear. I know where I am in life." She nodded slowly and looked out the window. She had felt old for a long time now, and she was aware of her body sending out signals to get her ready for the end.

It was quiet for a moment and Cecelia wasn't sure what to say. "Are you scared? Of dying?" she asked finally.

"No. Not me. I've spent my whole life in God's hands. I figure I'll go into the next life in them as well, God willing." She made the sign of the cross, her old hand graceful and sweeping as it lightly touched her forehead and came down, then went across her shoulders, left to right.

Cecelia leaned forward in her chair. "That must make you feel safe, secure, you know? Your faith? That you know in your heart that there is a higher power beside you, inside you?" Madonna tilted her head with a small smile and nodded almost imperceptibly but didn't say anything, so she continued. "When you were my age, finishing high school, did you already know you were headed for the convent?"

Madonna looked out the window, her hands clasping together tightly the only sign of distress. It was a minute before she replied, and she turned away, her eyes watching Cecelia out of the corner. "It's not something I talk about often, but I didn't get much schooling. I went into the service of the Lord early in life."

"I'm sorry. I hate to be so pushy. I am a very private person too. Believe me. I hate it when people ask me personal questions. It's just that so many of us, my classmates and me, we don't know where to go, what to do. There's no simple answers today, and I'm trying to figure out what I'm going to do with the rest of my life. It's so much to think about. Why don't you ask me something? That would only be fair."

"I don't even know what to ask, it's been so long since I had a conversation with a youngster. Let me see ... Oh, I don't know. Do you like school?"

"Madonna, Madonna. What kind of a question is that? Boring. I feel that school is something I have to do. Check it off the list, go through the motions. I'm not a horrible student, not top of the class either, mind you. It's different here than in Sydney and I miss my few friends from the other side, but I never really liked Sydney. It's much prettier here, and I've made a few friends. Amanda, mostly, Bridget." She shrugged her shoulders. "I'm sorry. I shouldn't have said it was a bad question. My mother would say there is no such thing as a bad question." Cecelia stopped for a minute, thinking, then said, "What was your mother like, Madonna?"

"You're right. Your questions are much tougher. My mother?" She stopped for a minute, collecting her thoughts, almost as if she were reaching back and whisking the cobwebs off them. "She died when I was a bit younger than you, and I try to remember her, but she seems like a blur. I can never get her face right, though I know she had dark, thick hair, like mine. There was gray in it, but it was still a striking colour. That's what I remember most about her, her hair, and her telling me what work needed to be done."

"My hair! In Sydney it was a cross to bear, let me tell you. Sorry, Sister! Here, there are more gingers on this side of the island, so I fit right in. A lot of girls are dying their hair now, every colour in the rainbow. I don't get it. Some girls' hair is already dead, you can tell."

Madonna asked, "Do you have any brothers or sisters, Cecelia?"

"None. Only child, me. Mom was like forty-five when I appeared in her womb. Scared the living daylights out of her and Dad and their retirement plans, let me tell you! My dad is really old. He's like seventy-eight now." Cecelia laughed.

"Seventy-eight? That's old, is it? That's my age too, you know." Madonna looked at Cecelia, wondering how she would take that news. Would she seem older or younger than her father? Probably older. She had felt old for so long. She looked around and thought that being in the Convent didn't help the age creeping into her brain. Cecelia's father was lucky being surrounded by youth and vigour.

Cecelia was taken aback but didn't want it to show. Her father was young for his age, everyone always said so, and his mother was still going strong at ninety-five. "What about you, Madonna? Do you have brothers and sisters?"

"I had four older brothers who worked on the farm. It was an old place but on the water, close to Dominion." She paused, her blue eyes looking glassy with unshed tears. "It was hard work for my father. A nice man, a gentle man, he was." She paused again and Cecelia let her gather her thoughts. She was used to how much time it took older people to talk sometimes. Her dad's mom was like that too. "And I had two younger sisters, much younger than me, I remember. I always had to comb their hair, wash their faces, Ma was always so busy. We had a farm, you see, though not much of one. A few cows, the pig, a few chickens. We had our own milk, and I'd have to go get the eggs." Madonna's voice seemed thin, as if reaching back for the memories stretched it too much.

"I suppose that's why you didn't get to school much, between everything," Cecelia said.

"Yes, I suppose." Madonna turned to look out the window. "We didn't stay in touch. You know, after I joined the Sisterhood." There was a long space of silence, with Madonna staring out the window and Cecelia not sure where to go from there.

"I'm going to Sydney for the weekend, staying with my friend Jennifer. I haven't seen much of her this year and summer jobs start soon, and then we'll be off ... to university or wherever. We're going to the movies. Do you like the movies, Madonna?"

The old lady shifted in her chair and turned to look at the girl. "Never been much of a one for movies. Before joining the Order, I think I was only to one movie, a special movie, but that movie, well, it may be another one of the reasons I became a nun." She settled back in her chair, remembering, wanting to bring back a feeling that she hadn't felt since she was a child.

"My mother, she was religious to say the least, and the movie *The Song of Bernadette* came to Sydney, and she insisted on going, so I got to go with her and my father since she didn't drive. Only me. The boys wouldn't have been seen dead going in to see a movie about a nun, though they were going to town often enough by that time, to dances and such. It was a special night for me, just me and my parents. Oh, I dreamed about that movie for years! Sister Bernadette on her knees, persecuted for her faith, but never giving up. She was the kind of nun I wanted to be." She seemed to enjoy the memory, tired but smiling at the same time.

"*The Song of Bernadette*? That's the name of the movie? I wonder if they have it on Amazon? I can check when I get home and if they do, I'll get Mom to order it. I can bring it over and we can watch it." Cecelia took her cell phone out of her pocket and typed the name of the movie into her notes.

"Oh, that would be too much bother, for you and your mother." Madonna's hand came up, brushing the air as if she could sweep away the notion.

"No, I'd like to see it. Really. Mom is always ordering books from Amazon. She'll tack it on an order and won't even have to pay shipping. When she gets it, I'll bring it over and we can watch it together. What do you say? I'm not being too pushy, am I? Just tell me if I am."

Madonna could feel her heart thumping a little faster, and she wondered what it would be like to see that movie again after all these years. Would it be a good thing or a bad thing to see it? She could tell that Cecelia was thinking the same thing, but the girl had a curiosity about it, about her, that made her feel important, needed, and she hadn't felt like that for as long as she could remember. After a minute, Madonna nodded. "I'd like to see it again. I would. That would be nice, if it's no bother."

"No bother at all. I'm off then, Madonna. I'll be back, movie in hand, in a week or so." With that, Cecelia touched Madonna's hand in farewell, slung her backpack over her left shoulder, and turned to leave, her eyes taking a swift glance at her phone as she walked away, her long auburn hair wafting close enough that Madonna could have reached out and touched it, if she had allowed herself to do it.

Madonna sat in the wake of quiet afterwards thinking back about her life, visiting alleyways of thoughts she hadn't ventured near for years. She had always known that she was a part of God's plan. Ever since she was a little girl, and she'd go down to the intervale and lie in the deep grass of the furthest pasture. She'd lie still, with the ants finding their way over her on their journeys for food and the mosquitoes buzzing around her closed eyes, feasting on her blood while she lay prone in the field. She'd wait on those special days while the clouds made their way across the sky, down from the hills, slowly drifting across the field, until she'd feel the darkness cross her body. Then she'd wait, scarcely breathing, and she'd imagine God's fingers reaching out to her, through the clouds, the sun's rays touching down like they did in the Catechism books with the angels with their golden wings sitting on top, looking down, and she'd know that she was one of God's chosen.

Chapter 3

Visions

No one believed what she had seen; No one believed what she had heard.

— Jennifer Warnes, Leonard Cohen, and Bill Elliott

"Do you think you are really going to find your way by talking to an old nun? Don't you think you should be researching what this whole Mary's Maidens is doing now?" Elspeth asked as she reluctantly pulled her credit card out of her wallet. "I don't know why you can't just try university, give it a year or so, and then do what you want. Why rush into all this now?"

"Oh, Mom. It's only a movie. I know you have an order going and it's right there. All you have to do is click on it." Cecelia's voice sounded impatient. She didn't want to go through another round of this argument. "I've got to start somewhere, don't I, and, I mean, her name is Madonna, which I think is a sign or something, you know? She's the real deal, a real nun, and I can ask her things once I get to know her. I can't just start asking her really personal questions out of the blue. I feel comfortable with her, though, like with Gran, though she's the total opposite of Gran." Cecelia pulled a chair up beside the computer. "It seems like a quiet world up there, at the Convent. Frozen in time. I like it."

"Your grandmother in a convent!" Elspeth smiled at the thought of Andrew's mother, the life of the party, with "I'll love ya and leave ya" on her lips and off she goes to the local for a small one and a gab with the neighbours. "You've always been an old soul, my darling."

"I think she likes my company, Mom. Really. I can tell. She's lonely."

"I suppose she is. Lots of older people are. I know my parents were." Elspeth shook her head but it really meant that she was going to do it, which made Cecelia happy as she watched her mother complete the transaction without making any suggestions, fighting her teenage eagerness to take the mouse and do it in a more efficient way. Elspeth couldn't help but be sad and proud at the same time, and she could feel herself getting emotional, suddenly missing her own mother.

Cecelia followed her out of Elspeth's office to the kitchen and perched on a stool. Through the window, the fast-flowing water of the Mull River swept down towards the Gulf. The spring thaw had made the river wide, drowning the green marsh that waited patiently for the water to recede so it could breathe air again.

"I want to find out why she became a nun. Was she feeling the same way that I am? Did she feel that her life was worthwhile, you know? Like, did it turn out the way she thought it would be when she was my age? Or is she sad that she made that choice? I don't know. I don't know if I can really ask her those questions."

Elspeth kept straightening up the kitchen, glad to hear her daughter talk, and she tried to restrain herself from jumping in with her own ideas in case it would make her stop talking. She didn't want her to retreat to her room. The house had been so quiet, studious and book filled, until Cecelia burst into their lives, and she would not have given up being a mother for the entire world. "You are not usually the nosy type, that's for sure."

"I know. It's not me to burst in and ask about personal stuff."

"No, you don't." Elspeth held back from filling in the spaces of the conversation for her daughter. She was usually so reticent about talking that this was a bit of a breakthrough, and though it showed that it was important to her, it also frightened Elspeth.

"I mean, maybe I am just scared of it all, you know. Taking a chance, but at the same time, I know what I feel, and I feel excited about it. The thought of working for something ... big, you know?" Cecelia rolled her eyes. "I sound stupid." She sighed and took a second. "There's just so many decisions to be made right now."

Elspeth kept her silence, waiting to see what came next.

"What about you, Mom? When you finished high school. Did you feel like this?"

"It was a simpler time then, even though it wasn't that long ago. No jokes allowed." She smiled at Cecelia, who smiled back. "The world has become much more complicated in a very short time. I mean, I grew up on the mountain in Glencoe. When I left there and moved to Sydney at your age, it was like going ahead two centuries! It's not like it is now. There were so few options for women. I mean, I don't know where I would have ended up if the Celtic Studies program and the Beaton Institute hadn't been starting up when I was heading to university. It was perfect timing for me."

"How old were your folks when they had you?"

"They were as old as I was having you, my dear, older even." Elspeth leaned back against the kitchen counter. She loved living in her house in Mabou, watching the delta below as it flooded and receded, the sea coming up to meet it and then flowing away. Feeling the life of the village pulsing behind her. Being able to walk to the Red Shoe Pub when it was packed in the summertime. She had longed to be back on this side of the island for so long that it still felt like she was living in a dream. She had the feeling that time was flowing along as fast as that current. Her past and her future meeting like the tide and the river.

"But you were forty-five having me. That's old."

"Thanks. I know that. I was the laughingstock of the maternity ward, that's for sure!" Elspeth turned to the dishes in the sink. "My parents only spoke Gaelic, and that was what I grew up on. The

Gaelic, the stories and songs. It was my TV, my Internet. It must have been a shock to them, just like you were to us, but life was simpler then." Inside the house, even now, it was only Gaelic between Elspeth and Andrew, which kept them fresh and challenged in the language. They had tried to teach it to Cecelia, but she said her friends would laugh at her speaking like that, so they had given up early, and then they found it easier to talk about some things without little ears hearing as she grew.

"It must have been neat though, with the old folks, living like it was a century back up there in Glencoe." Cecelia took an apple from the bowl on the counter and took a bite. "I'd love that. Going back in time."

"Well, isn't that interesting? That wasn't your take on the Gaelic a few years ago! How things change." Cecelia shrugged her shoulders and smiled at her mother, so Elspeth went on, "Yes, it was a good way to grow up. Lonely at times, but there was a lot of activity, lots of big families, up on the mountain then. Lots of dances. It's sad to see all the homesteads deserted now." Elspeth felt tears coming close again and got cross at herself for being so emotional. Must be hormones. She didn't use to tear up like this over nothing. "Too bad they died so early in my life. Your dad never even met them, let alone you. You would have liked them."

Cecelia put her apple down and looked out the window as a bald eagle flew along the river, heading to its nest around the bend. "Don't be sad, Mom. It was a long time ago and they are at home with the Lord."

Elspeth fought the instinct to snap back at the last comment. "Ma's biscuits. They were the best. I could never get the feel of them like she had. Mine are always hard as rocks in no time." She looked down at her hands as if she blamed them for her poor baking skills.

"You'll see them again," Cecelia said, with a youthful certainty. "In heaven."

Elspeth stopped, and caught herself before she responded inappropriately or rolled her eyes. She felt the urge to lean across and take Cecelia's face in her hands, and for once, Cecelia didn't shrug her away. Elspeth fought back tears, wishing she wasn't an emotional old woman all of a sudden. "We shall see. They were my parents, they made me who I am, and they were so good to me. Look, my darling, sometimes, life puts challenges in your way, I guess. Challenges and decisions. Something that may seem like an ending, a terrible curse, could end up being a gift. In the end."

"You mean graduation? Deciding what to do?"

"Life, in general. You know, it wasn't easy, finding out I was pregnant at forty-four. I was so set in my ways, and there I was, pregnant. I was a professional woman, with students and my career. I was used to doing things a certain way, and your dad and I, we had always given each other the time to do our thing. He did his projects; I did mine. He stayed out of my way; I stayed out of his. For us to do research together was like having two cooks in the kitchen fighting over one knife. We were shocked, and we had decisions to make ... You know." She dropped her hands from her daughter's face, ashamed.

"Like an abortion?"

"Let's not talk about it. It was a tough time. I wish you had come earlier in our lives, not stuck, like you are now, with old folks like us bringing you up." She paused, wondering how honest she should be with her daughter. "No one was sure how it would turn out."

"How I would turn out, you mean." Cecelia's eyes grew big, a little slant of her head, her mouth tight, putting her mother on the spot. "You were afraid I'd be Down's syndrome or something, weren't you?"

"We were scared. It happens, and we could have turned our nice little life into a huge challenge, and we would have been fine I'm sure, but you didn't." Elspeth wiped tears from her eyes. "And, I guess, I want you to know that we are here for you, when those tough choices come up, because those tough choices are what makes your story, for good or for bad. And above all else, we want you to be happy. We really do."

"And you are afraid that the Church is the wrong choice?"

"I don't know. We don't know. But we are afraid of it. Afraid of losing you." Elspeth took a deep breath and rolled her head, feeling the tightness in her shoulders. She knew she was laying it on a bit heavy and didn't want her to shut down on her. "We only have so much time in life. It will be hard if you go so far away. Look, I'm sure it will be fine, whatever you decide, but we want you to be sure about it. That's all."

Cecelia didn't know what to say. She didn't want to lie to her mom, so she sat there for a second saying nothing. "I've got to do some studying. Huge tests this week." She jumped off the stool and retreated to the safety of her room.

* * * * *

It was a warm June evening, a Friday night, and Cecelia had promised that she would join the crowd down at the Point for a bonfire, but she was determined to watch the movie with Madonna before that. Grade twelve life had become busy with final exams and Grand March practices, and girls' get-togethers where she had to listen to endless girl talk about boys in grade seven who were so gawky and now were the tall, handsome hockey players. She ran up the hill to the Convent, climbing up to the U-shaped brick building. It always felt a bit haunted with only a handful of retired nuns wandering the empty hallways, so Cecelia felt intimidated walking through its doors. She had the DVD in her backpack, along with a few beers for the bonfire she had slipped out of her dad's beer fridge in the basement. The movie had come in two weeks ago, but it was only now that she was getting back to watch it with Madonna. She stopped to look back at the sunset, knowing that these evenings on the west side of Cape Breton would become scarce if she made the Brazil choice.

Madonna had the DVD player and the old TV set ready to play when Cecelia came into the room like a gust of fresh air. Madonna had not told the other Sisters about the movie for the evening, not wanting to share her young company with the rest, and not admitting to herself that she wasn't sure how she would respond to the film, so she didn't want a large audience.

"I bought some chips for us, for the movie. That's what you do, right? With a movie? I didn't know how to deal with popcorn," Madonna said nervously as they sat beside each other on the dark brown sofa, the dated pattern of wagon wheels and a country scene supported by strong, dark wood. It was solid and would last forever. This was the lounge as they called it, and only used by the few who liked to watch *The National* at ten o'clock or *Coronation Street* at 6:30. Madonna had arranged to not conflict with either of those set-in-stone commandments.

Cecelia inserted the DVD. "I'm so curious about this movie. I've been listening to the song, you know, Jennifer Warnes' song?"

"There was a song?" Madonna's puzzled look made her long white eyebrows extend out prominently.

"Yes, she wrote it with Leonard Cohen. She's got an amazing voice, like an angel. You'd like her. You know Leonard Cohen?" Madonna still did not show any signs of recognition so Cecelia continued, "Anyway, I've been listening to it, over and over." She sang the last bit. "'Come on let me hold you … Like Bernadette would do …' That's a line from the song. I found it when I was doing some research on the life of Bernadette." Madonna didn't say anything to this and Cecelia awkwardly sat on the couch. "Wow, this film was made in 1943," she said as the credits rolled slowly on. "This is so neat. Look how little information there is on the screen! You can really read these credits, they are so slow."

She took a handful of chips and then noticed how loudly she seemed to be chewing. She took the remote and turned it up, aware that Madonna had not said anything since the movie had started. She looked sideways toward her and was surprised to see a single tear slipping slowly down her cheek, sliding over the ridges and valleys of the creases of her wrinkles, the old lady's eyes glued to the screen.

Madonna was lost in her memories, brought back to the comforting smell of lingering pipe smoke and years of sweat ingrained in the wool of her father's suit as he sat beside her in the theatre in Sydney, waiting for the movie to start. She remembered the excitement she had felt, her mother sitting beside her and her small, hard-working hand had reached over and taken hers. It was the first and only time she could remember her mother holding her hand. And then Bernadette came on the screen, so simple and quiet, soft and serene, in the chaos of her family.

Madonna could not separate the memories from her reality, sitting on a couch with this strange teenager, an old woman living in the mind of her childhood. She couldn't stop the tears coming to her eyes as the years stretched back and forward, taut and tense. She didn't know what to say, or do, so she sat there silently, lost between then and now.

Cecelia realized that she was watching Madonna more than she was watching the movie, but she didn't miss much since there was a lot of time spent on each scene, with no music track and it seemed like they only had one camera to do the whole thing. She checked the back of the DVD case and realized it was going to be a three-hour movie. Amanda was going to be wild, wondering where she was. Brittany would probably be loaded by the time she got there.

Madonna held her breath when Bernadette saw the Lady, knowing the choices that she had to make in the days ahead, knowing the pain and suffering coming her way. The movie was so much simpler than she had remembered for she realized that she had coloured the Lady in her head, putting the yellow and blue in Her clothes, and imagining the flowers on Her feet. She was shocked by the starkness of the black and white, so different from her memories. Bernadette was asked to do something she didn't want to do, not really, but she had had no choice, just like her. She suffered for it too, though she never complained, and Madonna sat, watching the parallels of her life move across the screen. The world did not necessarily understand, but maybe that was enough for Bernadette.

It came back to her so clearly: that sense of lying in the grass on a summer day, when she felt so strongly, so certainly, that God was right there, reaching down through the clouds to her, making her special, choosing her. She could feel it now, His light shining upon her from the TV screen, making her a part of His bigger plan. Because of those moments, she had not hesitated when Father told her she should be a vessel for God and lie on the floor of the vestry.

Her mind went back to the vestry, and the feeling of Father on top of her, and how close she had felt to God and holiness during those Saturday sessions when she was supposed to be cleaning for Sunday. He kept whispering in her ear that she was a vessel, a vessel for God, and what she was doing was holy and God's wish for her. Bernadette had not wanted to dig in the dirt or eat it, but the Lady, her beautiful lady, had wanted her to do it, and it was what she had to do. And she suffered for it, giving up her life. Giving up her life.

Cecelia was nervous and the hours ticked past and Madonna's eyes never left the TV. Was she having a stroke? As the movie continued, and Madonna barely blinked, Cecelia could feel her own pulse race, wondering what the old lady was thinking. She didn't know what to say. As the ending credits rolled, she started to get up to turn off the TV. Madonna's hand reached out and grabbed her wrist, tightly pulling her back down.

"Don't turn it off. Not right now. Can we sit here for a minute?" Madonna's voice was low, and it seemed like she wasn't quite awake. It spooked Cecelia a bit.

"Sure, Madonna. Sure." The light from the television was the only light in the room since the sun had set. Cecelia knew the crew would have the fire going down on the beach now, but she didn't feel that she could leave the old lady. It felt like she was praying, sitting there in the dark with the nun, the quiet of the space around her filled with a powerful energy.

Madonna slowly came back to reality, sitting in the chair in the lounge and losing the sensation of her parents beside her. She thought about watching Bernadette die, with no complaints, living her life day by day, simply wanting to see the Lady one more time.

She wondered if her service to God had been done with no complaints or when she was on her deathbed, which was so close now, would she not be afraid, or would those ghosts from the past tell her that she had not followed the right path, the one He had chosen for her by making her His vessel?

It didn't feel like long to her, though it felt like an eternity to Cecelia, before she finally spoke again. "Oh, dear. It's dark in here, Cecelia, and I'm boring you. An old lady lost in her memories, not even talking to you."

"That's okay. I'm glad to be here. It was an interesting movie, and I'm glad I got to watch it with you. Maybe we could talk about it some time. After." Cecelia didn't know how to say it but she wanted Madonna to recover or something. "It was a powerful movie, for sure."

"Really? It's a strange thing for a teenager to want to do, sit on a Friday night in June and watch a movie about a saint with an old nun."

"You're not that old." Cecelia wondered if this was the opening to talk about what she really wanted to talk about, knew this would be a good opportunity to ask a few of the things on her mind, but Madonna had been so moved by the movie, she felt that she should not push her too much. Besides, she knew they were waiting for her down at the beach – they'd be thinking she was not going to show if she didn't get there soon. She'd look even weirder to her classmates, blowing them off again by not showing up at the beach.

"Yes, I am. We both know I am." Madonna wiped the tears finally with a Kleenex that she pulled out of her sleeve, though she did not acknowledge them to Cecelia. Some had dried and left little white specks of salt in the wrinkles, highlighted by the glare from the TV.

"Well, you are old, but it's still nice to hang out with you. I think nuns are interesting."

"Why?"

"Well, they made choices. Like Bernadette there ... She could have married that guy. He seemed sweet, but she chose a different path because she felt part of a bigger plan, and the water at Lourdes, I mean, even I've heard of it. She did what she had to do, even if people told her it was crazy. You know, that still means something today. I feel like that sometimes. Actually, a lot of times."

"You'd make a good nun, Cecelia," Madonna said, patting her hand.

"Well, I'll take that as a compliment, although I'm on the way to the beach for a few beers right now." Cecelia was glad that the evening was ending on a light note.

"Some nuns like a beer now and then too, my dear."

"Really? I'm shocked! Would you like to keep the movie, Madonna?"

"Oh, I couldn't do that, dear. It's your movie." Madonna shook her head sharply from side to side, not used to taking gifts, though a part of her wanted it badly, which she felt sinful about, that strange pang of selfishness.

"No, take it. It will mean more to you, and maybe we can watch it together another time." Cecelia took the movie out of the DVD and put it in its case. "Maybe the other Sisters would want to watch it."

"That's very kind of you. Will you be coming to the graduation dinner we put on?"

"Yes, I'll be here. I think most of the grads signed up."

"That's so nice. I'd like to meet your folks, if they are coming. They have a very special daughter." Madonna took the DVD and held it to her chest. She felt a heavy feeling in her stomach, as if she was going to be sick, and felt glad when Cecelia left the room and she was alone again with her thoughts that were flooding back.

Life had always swept her along, from the beginning. People had always told her that at her birth, her mother had been so overjoyed to have a daughter, and had prayed so much to the Virgin Mary for a girl, that she was named Madonna as soon as her gender was confirmed. Madonna, with four older brothers to slave for as soon as she could walk. Fetch, carry, clean, sweep. The boys dragging mud and sawdust and manure into the house, and her sucked along with a broom or a mop behind to clean up the mess. The noise, the jostling, the pushing for space at the table. She had stood, removed from so much of it. And then, after a long time, the girls came, and Madonna was the monkey in the middle. A brood of brothers above who seemed to holler her name as if she were a dog, and hair to comb and braid, buttons to do up, and ribbons to tie for the demanding sisters below. She was given her own small room, since there was nine years between her and the girls, and the two of them, squabbling and laughing with their little child voices, with her on the other side of the wall, alone.

Madonna had never minded being alone. She'd get down on her knees and pray quietly, listening to the battles raging through the house, glad to have her small space of quiet. She'd speak to God and hope that He heard her, feel that she had one true friend who would always be there for her.

Ma spent a lot of time, especially on the Saturdays, cleaning the church and the Glebe House for Sunday mass and the visitors it would bring. That left Madonna with the brunt of the work at home, and then Ma went and died, and so Madonna ended up cleaning the church too. Madonna never asked Pa what Ma died of and no one had ever told her. She thought it was probably a heart thing, but she was never sure. She just knew she couldn't go to school anymore. She had too much work to do at home.

Madonna felt a sharp tightness in her chest, and realized she was squeezing the DVD against her body. She felt exhausted from the hazy, unclear memories that had filled her brain, mixed with the scenes of the movie until she wasn't sure which scenes belonged to her and which belonged to Bernadette. She slowly got out of the chair, made sure of her footing when she got to her feet, and made her way to bed.

Chapter 4

Departure

Guard your heart above all else, for it determines the course of your life.

– Proverbs 4:25

"You watched a movie? At the Convent? With a nun?" Amanda took another swig of her hard lemonade and sat back against the log they had found to make a bench around the bonfire.

Brittany had been trying to keep up with the boys and had been sipping from the pint of whisky that had been passed around, so her speech was now quite slurred and her eyes were struggling to get more than half-open. "What's wrong with you anyway? Are you gay or something?"

Cecelia was not a big drinker, and coming late to the party, she felt like all of them were in rough shape. All the boys within earshot shut up with the gay comment, turned, listening, their faces shining in the reflection from the fire, still unsure of this new girl and why she seemed so hard to get to know. If she was gay, it would explain a lot. All of a sudden, it was only the murmur of the waves on the beach and the crackle of the fire that could be heard, waiting for Cecelia to respond.

"What's it to you? You wouldn't be my type anyway," Cecelia came back at her. Amanda smiled smugly at the answer and the boys laughed. "I find them interesting, nuns, I mean. Boys can be interesting too," she said, pointedly emphasizing the words while trying to ignore the boys. "I think Sister Mary Jerome is sweet. She was so moved by the movie tonight. It felt like a spiritual experience watching it with her."

"She's the quiet one, right? Little? Kind of mousey?" Amanda asked.

"Yeah, she's quiet, but I don't know. She's sweet." Cecelia took a sip of her beer. "I find it easy to talk to her, which is not like me at all."

"That's for sure. She seems more like a nun should be than the others, if you ask me, like the rest of them are kind of playing the part, could be female impersonators, some of them. Transgender when transgender wasn't cool." Amanda snorted, some of her hard lemonade coming out of her nose.

"God is going to hear you, Amanda! I was at Challenge too, you know, and it changed my life. It did. It changed my life." Brittany hiccupped and covered her mouth, her eyes growing wide as she struggled off the log and headed for the bushes.

"God's gonna hear that too, Brittany," Amanda hollered. "You better make sure you don't get any on my shirt, 'cause then I will hear it from my mom and I'm not covering for you again! She's already changed once this evening. She should know better than to be drinking that whisky. The boys only want to laugh at her."

The boys had been searching the beach for more driftwood. They all seemed to be pyromaniacs to Cecelia. The flames from the fire were about five feet high now. There were only a few of them on the beach tonight. The grade twelves were trying to lay low so their folks would be okay with them partying for a good solid week once exams were over. It was only the kids who could walk to the Point and back home who were there.

"But think what it was like, when as a woman ...," Cecelia said.

"Which we are, full-breasted, full-blooded women," interrupted Amanda, smiling over at Jack, who was throwing another driftwood log on the fire.

"Yes, all that, but back then, I'm sure they were too, but the only choices they had were to be married, single, or a nun, that's what Sister Mary Jerome said. The three choices. Married, single, or be a nun." Cecelia took a drink and looked out at the reflection of the moon on the water stretching, searching towards the blackness of the sea. She didn't want to talk to Amanda about Brazil. She'd talk to Bridget, but she wasn't going to bring it up to Amanda. "Now, we have so many choices, it's hard to know which path to take. There are so many, the right one is lost in there somewhere."

"Kind of like trying to pick a show on Netflix. You know there's got to be a decent movie in there somewhere, but it's buried under a bunch of mindless crap."

"Exactly, Amanda! That's exactly it! Even my mom, she knew what she wanted from day one. She was like Madonna, sorry, Sister Mary Jerome, was like about religion, I suppose. She knew she wanted to dedicate her time and energy to the culture." She took another sip of her beer, a feeling of unlimited freedom flowing into her veins. She felt she could spend the whole night sitting there, thinking about the movie, and Madonna, and what she could do if she had the chance. "Do you have a passion that you need to follow? I mean, besides Jack, of course."

"I don't know. I'd follow Justin Trudeau a few blocks … Maybe even a few miles. Ryan Gosling. I'd follow him somewhere. He's pretty cute." Amanda squinted her eyes, thinking about her options.

"I mean, in life. I'd like to do something that really helps people, makes a difference. You know?" Cecelia's voice was rising, and she caught herself before she went too far. She wasn't ready to talk about it yet.

"No, that's too deep for me. You Sydney chicks have too much time on your hands, thinking like that. Spending your time with nuns." Amanda got up to join Brittany and the boys at the fire, leaving Cecelia to think back over the evening with Madonna in peace.

She looked out at the waves lapping gently into the shore along the sheltered harbour, a long way from the crashing gulf waters. She lay down on the beach, looking up at the lit spire of the church above her pointing straight to heaven.

* * * * *

Elspeth was at a loss. She was trying to fit in with all the younger mothers as they talked about the prom dresses their girls were going to wear, and where to get the nails done the cheapest. They were also keen to get the after party organized, which totally confused her. She was wishing she had stayed back in Sydney where none of this would have been part of her responsibility. She sat around, wondering why there were no actual grads at this planning session, only a bunch of hair-dyed women wearing the same clothing their daughters' bought so they would feel like they were still young. She looked down at her woollen, formless sweater and pulled back a strand of gray hair out of her eyes, feeling a million years old and in a world where she just didn't belong.

"I think we should simply hire a bus, straight from the prom, so that there won't be any cars at all coming to the party," said Angela, the mother who had stepped up to host the after prom party, commonly known as the "piss-up." "That will save you all from getting them from the school to the party, and you'll only have the pick-up to worry about."

Nods of agreement seemed to be the predominant response to the suggestion except for one mother. "No way will Gloria stay until the end. I know she won't. She already has it in her mind that she's chucking the dress as soon as the march is over and she's heading to Jack's to start partying."

Well, what's the prom for, Elspeth thought, but she didn't have the guts to bring it up.

They had already discussed the schedule of chaperones and who should be where, and who was going to bring the vests that glowed in the dark. We haven't discussed who's going to help them put on the condoms when the kids are absolutely loaded, Elspeth thought, a wicked smile crossing her face.

Finally, the meeting came to an end and Elspeth started milling out from the school with the rest of the parents. They were mainly mothers, though there were two fathers who had come since they were in charge of putting the tent up. Elspeth couldn't help wondering if Cecelia was right about all this. Maybe she was the smart one, seeing the flaws in all this strange adoration and celebration of excess. Excess in every direction, spreading out, infecting and changing people, not for the better. She could definitely empathize with her and felt a strange sense of pride again that she was seeing through the phony fabrication of it all. But surely that didn't mean that she should become a nun.

"So, is Cecelia excited about the big night? Who's she doing the Grand March with?" a petite, brown-haired woman with strategically placed blond highlights asked her, breaking her out of her thoughts.

"Grand March? What's that?"

"Oh, my God! Hasn't Cecelia been talking about it? They've been practising for months after school. I think it's going to be the best ever this year. The grads all pair up and are presented to the community with their gowns on, oh, and the boys in their tuxedos. They look so nice. It makes me cry every year, it does. Then they dance, and I think they're going to end it with a Cape Breton mash-up this year. They're going to start with the 'Mull River Shuffle,' then go on to Minglewood's 'Me and the Boys' for the boys, and then the girls will dance to 'The Girls of Neil's Harbour,' and they end with 'Go Off on Your Way.' I've been working on it with Kelsey for two months now. Oh, I'm going to have my Kleenex ready, let me tell you!" She was actually already tearing up as she talked about it.

"Whose mother are you?" Elspeth hadn't been able to get all the names straight yet.

"Oh, sorry! I'm Kelsey's mom, Cathy. My husband works away, but he's going to be home for the Grand March. You do know that the girls dance with their fathers at the end of the dance, right? And the boys dance with their mothers. You do know that, right?" Cathy was very serious all of a sudden.

"No. I didn't know that. My husband, Andrew ... he won't be home for the prom. He'll only get back for graduation. He didn't think the prom was such a big deal."

"Oh, he'll have to get back for Grand March," she said with a finality that shocked Elspeth.

"We're not going to switch his ticket from Scotland now," Elspeth responded with a similar finality. "He's got his mother to take care of, and her birthday besides. We'll send him pictures of her all dressed up." She stopped herself. Why was she explaining all this?

"Well, don't you think Cecelia will look, well, out of place if she doesn't have her father to dance with? Won't she be sad? Embarrassed?" Cathy's eyes were wide with disbelief. "Everyone else will have a man to dance with."

"She hasn't brought it up to me, so I guess it's not bothering her too much. She's not into this prom stuff too much either, to be honest." Elspeth was fighting back the urge to be blunt. She was known for being straight to the point in her work, cutting through to the heart of an argument in order not to waste a lot of time. She was trying to fit in here, so she didn't want to mention what she thought about all the energy going in to the big "piss-up" idea either. "We're only going to Sydney to get her a dress on the weekend."

"She doesn't have her dress yet?" Cathy looked as if she had been told that Cecelia was going to come naked to the prom.

"No. And we might even get it second-hand." Now Elspeth knew she was teetering on the rude.

"Well, isn't that financially responsible of you," Cathy replied quickly, her eyes searching quickly to find an escape. "I have to ... eh, I have to check something with Laurel," she said as she rushed ahead to catch up with someone else.

Elspeth was left thinking once again of how she would feel if she was Cecelia, daily dealing with the dribble of this modern view of things. She may have ended up thinking about joining a convent herself. She remembered when she had headed off to university, how different things had been then. She walked slowly home from the school, the fresh green flush of the leaves on the trees sheltering her from the setting June sun.

Her mother's voice came back to her from the bottom of the stairs in the old house, and she smiled, feeling her presence. "Elspeth! Elsie! Thig sìos an staidhre. Feumaidh sinn bruidhinn riut."

Come downstairs? Now? Elspeth remembered she had been packing for university for weeks, picking and choosing between her treasures to find the few that she was going to take up to Sydney. At eighteen, her thick, auburn hair had been freshly trimmed at shoulder level, though she knew that it was too thick and didn't settle nice and smooth like so many of the other girls' hair. Her glasses were the cat's eye style that was all the rage and made her feel quite cosmopolitan, ready for the city even though she'd be going by the rickety old army truck which was Pa's pride and joy down the mountain to Whycocomagh. There, she'd get a drive with the mail truck to meet the train in Orangedale. She'd never been past Whycocomagh, so the thought of heading to Sydney both frightened and excited her.

"Elspeth! It's important!" Her mother's impatient slam on the stair banister made her look up suddenly. She was serious. Her parents were old, really old, and everything was important in their eyes. Their only daughter, a gift in their old age, was heading away from home and they had both been tense and cranky for the entire summer. The house had a sense of foreboding, and she was sick of the feeling that she was doing something wrong by going away to school. Did they really expect her to sit here forever?

She snapped the case shut, though she knew her mother would be going through it, neatening and folding everything again, before she'd be able to get out the door. She looked around at her room, bright and white from the fresh coat of paint her father had applied in the spring, as if by sparkling her space she'd be more apt to stay or at least want to come back home. She knew they were thinking that once she left, she'd never come back, but they didn't realize how peaceful she found the mountain, walking through the woods. The natural power she felt sitting in the old kitchen with the folks telling stories about the struggles of the people who had come before them. She'd never stray too far from them, for they gave her strength, though she wouldn't admit that to them.

When she came into the kitchen, she knew that her mother had been crying. Ma quickly stashed her soft, red chequered handkerchief inside the pocket of her apron and looked out the window. Elspeth knew that she had been crying for weeks, trying to hide it in the pantry or bending to check the biscuits over and over. No one wanted to talk about it, but the changes coming were going to be tough on all of them.

"Dean suidhe, caileag," Pa said, gesturing to the chair at the little table pushed against the wall to give a bit more space to the small kitchen. "Agnes, let's have some tea."

"I'll get it." Elspeth went to go to the pantry, but both her parents waved her away, gesturing towards the chair. She sank down into it, willing to wait. She had learned patience, growing up in an old house with arthritic knees and crooked hands making everything a bit slower. Through her entire childhood, she had been running and fetching, opening and helping, and she felt a wave of guilt pass over her as she knew that they would miss her, in so many ways.

"You are a young woman now, Elsie," Pa started, "and a handsome girl." His voice rose at the end, choking with the effort and the emotion of speaking.

Ma put the tea in front of her, and a plate with a biscuit covered with butter and jam, a slice of cheese beside it. She felt like company, company in her own house. "Ìos, Dòmhnall. That's no way to start it."

"Well, how would you start it, then, Agnes?" Donald took his cup of tea so suddenly it sloshed over the top of the cup into the saucer. His hand seemed so large taking the small handle between his thumb and forefinger, but Agnes liked her tea in a proper cup, so the good china was always in use.

Ma sat at the table by the window, across from Elspeth. Pa took his tea and sat in the rocking chair, putting his cup and saucer on the back of the stove. "It's an exciting time, leaving home, and we want you to do well. We do."

"I will, Ma. I'll work hard. I've got a passion for the Gaelic, you know I do, and Sydney is not very far away. Still on the island." She took a sip of tea. She wasn't sure what this was all about, but she knew there was something coming.

"You've always been a good girl, Elsie, right from a baby. You were sweet and kind, and thoughtful." Agnes stopped, her hand going instinctively for the handkerchief.

"Dhia fhéin, Agnes, don't you start now." Donald sounded like he was about to crack himself, again, his voice lifting towards the end and spoken on the inhale, so that the word "now" was spoken with no breath left, barely heard.

Elspeth loved to follow the rhythm of the Gaelic speaking voice. She instinctively knew it was a sound that was going out of existence, like a rare and exotic species.

The clock on the shelf above the kitchen table struck eleven, the singsong chime filling the silence. Elspeth loved that clock, waking in the night to listen to it, quietly telling her when every fifteen minutes had passed with a different chime. She looked around at the pictures of her decorating the room. Had they always been there or had her folks been making a shrine out of the space to make it full of her before she left? She was the only person she knew with real baby pictures taken, her parents proudly holding her stiffly in their black and white finery.

"You are leaving our house, which will always be your home," Ma said, as if she had been practising.

Pa jumped in, "Yes, it will always be your home. You can never forget that, no matter what happens."

"Yes, everyone is leaving home. Well, most of us." There had only been seven graduates from Glencoe Mills of the thirty of them who had started in grade primary up on the mountain. Not many in the community made it all the way through the high school program, most stopping to work in the woods, or help on the farm, or head west, long before they finished grade twelve in Mabou. But then again, the mountain farms were being deserted, left and right, as more people found life increasingly challenging in the remote rural area. Of the seven graduates, five were going to St. Francis Xavier University in Antigonish and only she and Dougall Arthur were heading to Sydney to Xavier Junior

College, an offshoot of St. FX. Elspeth knew she didn't want to leave the island. It would be too strange, living away from her culture, the Gaelic. She couldn't imagine living anywhere else. Her best friend Martha Jessie was already pregnant so St. FX was out for her, but Ma and Pa didn't know that and Elspeth was not going to spill the beans, that was for sure. The wedding banns would be coming out next week and people would be talking soon enough when she didn't leave for school. Too bad. She was a smart girl, smarter than I am, she thought.

"Things can happen, girl. That's all we're trying to say. Maybe you don't like it. The city. The courses you have to study. You don't have to do it. You know." Pa seemed to want to say something more, but stopped suddenly. "I'm going to the woodpile. Call me for supper." With that, he grabbed his hat from the hook by the door and swung out, the latch of the door rattling behind him.

Elspeth and her mother sat in silence for a minute. Finally, her mother took a deep breath and started again. "We don't know much about living away from here. We were both born up here. But it's a big world out there, and there're too many girls that leave from the mountain and, well, things happen. And then they find themselves in a spot of trouble, and then what do you do?"

She looked at her mother and asked hesitatingly, "You mean ... Do you mean, if I should get pregnant?"

"Elspeth! Is that any way to talk?" Her mother looked away, blinking, unwilling to really talk about what needed to be talked about. She took another breath. "We want you to know ... well, we want you to know that whatever should happen, not that it will happen, but if something should happen, God forbid, and He does forbid, but men will be men and girls will be girls, and, well ..." She took another breath. "We just want you to know that our door will always be open."

"Thanks, Ma. I understand, and I appreciate it. I really do."

"A child is a gift, Elspeth, and you have been such a gift to us, all these years. You'll never know ..." Agnes's shoulders went up and she looked away. "We suffered, you know ... Trying to conceive a child. For so many years. Everyone else's families growing while Dòmhnall and I sat here alone. Lookin' at each other. Blamin' each other. But then you came along." She hesitated, as if she was going to say something else.

"I'll never forget the first time I saw you. When I held you. You were so beautiful and you needed us."

There was a strange feeling as if there was going to be another foot drop, an expectant wait. Elspeth looked at her mother, so sturdy and round, gray hair cut above her shoulders. She had Elspeth cut it once a month at the same blunt angle. Another thing she would not be there to do for her family.

Agnes opened her mouth, started to talk, and then put her hand over it. She shook her head, as if deciding something. "Ach, to hell with it."

Elspeth was shocked and confused. There was a long pause. An expectant silence. Ma was shaking. What could be so hard to say? She urged her mother on: "Siuthad. Siuthad."

Agnes swallowed and firmly shook her head again in finality. "That's it. That's all we wanted to say." She stood up and headed to the pantry. "I have to get the supper on. Can you peel the potatoes? Get some good big ones, if you can find any decent at this time of year. They're all full of rot down there. I can smell it. We'll have to biff the whole lot and starve until the fall if we don't finish them off soon."

With that, Elspeth knew that she had come as close as she ever would to having her parents tell her that they loved her.

Chapter 5

Romance

Kens the pleasure, feels the rapture,
That thy presence gi'es to me.

– Robert Burns

"Look, it's no skin off my teeth if you don't go to the prom or that stupid piss-up of a drunk. In fact, I'd rest much easier knowing that you weren't there. It's just that I don't want you to regret not going later on in life and feel like you missed something." Elspeth was sitting on the edge of Cecelia's bed after a day of useless dress shopping in Sydney. There had been nothing that didn't feel like a coloured marshmallow, or a fairy queen want-to-be, on any of the racks there.

Cecelia drew her blanket over her head, unwilling to talk to her mother any more about the subject. She had felt out of sorts all day, looking at the price tags and the colours and the uselessness of it all. They had tried to find a suitable dress at the consignment stores and Value Village, but there had been nothing that caught Cecelia's imagination. She was tired and cranky and wanted her mother to leave the room. She wanted to be alone. To think, for God's sake.

"What about this Grand March thing? Don't you have a partner or somebody that you have to go through that with? Won't they be left out if you don't show up?" Elspeth knew she was grasping now.

Cecelia stuck her head out, more for air than anything. "Uh, that's another thing I don't want to face. I have to walk and dance with Nathan Beaton."

A name to the mysterious partner, Elspeth thought. Interesting. "What's Nathan like?"

"He's short like me, so the girls have been trying to fix us up for the whole year and he's cute, I guess, but he's got this feeling that I should be pleased as Punch to be his partner. As if he's God's gift to women or something." Cecelia looked up at her mother. "And I think he likes me or something."

"Why do you think that?"

"Because he told Sarah who told Ella who told Amanda. So that's not even gossip, really. That's practically from the horse's mouth."

"Is that a bad thing?" Elspeth felt like she was walking on eggshells now. "I mean, do you not like boys?"

"Mom!"

"Well ... In this day and age ..." She hesitated before going on, "We just want you to be happy, Cece. But it's nicer in life, if you have a partner. I mean, I know you haven't dated much, but how much experience ..."

"Mom!" Cecelia cut her off and buried her head under the blanket again.

Elspeth rubbed her daughter's leg through the blanket, hoping that touching her would somehow transmit how much she wanted her daughter to be happy. She thought back to when they had found out she was pregnant, and in spite of herself, she remembered the wave of embarrassment and breathtaking excitement that had filled her that day. But, of course, it had all started with Andrew. Oh, God, she wished he was home right now. Maybe he would have been able to help Cecelia see some light in the situation.

She had been past her best before date getting married. If she hadn't had that trip to Scotland, that trip, that time, things would have been different, but then she looked down at her daughter, miserable on the bed, and she smiled. She had been fed up then too.

"I don't get it. There's no money in this, there's no future, and yet, here I am working towards a master's degree in a culture that is dead and gone," Elspeth remembered saying to herself. She had been sitting against a rock wall on the Isle of Skye, talking to herself. The wind had picked up and her hair whipped around her face, slapping her as if she needed a wake-up call. She pulled wet strands out of her mouth and couldn't help but laugh.

She walked back down to the hotel, washed up, and changed her clothes. The group that she was working with, going through endless documents and rubbings of old tombstones, looking for connections with people who had left these islands centuries before, were a dry bunch for the most part. They loved the challenge of dates and facts, searching through their memory banks or in the old books they all seemed to have in their luggage to prove a point. She got out of the shower and dried off, feeling a bit guilty about the government money that was helping pay for the cost of this beautiful hotel above Portree.

She took a deep breath, chugged the last bit of her glass of red wine for strength, and went down to join the crowd for supper.

As she sat, Arabel Burns, glasses suspended on a gold chain on her abundant breasts and her stringy hair obviously puffed and fluffed for the occasion, leaned over towards her. "Andrew MacLeod is going to be joining us for supper tonight. I have been dying to see him again since we worked together on the latest edition of the Modern Scottish History series. Have you read it?"

Elspeth pulled in her chair. "No, I haven't had a chance yet. My night table has been pretty full. It must have fallen off the back."

Arabel, not sure what to make of her response, sat back in her chair and picked up her glass of sherry. "Well, you should. We dug much deeper than Feswick did in his, and our prose is much more palatable." She grimaced at her sip of sherry. "Much more palatable than this wine, that's for certain."

For the second time that evening, Elspeth felt like she had been slapped in the face with reality. She had no desire to be in this company of historical pomposity, and if it hadn't been for the good graces of the Nova Scotia Department of Culture and her ability to write a pretty decent grant proposal, she wouldn't be here, forced to sip sherry with upper-crust Scots. She was wondering if she dared to leave, and spend the evening with a nice glass of Merlot and the documents she'd left open on her desk, searching for tidbits of new knowledge like dust bunnies hidden for centuries, when Andrew MacLeod came in.

The whole table seemed to rise as one, as if a wave's rush forced them to their feet. Elspeth couldn't help but be pulled along in its wake, for to be the only one still seated seemed even more bizarre than to stand for a person she didn't know and didn't care to know. He seemed very gracious, however, and started making the rounds of the table, shaking hands and saying hearty hellos.

"You must be Andrew MacLeod," Elspeth said when he came to her. "Arabel here was telling me about your work together on the Modern Scottish History series. I'm Elspeth MacKay. I'm from Cape Breton, over with the Researching Our Past, Planning for the Future grant." She nodded formally and prepared to sit, but Andrew hadn't released her hand, so she had to keep standing as it became a bit more awkward with each passing moment. She thought to herself that she was much too old for this.

"Elspeth MacKay. From Cape Breton. So nice to meet you, mo ghràidh." His Gaelic was smooth, well, as smooth as Gaelic gets, thought Elsepth. He's really too old for this too, with his well-groomed moustache and the gray hair trimmed to an almost military shortness. Finally, he let her hand go and went on to Arabel, who was pretty much drooling by the time he got there.

The evening went by in a murmur of chatter and clink of wine glasses. Thankfully, the red wine was much better than the sherry, and the meal was wonderful. Elspeth felt enchanted, like a princess, though that was probably the glow from the wine as she thought back, sitting in that ancient hall, looking down on the sparkling lights of Portree. She could name all the families that left Portree for Cape Breton from the beach below, and she had spent a good part of the evening imagining what it was like two hundred, three hundred years ago within these stone walls. She knew that was what drew her to this life, this work. Going back in time and imagining people's stories as they decided to leave or to stay. It fascinated her, and she felt that piecing together people's history gave meaning to her life, as if by remembering them she helped to keep their souls alive.

"Will you stay for the music, Elsie, or are you too tired? You don't mind if I call you Elsie, do you? Elspeth is so formal," Andrew said, suddenly at her side as she stood from the table.

"A Cape Bretoner will never admit they are too tired to hear music, Andrew," Elspeth replied, purposely using his given name.

"Ah, that's good to hear. Good to hear." He guided her to a stool looking over the great hall where the fiddler and the bagpiper were tuning up. "It's gonna get loud soon, I'm afraid, so I want to ask you this now. Will you come for lunch with me tomorrow? I have to do a drive out to Dunvegan. I'd like to visit the castle and take a few pictures for a bit of context I need for a project I'm working on."

"I am a MacKay. There won't be a problem, do you think?"

"Oh, I think the MacLeods have forgiven the MacKays for almost wiping them out, but that was back in the fifteen hundreds or so."

"1406. Nasty business for sure. None of my doing," Elspeth said, enjoying the historical exercise.

"When we get to the castle, I won't even tell them you're a MacKay. I'll simply tell them that you're my new wife. They'll be nice to you then. I've got lots of MacLeod blood in me. Enough for us both." He laughed, a loud explosion that shocked her enough to bring a smile to her face and made others turn and smile as well.

"How many wives have there been then, Mr. MacLeod?"

"Only the two. None currently." He looked at her suggestively and she couldn't help but roll her eyes. He winked back. What a flirt. Why did she feel like a teenager all of a sudden?

"None currently. Sweet." Elspeth scoffed at his attitude. At thirty-five, she had had romances, but they sparked and died, sparked and died. She had become a bit more jaded than she would have liked to be, but at thirty-five, one becomes more pragmatic.

"I was young, and horny, to be honest. They didn't last long. But

I'm older now, and much, much more mature. Look, this is lunch, not an elopement, mo ghràidh. I don't get married that often. Too expensive." His guttural, barking laugh brought everyone's attention to them again and it caught Elspeth off guard. He leaned in. "Actually, I thought you'd be interested in the castle. It's a grand spot to walk around in, soak in the Scottish fog of history. I feel like it's a blanket around me." He looked away, standing quietly, waiting for her answer. The squawking of the instruments added a bit of drama to the situation.

"Yes, I'll go. I don't have a rental so it may be the only chance I get to get off public transit and get away from tours." She had almost had enough of the group, walking in staggering unison through the day, meal by meal, castle, and village.

"I'm so flattered," he said, graciously bowing and reaching across for his glass of brandy. "Gun a-màireach," he toasted.

"Gun a-màireach," Elspeth had replied, an unwanted tingle coming down her fingers as their glasses touched.

"You don't have to be embarrassed, Cecelia. Talking about boys, sex. It's not like I was a nun, or anything. Oh dear, you know what I mean. And your dad," she scoffed. "Well, three wives. Let's not even think about his past." Elspeth hoped talking about her father would at least bring her out of the blankets.

"Mom, I have no boobs for those stupid dresses. They are going to hanging off me like a sack or something. I don't fit in anyway and everyone in the whole world is going to be there looking at me. It's going to be embarrassing!" Cecelia's voice was muffled, coming from where she had her head stuffed between two pillows.

Ah, at last something that Elspeth could actually help with. "Let me look online. And see what I can find." She patted her daughter's leg once more and left the room.

Cecelia grunted, glad that her mother was out of the room so she could turn over and not totally suffocate. She felt so confused by it all, this bizarre range of emotions colliding inside her head, making her heart pound faster. The whole event was building and building and building and she desperately wanted it to be over. Every time Nathan put his arm around her waist, as if she belonged to him or something, she felt both a feeling of anger and a twinge of pride. She didn't want to be one of those girls who thought boys were everything. She also knew that a part of her wanted to fit in, be able to laugh and sing and have those memories that movies are made of, but she didn't know if she was going to be able to do it. It all seemed so fake and childish. She wanted to stay under the covers and hide. She felt a tear slide down her face and settle in her ear.

* * * * *

Elspeth sat at the computer and logged on to Amazon. She would never have thought in a million years that she would have been looking online for a daughter's prom dress, and here she was at sixty-three trying desperately to find the right one. Andrew should be here. He'd be laughing at her, saying she was way out of her bailiwick.

He had been the one who came looking. It was his fault she was in this situation.

"*Andrew MacLeod was calling again,*" *Tracey, Elspeth's grad student assistant, called from her desk.* "*I heard your phone so I went in and grabbed it, in case it was important.*"

"*Thanks, Tracey. I'll call him back tomorrow.*"

"*Tomorrow?*" *Tracey came and leaned against the door.* "*He's an interesting guy. A bit past his prime, maybe, but good-looking, personable.*"

"*Mór ás fhein? Did you add that?*"

Tracey smiled and replied, "*Well, maybe a bit full of himself, but he's done a good amount of work to be proud of, Elspeth. He deserves a bit of pride.*" *She waited expectantly then asked,* "*So?*" *Her eyebrows rose with the question.*

"*We're just friends! Honestly. We met five years ago now and we chat, drink some good whisky, and imagine historical romances. And yes, sometimes, we act them out ... once in a while, but basically, we are good friends. Very good friends.*" *Elspeth couldn't help but smirk.*

She had turned away, but she smugly thought about the shock on Tracey's face behind her. She had turned to file the books in her arms in the right place in the bookshelf. *The girl probably thought we were too old for that go-ahead.*

"Well, you can't put him off this time. He's in Sydney and he's in the building." Tracey had plunked herself in the one decently comfortable chair in the office and had her own smirk on her face when Elspeth turned around.

Elspeth's hand instinctively went to her hair, wondering how much gray was showing along her part. She hadn't been able to get to the hairdresser to do a decent dye job and she was a week overdue for her regular appointment. "I can't see him today! I'm a mess!"

"I thought you were 'just friends'?" Tracey asked innocently, picking at her nails, holding back from making quotation marks in the air.

At that moment, Andrew appeared at the door. Tracey quickly got up. Both Andrew's height and his many prestigious publications made it important that she not be slouched on a chair when talking to him. "Andrew! I was telling Elspeth the good news that you were in Sydney and here you are in the flesh. It's good to see you again!"

"You too, Tracey, and as always, Ms. Elsie MacKay, *tha e math d' fhaicinn.*" Andrew bowed slightly, gallant as always.

"Oh, lovely to see me! I'm a mess! *Dùin do bheul agus pòg thu.* You should have told me you were coming to Cape Breton!" Elspeth shook her head, but came forward for a quick hug and a peck on the cheek.

Tracey said, "I've got some work to do. I'll let the two of you catch up." Neither one of them paid any attention to her as she went back to her desk. She knew the score.

"And not get to surprise you? Get to see you in your natural element? Why would I miss up on that opportunity? Are you free for lunch?"

"Of course I am, for you. Any time. What brings you here?" She pulled her coat down from the hook on her bookcase and grabbed her purse. "Let's go now before the phone rings and something ends up on my plate. Tracey, we're heading for lunch. If you need me, you have my cell number."

Tracey smiled knowingly and winked at her when she walked by. Elspeth gave her the finger behind her back as she went out the door behind Andrew.

They went to Governor's Pub for lunch, and both ordered a Guinness. They had taken a small table that was inside a window alcove so they could not be seen by anyone in the pub unless they came right up to the table. Andrew took a drink of his beer when it arrived, wiping his mouth afterward to get rid of the froth that stuck to his moustache.

"So, this is a pleasant surprise. Celtic Colours isn't for another week or so, and you hadn't even said that you'd be over for it this year. Why the secrecy?" Elspeth found her hands were shaking a bit, and she put them around the glass, warming her beer and settling her nerves.

"I am going to retire, Elsie. Early." Andrew took another drink. "Maybe I'll do some summer sessions, or some distance courses. They're getting pretty popular. I've thought about it long and hard, and between it all, I think I can make it work. I want to spend more time writing and less time wondering what I'm supposed to be doing with my life."

"Well. I always thought you knew exactly what you were supposed to be doing with your life." Elspeth sat back in her chair. "That's interesting. I suppose I can see why you'd do it though. The teaching schedule makes it hard to concentrate on any of the projects that I really want to do, and the students are, well, they are not as focused as they used to be. Your mother will be pleased. Would you use her place as a base, back to Skye and Portree, move out of Edinburgh?"

"Maybe. I don't know. Maybe some of the time. Elsie, I'm looking fifty in the face pretty soon, and I know I'm so much older than you, but we've been friends a long time now, and I enjoy your company. I'd like to take it past the friends thing. I'd like to date. You. Bu mhath leam a'bhith comhla riut." He took another sip of his beer and he sat back. He felt more nervous than he had in years, and he was uncertain of how she felt so he concentrated, watching her face to gauge her reaction.

"Date? With that distance? That doesn't work. I can't retire for fifteen years at the least. I can't see how that would work, Andrew."

He leaned towards her. "I've rented an apartment in Sydney for the winter."

"You did what?" Elspeth was shocked.

"Six months. Let's date for six months and see what happens." He looked at her, not letting her gaze slip from his.

"A winter in Sydney? You set yourself up to live a winter in Sydney?" She had to laugh. She knew he hated Sydney, let alone in the winter.

"I'm serious. I'm staying for six months. It's a done deal. Let's date."

"People our age don't date." She shook her head. "That's crazy!"

"Sometimes, you have to start on a road, even if you don't know where it's going to lead. Right? I've made two mistakes, well, marriage excursions, shall we call them, already in life. I want this to be the last trip up the aisle, not a dead end, so I want to be sure." Andrew smiled and reached across the table and covered her hand with his. "I think a winter in Sydney is a great place to start. Nì sinn ar dìcheall, a ghràidh."

Ach, and the rest is history, Elspeth thought and rotated her wedding ring, a silver Celtic knot encircling her finger, missing Andrew once again and wishing he were here to help her. His running commentary on the dresses would have been fun. Sure enough, there were plenty of dresses on Amazon. Elspeth looked over at their wedding photo, her in a simple green dress, flowing to the floor, and Andrew in his MacLeod kilt and finery. She knew the same colour would look perfect on Cecelia. It wasn't long before she found the perfect dress – plain green, a pleated A-Line gown, with a built-in bra and a nice wide-banded waist. She could even shorten it and Cecelia could use it again, and it was only $150. Sold!

Chapter 6

Blessings

Mistakes are blessing, not burdens.
Lights in the path of life.

– Priya Sharma

"Are you ready to go, Cecelia?" Elspeth said, her forehead resting on her daughter's door. Things had been so tense these past few weeks between the dress and the praying, and the debating, and the cursing. The praying had been on Cecelia's part. Elspeth had been doing the cursing. She was wearing a loose, cool summer dress, a bit of red and orange, to hopefully distract from her gray hair as she sat at the Convent with all the young parents of the graduates. She didn't want people to think she was Cecelia's grandmother.

Unfortunately, Cecelia had negated Elspeth's elation about the dress with a turned-up nose and a hasty retreat to her bedroom saying that she just couldn't face the prom and all the fake frivolity of it all, and she didn't want to look like a slut. The whole thing was bullshit. Both of them weren't sure if they were fighting over the dress anymore, or using the dress to argue over the Brazil idea.

Elspeth remembered the shock of her pregnancy after four years of marriage. She pulled back and looked at the door, festooned with pictures of Cecelia at different ages, as if she could go back in time through them. Her finger traced her little girl's grade primary face with her golden red hair, two bushy pigtails sticking out. She could still remember that purple velvet dress with the lace collar that Cecelia had started wearing when she was four, stumbling over the length of it, and wore it constantly until it was above her knees when she was nine. Maybe she could sell her on the idea of wearing a dress like that to prom, for old time's sake. Elspeth shook her head. She knew that her daughter didn't want any more of her suggestions, her help. She was sick of them. She'd have to find her way on her own.

"So, you haven't been feeling well, you say?" Dr. Zinc had asked from beyond the curtain pulled around Elspeth.

"No, that's why I wanted the blood work. I've been tired, and I don't know, my hair seems to be falling out. How weird is that? I think I might have started menopause because I haven't been having my period either. Maybe I need hormones. What do you think?" She finished buttoning up her blouse and zippered up her pants. She really needed to get back into the sit-ups. All her pants seemed tight these days. She had gone past her "fat pants" and had resorted to sweatpants today. Nice sweatpants, but sweatpants none-the-less. What would her mother have thought? It would have been like wearing your pyjamas in public to her.

She pulled back the curtain and sat in the chair beside her doctor. She was so glad that she had a female doctor. It made it so much easier to talk about things like menopause and periods. Dr. Zinc seemed puzzled by the blood work report.

"There's nothing wrong, is there?" Elspeth suddenly felt worried. Every day there seemed to be another person diagnosed with cancer or something equally horrible. It was an age thing, she thought. Getting older, more friends sick. ALS. MS. She could feel herself getting riled up and emotional. Here it comes, she thought, and braced herself for the bad news.

"Well, I didn't even think to look there, to be honest, but it is very clear by this blood report that you are pregnant." Dr. Zinc put the paper down and she tried to cover her mouth with her hand, as if she was being concerned, but Elspeth could tell she was smiling. Her dark brown eyes were wide with surprise.

"Pregnant? I'm in my forties. I can't be pregnant." Elspeth seemed to lose all feeling in her legs, and was glad that she had the back of the chair to support her.

"You are pregnant, Elspeth," the doctor repeated.

"Maybe the tests were mixed up, you know. In the lab." But she knew as she said it that the tests were right. The nausea she had blamed on the two glasses of wine that didn't usually bother her. The tight pants. Her breasts, nipples sore. Of course she was pregnant. If she was sixteen and didn't know any better it would be one thing, but to be an educated professional and not recognize the signs. How embarrassing!

"When did you have your last menstral cycle?" she heard the doctor asking. She was in shock. This can't be happening. She's got a paper to finish and the students are all working on their theses. She'll have that conference next fall to organize during Celtic Colours.

"Oh, I don't know. It's been a while. I thought it was menopause, right? That's what I thought. I enjoyed the break to be honest." She took a deep breath and tried to remember. "It must have been back around New Year's. We went to Scotland to spend Christmas with Andrew's mother, and I remember I had a wicked period when we got home. I blamed it on the plane, the gravity sucking it out of me." She paused, then said almost to herself, "That was the worst one. There were a few lighter ones after that ... "

The doctor looked at her, patiently waiting for her to do the math. "Oh, my God. That makes me, what, five months along? I'm even too late, aren't I ... You know?"

"Would you want to? I mean, would you want to get rid of the baby?" Dr. Zinc seemed surprised.

"Well, I'll be high risk, won't I? And my husband, well, he's older. What kind of a sperm would he have left over? They're ancient!" She felt that she was drowning, water coming up over her nose. "Work is so busy right now, and Andrew – I don't know how he'll deal with this, and if something does happen to him, and he dies, or he gets MS or whatever, and I have a baby, a child, a teenager, I'll be doing it on my own. I mean, dealing with young adults in a classroom is bad enough. I'm not sure if I can deal with a teenager when I'm what, in my sixties? Oh, my God!" Elspeth felt tears coming. "This is crazy! It can't be happening to me!"

She thought she was smarter than that. Martha Jessie, we finished high school together and she's a grandmother, her daughter, Cara twenty-six now, and for God's sake, she's expecting her third child! They could do maternity classes together. Oh, Dhia fhéin. Tracey and Beverly at work. How would she tell them? And the Gaelic Development Steering Committee? Nach fhaigheadh iad geir air á seo? She and Andrew would be the laughingstock of the Celtic world.

She didn't feel that she had grown any wiser with age, impatiently waiting for her daughter to open the door. Finally, it swung open and Cecelia flew out in a hurry, rushing out of the house past her mother and letting the screen door slam, which she knew would bug her mom. "C'mon, Mom, Amanda's there now. She's waiting for us. The dinner will be starting so if we're walking, we better get going." Cecelia sprinted off ahead, with Elspeth once again cursing Andrew for being away.

"There you are," Amanda said to Cecelia when she finally got up the hill. Cecelia had left her mother to walk up the road rather than the grass slope. "I thought I was going to have to go in and sit with Brittany, and I've had enough of her today. She took forever with her hair and makeup for this ordeal. I'm dreading to see what Monday night is like. She'll be like a Bridezilla. We must have taken a gazillion selfies. You'll see them all over Facebook so no need for me to show them to you now." Amanda grabbed Cecelia and started in to the Convent.

Cecelia clutched Amanda's arm when they got to the basement with its red and black tiles leading the way to the cafeteria. "How old do you think these tiles are, Amanda? I feel like I'm in an American diner from the '50s, they're so clean and bright. As if no one has ever stepped on them before."

Amanda peeked down the stairs to the gym with its gleaming wooden floor, which was softly golden with the evening sun streaming through its high windows. "Jesus, this place is spotless. Mom needs to take lessons up here. Supernatural cleaning abilities, I'd say. By the power of God, these floors shall proclaim your glory, and so it was!" Her arms spread out to both sides of the hall with the commandment, the spaghetti straps on her dress loosened up, and one fell over her shoulder.

"Amanda, behave yourself! Remember where you are, and don't embarrass us," her mother, who'd come in behind them, said sternly. Elspeth had joined up with Amanda's parents, glad to see someone she knew, aware that she was sweating more than anyone else.

"I hate these things, myself," Amanda's father said. "How did Andrew get out of this?"

"His mother's ninety-fifth birthday. He went over a couple of months ago since she had some health issues, but I think he was pretty happy to avoid all this hoopla as well. He'll be back for graduation." Elspeth followed the crowd as they were taken in to the cafeteria. There were name tags on the table, and since they were the last ones coming in, it was easy to find their seats.

"Before we eat, we want to congratulate all the graduates, and their parents, because it is a partnership, you know. Getting someone through school." Sister Mary Augustine's voice was deep and commanded the room to listen. All chatter stopped and eyes turned towards her. "So together, we must give thanks to the Lord our God, who is also a part of the partnership, for without His love and support, none of this would be possible today."

The heads, blond, black, brown, and the few gray ones in the crowd, tilted forward as Sister Mary Augustine's voice said grace. Amanda tried to kick Cecelia under the table, but ended up hitting her mother's shin instead. If looks could kill, Amanda, you'd be dead, thought Cecelia, glad to notice her own mother was stifling a giggle at the scene.

"Which one is your Madonna?" Elspeth whispered to Cecelia.

"Mom! I told you. She doesn't go by that name," Cecelia whispered back. Amanda had a puzzled look on her face, wondering what they were talking about.

"Well, whatever her name is, which one is she?"

Cecelia looked around. The nuns seemed to have taken one table at the head of the room, but Madonna wasn't there. "She's not here, Mom. She was going to be here. That's what she said."

They started calling tables up, one at a time for the meal. They were called third, and still there was no sign of Madonna.

"That's strange, Mom. I'm worried about her. We'll have supper and if she hasn't shown up by that time, I'm going to have to ask someone. I'd like you to meet her." Cecelia started eating her turkey dinner with all the trimmings, but something didn't seem right and she didn't have much appetite.

"Excuse me, Sister Mary Augustine?" There was a lineup of parents, and parents urging teenagers, shaking the Sisters' hands at the end of the meal. People were eager to get back out to the lovely June freshness since the room had gotten pretty stuffy between the hot meal and the warm evening.

"Yes?" Sister Mary Augustine's bushy eyebrows rose in surprise. She hadn't expected conversation of any sort from the students.

"I was wondering about ... Sister Mary Jerome. She was going to be here tonight and I was going to introduce her to my mother, but she never came. Is she okay?"

"She wasn't feeling well the past few days, so we took her to the hospital and they are keeping her in for some tests. That's why she's not here tonight. Nothing to worry about, I'm sure." The nun turned away to greet more of her public. This was an event the Convent looked forward to every year, and Sister Mary Augustine was not going to waste the chance to enjoy the evening.

"Mom, Madonna's in the hospital. For tests." Cecelia caught up with her as she got to the stairs. "We should go and visit her."

"Oh, Cecelia, really? It's such a nice evening out, and I was going to finish putting the perennials in the front garden bed."

"It's only in Inverness, Mom. Fifteen minutes away. It won't take long to go there, drop in for a quick visit, and get back home."

Elspeth looked back at the Convent and down at the church, and couldn't resist standing for a minute to look out at the water, her daughter's red hair blazing in the light of the sun. She looked at the other graduates, posing for suggestive selfies with their classmates and marvelled once again at her daughter's thoughtfulness. "You're right. The days are long now. We'll be home well before the sun sets."

* * * * *

Elspeth fought her nerves as she drove the fifteen minutes it took to travel between Mabou and Inverness. She was surprised that she was so riled up. It's not like she hadn't been to Inverness ten times a year since then, but she hadn't been back to the hospital since her parents had died there. But it would be the new hospital, she reminded herself, so it should be better. She had avoided thinking about their deaths for so long. She told herself again that they had lived good lives, long lives, and the cancer had eaten them away, though even that didn't stop her from feeling a little ache for them.

She shook her head to clear it of the images of them in those hospital beds. First Ma, then Pa, which seemed especially sad since Pa had been the smoker and Ma never touched a cigarette in her life. Each of them in turn, lying on beds while they struggled to breathe one day more. The clatter and clang in the hallways when you just wanted, needed to rest. The smells that made her gag while she tended to her parents as if they were children. She had sheltered herself from hospitals since then. Cecelia's birth, Andrew's hernia operation. She could count on her fingers how often she'd been in a hospital since their deaths.

She looked over at her daughter. Cecelia seemed to be in her own thoughts, and Elspeth felt another pang of worry. She felt she had no way of getting to her, of getting her to talk. Maybe this nun, this Madonna, would be a way for them to connect. The sun was starting towards the horizon as they drove up the hill to the town, and Elspeth fought the impulse to look at the ocean to watch it. She didn't want to take her eyes off the road since there was always a steady stream of traffic in Inverness. She steeled her nerves and took the right-hand turn up to the hospital.

"Gosh, so much has changed since the last time I was here, but of course that was, what, thirty-five years ago now? That's amazing. Thirty-five years since Pa died." Elspeth parked and looked over at the old white building which had been the hospital, and once again the feeling of dread invaded her body. She had felt so young, and so alone. An orphan. She had only been ten years older than Cecelia when her world crumbled. She felt a sense of panic come over her, realizing how real the possibility was that her daughter would have to live through that pain.

"Life can serve you some hard times, you know, Cecelia. It has them in store. Curve balls. Things you aren't expecting but you have to deal with. Are you sure you want to get deeply involved in this woman's care? It's not easy to walk away, you know."

"I want to check on her is all, Mom. It didn't sound too serious."

"Okay. I had a few curve balls come my way and I had to work through them. A few times, I realized that I had started on a path without even knowing I was on one, and then it was simply easier if I stayed on that set track. I see a lot of myself in you in that way. When you make up your mind, you aren't going to change it easily." Elspeth wasn't sure if she was talking about Madonna or the church anymore.

Cecelia looked at her mother and asked, "Curve balls? What kind of curve balls?"

"Your father, for one. He was a curve ball." Elspeth laughed, trying to lighten the situation as they walked to the door of the hospital.

"He'd probably like to be called a curve ball. Suits him." Cecelia noticed how her mother sparked up when she talked about her father. She wondered if she was right, thinking about giving up the chance to have someone like him in her life. It could be, it would be, lonely.

"Life is so complicated, and that's what life is full of. Curve balls. And it's how you deal with them that makes you who you are. I can't believe we're going to visit a nun in the hospital. Where has my life taken me that my teenager daughter is more concerned about an old lady's health than a party on the beach?"

Cecelia straightened her dress as she walked towards the door. "There's no party tonight. Everyone's keeping their stash to make it an even bigger drunk on Monday night, thank you very much."

Elspeth looked over at her daughter, her clear face, fresh with a few freckles here and there, highlighted by her hair. "You are a good person, Cecelia. That's a nice thing for a parent to feel, you know."

"Oh, Mom. No need to get all soppy, for God's sake. There's something about Madonna. I think she has some answers for me, or something. I don't know. Maybe I feel bad about missing out on Nan's party in Scotland." She slowed down, looking around at the hospital beds, filled with lumps of people. "It's different for me. I don't connect well with people, and sometimes, when I really think about it, I get a little scared. I mean, you and Dad are old ..."

"Thank you," Elspeth paused for effect, "very much."

"Well, you are! But you're my parents, so that's weird. You're my parents but you're old enough to be my grandparents. It's confusing, you know? Though I do find old people interesting. Like, they lived in a different world, and they have something to say that people aren't listening to right now." Cecelia felt another twinge of something that she wasn't quite sure about, but she knew was important. She felt something but couldn't put it in words yet.

"I didn't have grandparents either, and when Ma and Pa were gone, I didn't even have aunts or uncles to turn to. Huh. I guess I transferred all that to history, genealogy. Did I ever tell you about Mother St. Margaret of Scotland?" Elspeth felt surprised, once again realizing how much Cecelia was like herself.

"The church up River Denys Mountain? Where we used to go for picnics?"

"No. I mean, that is St. Margaret of Scotland, but this was a nun. Sister Margaret Beaton, but she went by Mother St. Margaret of Scotland. Good name, eh? I'm pretty sure she was from here, Inverness." Elspeth looked thoughtful. "Maybe that's why I liked hanging out with her. You know, it just came to me that I spent a lot of time with a nun, when I wasn't much older than you. Isn't that strange? She was CND too – Congregation of Notre Dame, a teaching Sister, and she lived there in Mabou, at the Convent. Taught there too, which may be why she had such a soft spot for me, coming from the hills of Glencoe. She was pivotal in getting the library set up, saving countless Gaelic documents. I mean, the Beaton Institute wouldn't have happened without her. She played a big part in my life, when I was young."

Cecelia looked at her mother. "Well, there you go. I didn't know that."

"I haven't thought about her for years. I have a few mysteries of my own." Elspeth felt a little catch in her voice.

"Ah, don't give me that. You're my mom! No mystery there."

"She was a lovely lady. Sister Margaret. When I'd get home-sick, she'd sit beside me and tell me old stories about people in Gaelic. She was a smart woman." Elspeth felt another pang of loss hit her. She wondered if it was the thought of Cecelia leaving home that was making her feel so fragile. She took a deep breath and strode purposefully towards the door. "Well, I haven't been here since Pa died. Not even for blood work. I guess that's something to be said for my good health." She paused before going to the nurses' station to find out Madonna's room number. "It's so different now. At least we're not in the old hospital. No good memories there, I'm afraid."

When they came to Madonna's hospital room, both of them hesitated. "What are we doing here?" Elspeth asked.

"I'm not sure. But we're here." Cecelia walked through the open door and looked in the first bed. It was an old woman, but not Madonna. She went past the curtain and to the bed by the window. Madonna was there, a white buttoned-up pyjama top with small blue flowers peeking out from under the hospital blanket. Her eyes were closed.

"Madonna? Madonna?" Cecelia said quietly. If she was sound asleep, she figured they could sneak out and no one would know the difference.

Madonna's eyes opened in a flash. "Who's that?" She fumbled for her glasses on the tray suspended over her stomach.

"It's me. Cecelia. You know, from Mabou? We watched the movie together the other week? *The Song of Bernadette?*" Cecelia looked over at her mother, and Elspeth gently took her hand. "At the Convent?"

Madonna put her glasses on. "Oh, Cecelia! Yes, of course, my dear! I'm so sorry, there's just one person after another coming in here for one reason or another. It's hard to know what's going on."

"This is my mother, Madonna. Elspeth MacKay. We went to the dinner tonight at the Convent. You know, the one for the graduates? And you weren't there, so I asked Sister Mary Augustine where you were, and she said you had been taken here. So we decided to come over for a quick visit." Cecelia blurted it all out in a rush, as if she had to explain why she was intruding on the nun's space. "I hope that's all right?"

"Oh, it's more than all right, my dear. It's wonderful! It's nice to meet you, Elspeth." Madonna tried to push the tray away, to get her hand out to shake Elspeth's, but she winced in pain and stopped.

"That's okay, Madonna. Let me do that." Elspeth slid the tray out of the way and came close to the head of the bed. Instinctively, her hand moved to caress the hair out of the old woman's eyes, and they both caught themselves, surprised. Awkwardly, the old woman's hand came up and crookedly caught Elspeth's. It wasn't a handshake, more of a desperate plea, grasping and suspended in mid-air.

"It's so good of you to come, Elspeth, and you too, Cecelia." Her hand fell on the bed and Elspeth moved back to the chair close by.

Cecelia looked around for second chair but since there wasn't one, she perched herself at the foot of the bed. "Is it okay if I sit here?"

"I don't take up much room, dear, and neither do you. It's fine. They've got me strapped on to so many machines that you have to watch the lines and the cords, but I think you are small enough to find a space somewhere." Madonna smiled, happy to have company.

"You've got the ocean-view room, Madonna. The sunset is going to be beautiful this evening. It makes me glad not to be in Sydney," Elspeth said.

"Most places you have to pay extra for that ocean view," Cecelia said.

Madonna smiled again. "Oh, they are treating me pretty good here, really. Though I've been poked and prodded enough for my liking."

"Do they know what's going on?" Elspeth asked.

"Well, if they do, they aren't telling me much. I started having some chest pain, you know, heart palpitations. It's been coming on a few months now but I didn't think much of it. Old age. What can you do?" Madonna waved her hand as if she didn't want to talk about it anymore. "Enough of that. How was the dinner? Did they feed you enough?"

"Oh, there was plenty of food. All the girls are on some kind of a super diet, cleanse of some sort. Making sure they fit into their dresses," Cecelia said. "Is there anything we can do for you, Madonna? Anything?"

"I'm fine. Really. Just old. I haven't been feeling the best for a while now, and it's coming around to this, I suppose." She instinctively went up to caress the cross around her neck. "They make me take it off, you know, for chest x-rays. It feels strange, not to have it on."

"When did you become a nun, Madonna?" Elspeth asked.

"Well, I went in as a novice, young. Very young, fifteen or so, I guess."

"Younger than me," Cecelia observed, looking over at her mother.

Madonna's face clouded over. "I've been trying to remember it myself, ever since we met. Snippets come back to me, but –" and she stopped speaking, blinking quickly. "I know I went to that movie, with my folks, but I don't remember making the decision. To join, I mean. When I think about it, it seems like a bit of blur. The whole thing. Nothing seems definite or real to me."

"Where were you born, Madonna?" Cecelia glared over at her mother. Elspeth shrugged since those questions were her usual routine. Dates, parents' names. This was basic Cape Breton conversation and she rolled her eyes at her daughter's glare. This was where you had to start.

"Dominion, outside of Sydney. There was a big beach, I remember we'd go there a lot, but we lived on a farm. Outside the town a bit, but close to the church. Very close to the church. Like I said, I left early and no one ever asked me much about my early life after that. I was cloistered in Halifax and then I went to Honduras, and when I got old, I came here to Mabou. To the Convent and retirement, as it were. I remember the small farm, the smell of the barn." Madonna's gaze shifted from her company to look out the window. "I don't know if my family is alive or dead. It's like a black hole." The noise of the heart monitor filled the room.

Elspeth looked at Cecelia, puzzled. "I could do some digging for you, Madonna. Find out a bit about your family."

Cecelia's attitude changed suddenly and she said with enthusiasm, "That's a good idea, Mom. You are so good at that. She really is, Madonna. She can research like nobody's business."

Elspeth felt a proud smile creep onto her face. It was nice to hear her daughter say something positive about her for a change. "We all like to know our roots around here, Madonna." She stopped and took a breath. "It's the least I could do, to see if you have any family left."

"Oh, I don't want to be a bother, dear." Madonna shook her head.

"Oh, she lives for this stuff, Madonna!"

"Cecelia!"

"Well, you do! You love digging up census records and baptisms, the whole shebang. It will give her something to do, because to be honest, she's trying to garden and she's not great at it. She's been as cranky as a bear without her students and her papers and books all over the place. She's been trying to keep the new house like a magazine, everything glossy and polished, but she's not a natural at it. No one is having any fun." Cecelia smiled at her mother, knowing that she was hitting the nail on the head.

Elspeth was caught by surprise, realizing that Cecelia was probably right. Maybe she was part of the problem, the tension in the house. "She's probably right, Madonna. I'd much rather be sifting through details in genealogy than cleaning, though we have two absolutely gorgeous bathrooms now that I am spending far too much time polishing, something I've never been fixated on before. I didn't think retirement would make me a compulsive housecleaner!"

"And cranky. You've got to admit it ... And cranky. You never did like housecleaning!"

"Okay, okay, you've made your point. I need a project, other than the house." Elspeth took a pen and pad of paper from her purse, crossed her legs, and leaned the pad against her knee. She was pleased that Cecelia thought she could be helpful, and she realized that this might be a way for Cecelia to get her answers as well. "But I should be honest here. It's one thing to go through the archives of people long gone and it's another thing to find people today. Madonna, what is your full name?"

"Madonna Mary MacMillan. Lots of m's, I'm afraid. It would take a whole line of paper for me to write my signature, when I was little. I could never make my m's skinny enough to get it all on easily. Madonna Mary. No wonder I became a nun." She looked out the window. "What will they put in my obituary? I don't even rightly remember my sisters' names. I wouldn't know them if I met them on the street." Her pale blue eyes were glossy with tears and there was a look of strain on her face.

Madonna could remember her brothers clearly, but her sisters, they had been so little. They blurred into one. She heard her name ringing in her ears and looked out the door to see if someone was calling her. Then she realized it was in her head and closed her eyes for a minute, embarrassed.

"Madonna Mary! Madonna Mary! Let's get on our knees, Madonna Mary! Say one for us, please, Madonna Mary!" *The girls in the schoolyard had clasped hands and were singing around her, going faster and faster as they sang louder and louder. Finally, the slow, heavy one, one of the Italian girls, wouldn't be able to keep up and the circle would break and the girls would fall to the ground. Madonna tried to pretend that she liked the game, but she didn't. Tears started leaking out.*

Angus came up and put his arm around her. She'd only started school and Mama had told him to watch out for his little sister. "You okay, Madonna Mary?" He brushed off her knees when she had fallen in the dirt. "Don't want Mama to see you all messed up, now do you?"

Jerome came up to them. "What's goin' on? She okay?"

Madonna looked up at her big brothers, glad to see their faces. "It's fine. I'm fine." She looked over at Natasha, the heavy Italian girl, who was laughing at her.

Jerome watched her glance. "Is that Natasha girl makin' fun of you?"

Natasha's brother Alfonso, from grade five, could hear her name from miles away. He was big, practically shaving, and Jerome looked so small, only in grade three and skinny for his age. "What did you say? Are you picking on my sister?" Alfonso said threateningly.

"Well, they were makin' fun of my little sister, so it's only fair." *Jerome stood as tall as he could, and Angus made a beeline over to the older kids' playground. Jerome knew it was only a matter of minutes before his older two brothers arrived. "She's only little, and quiet, and they shouldn't be makin' fun of her."*

"It wasn't only Natasha though, was it? It was a whole pile of girls. Why do you love to pick on Natasha?" Alfonso grabbed Jerome by the shirt. "There were lots of other girls you could have accused, picking

on your simple sister. Look, you mooky little kid. No one needs that around here. Little farmin' kid coming around smellin' like shit and pretendin' he's a big shot."

By this time, Callum and David had arrived, Angus panting for breath trying to keep up with them. "Look, buddy, unless you want to lose the ability to chew your own food for a while, you let go of our little brother and go on your way."

Alfonso let go of Jerome's shirt and Jerome brushed off his chest as if to erase the dirty fingerprints. Alfonso kicked up some dirt as he turned to join the rest of his gang down by the end of the fence.

Madonna looked up at her four big brothers, who had already forgotten about her as they talked about who had done what. It was the closest she had felt to them in her life, but they never included her in the conversation.

"Do you remember your brothers' names?" Elspeth asked gently, bringing Madonna out of her reverie. She also glanced over at the heart monitor, which was showing a bit more activity. She looked at Cecelia to see if she was noticing it.

Madonna took a second before really registering the question. "The boys? Yes, I remember the boys' names. Angus was next to me, then there was Jerome. And the older ones were Callum and David. I remember the boys clearly enough. I picked Jerome's name when I became a nun."

"Pick a name, a saint's name, of course. And we'll put Mary before that, and that's what you'll go by." The old Sister, Sister Mary Patrick, who had the ledger in front of her, looked up at Madonna as if she should have known that this question was coming. "Do you have one in mind?"

"No. I don't. I didn't know that we had to know the saints." Madonna felt confused and overwhelmed. She had since she had come from the hospital, as if some part of her was missing, and she knew that she felt different, but she couldn't really understand why. It was all a part of His plan, wasn't it, so she should feel good about it all. She felt thick, simple, as if things were coming at her out of a fog.

"You don't know your saints? Didn't you study for your

confirmation?" the Sister asked, her mouth tight and stern against her teeth. Her face was tightly circled with the white cloth of the habit, the pointed peak of it rising like a house above her head, making her seem so big, so intimidating.

Madonna hadn't worn a full habit as a novice, just a long black kerchief with a white band around her head. She'd have to learn how to fold and iron well to fit in with the rest. She guessed they would teach her. She'd never been the best of students. She remembered that Bernadette hadn't known her catechism well either, and she'd been chosen. She had been okay.

The nun's eyes were almost closed because of the large bags under them, sinus-prone infections causing days of discomfort and headaches that made her cranky. She had one today and did not have the patience for this simple-minded girl who had got herself in trouble and was now joining their ranks. She wouldn't make it in the classroom as a teacher, that's for sure. The Congregation of Notre Dame might not have been the best choice for her.

"Do you have any brothers then?"

"Yes, four, but they are boys."

"Of course they are boys. Most of our saints were boys at one time. Were any of them named after saints?" Sister Mary Patrick asked, rolling her eyes towards heaven as if for strength.

"Angus was the nicest to me. He's closest in age to me." Madonna felt tears coming on suddenly, a wave of homesickness taking over.

"Not a saint. Any others?"

"There's Jerome, he's older than Angus, probably a year or two, then David and Callum is the oldest."

"You've got a choice then. Jerome and David are both saints."

"That's not what my father would call them."

The nun, surprised at the girl's insightful comment that didn't mean to be a joke, had to laugh in spite of herself. "Why don't you go with Jerome? There aren't too many of them around here. Sister Mary Jerome. Does that sound right?"

Madonna nodded. "Mary's always been my name, my second name. But, Sister, don't you think it's a bit strange that I have to change my name Madonna to Jerome to become a nun?"

The old nun grunted a response but didn't say anything. She hadn't thought the girl was smart enough to come up with that.

Madonna had turned away. Sister Mary Jerome. Her new name. Her new life.

Cecelia remarked, "Sister Mary Jerome. I can see that. Strange you had to pick a man's name."

Madonna shrugged her shoulders slightly. "That's the way it was done in those days. A man's name."

"A man's name in a man's world, I guess. What about your parents, Madonna? If I had their names, I could find them easily on the census, at least up to 1940, or maybe some other documents, I'm sure."

Again, Madonna looked out the window and it almost seemed as if she had fallen asleep with her eyes open. Cecelia reached down to rub the old lady's leg, a gesture that made Elspeth smile, thinking how recently she had used it herself. There didn't seem to be any response. When she spoke, it didn't make a lot of sense.

"I remember the house, the pantry and where I'd hang the broom. And I can kind of remember the pattern on the dustpan. It was a flower, and it was a metal dustpan, not like the plastic ones today. I had to be careful not to bang it around too much. If you did, then it would be crooked against the floor and you'd never be able to pick the sweepings up right. I think my mother told me that. It wouldn't have been my father."

Cecelia looked at the little woman, hunched in the bed, her eyes darting from side to side as her mind worked through the cobwebs in her brain. "Are you okay, Madonna?"

"Oh, sorry, my dear. It's not the Alzheimer's, honestly. I have been trying to remember things, and I have the feeling that there's something important there, and I'm trying to find it. Strange, isn't it? Getting old?"

"I don't know. I'm not there yet."

"No. You're not. You are just beginning to get old." The old lady smiled and reached out to pat Cecelia's hand with her knobby fingers.

"Your parents, Madonna? Do you remember them at all?" Cecelia once again shot her mother a glance to be quiet. Her mother's eyes widened as if to say, You were the one wanting me to do the research, for Pete's sake.

Madonna's breath went out of her as another strong memory rushed in. She couldn't stop the flood of it, smashing against her eyes, her mind, her heart, but they flashed so quickly that it was hard to make sense of it all.

It had been a rough night, when it all came out. She kept repeating that there had been no boy, no one getting around her, but the evidence against her was too large to be ignored any longer. Her father had been livid, his blood pressure sky high, his face blotched and red, as he pounded his fist again and again on the kitchen table, the plates and cutlery airborne for moments at a time. No one dared go near it to clear it off.

Madonna looked around the kitchen. Her big brothers gangly and embarrassed about it all, the priest's hands clasped together looking at the floor, and her father, ready to explode. The girls had been sent to their room, but Madonna knew they were at the top of the stairs by now, listening in. All she could do was sit there, and go somewhere else in her mind, so she started her rosary and felt the calm descend over her as she started the first Hail Mary.

"She's as thick as a barrel, and not just in the head. You can all see that. Now, someone has to be the father, and I know, sure as hell, that if we don't find out who did this, then we'll all be looking guilty about it. She never goes anywhere but home and church, and hasn't since her mother left us, God rest her soul. Boys, Jesus! Sorry, Father. Do you know anything at all about this, boys?"

"No, Da. Not a thing. Honest," David said, shaking his head. "Not a thing. She won't talk to any of my friends who come in. Scared, I suppose."

"No, she's never been a talker. I'll give her that." Da put his face in his hands. "That was a blessing, up to now." He looked over at her again. "Madonna. I'm asking you again, in the name of your mother and all that is holy, to tell us how you got in this condition."

Madonna could feel everyone's eyes on her. "I can't, Da. It just happened." She looked down. "I'm sorry. It's my cross to bear."

"Well, it may well be your cross to bear, but it will ruin the rest of us along with you if we don't know who made it. It wasn't a goddamned immaculate conception even if your name is Madonna Mary. Jesus, why did I ever let your mother give you that name? A slap in the face it is now." Da jumped to his feet, unable to control his anger.

Father Landon stood with him. "Now, Gussie. This is all a matter of nature, we all know that. Look, leave it with me. I'll make some inquiries and see where she could go. There are places, you know, for girls like Madonna here, and, well, once that part is over, she could simply stay in the convent. Cloistered, even. There are girls her age who go in as novices."

Da looked up. "Cloistered?"

"Yes. Some nuns only get home once a year, if that. Sometimes they never come home again." Father looked down at his hands.

"We'd miss her around here. With her mother gone, and all." Da looked over at Madonna, and she timidly glanced up to see his eyes get glassy. He swallowed and shook his head. "She's quiet, but she's always been there, it seems. Like an old soul, watching over us."

Madonna could feel all of them looking at her, as if they knew that she was disappearing before their very eyes.

"It's not easy for families, but it's a good life in the convent. She can read and study, and be of help to others. I always thought she would make a wonderful nun." Father looked at her, his smile making her heart beat a little faster.

"Me too. I was sure she'd be a nun … before this disaster." Da slumped back in his seat. "Don't think I'll get any priests out of this lot, that's for sure." All the boys muttered their assent on that score and Da shook his head. "I just didn't think she'd be gone until all the rest were out of the house. I'd have her here to help me."

"Well, Gussie, I think it would be better if she left sooner than later. I can make some calls and find a place for her," said Father.

"What do you think, Madonna?" Da got up and kneeled in front of her. He took both her small hands in his large, calloused hands and clasped them all together. "Would you like to be a nun?"

"Like Sister Bernadette?" Madonna asked, hopeful, still enamoured with the one movie she had ever seen on the big screen.

"Yes, like her, I guess." He squeezed her hands tighter, remembering the movie as well, and how the poor simple girl had suffered for what she believed.

"I'd like that very much, Da." Madonna breathed a sense of relief, thinking of the peace ahead.

Pa patted her hands and turned to Father. *"Let His will be done, then, Father. Let His will be done."*

Madonna took a deep breath. "His name was Gussie. Gussie MacMillan. Mama was just Mama to me, but she must have had a name." She started to cry. "I don't remember it. I can't remember it. Not right now." The heart monitor started to beep and a nurse came from the station and told them they should leave so she could rest.

Cecelia and Elspeth didn't want to leave her in such a state, but the nurse assured them that she would be fine. It was basically the end of visiting hours anyway.

"I'll be back soon, Madonna," Cecelia said reassuringly as they left the room. "And I'll be praying for you."

"Thank you, my dear. Thank you both for coming." Madonna closed her eyes and took a deep breath, surprisingly glad to see them go.

Chapter 7

Struggles

I felt a Funeral, in my Brain,
And Mourners to and fro
Kept treading – treading – till it seemed
That Sense was breaking through –
                              – Emily Dickinson

Cecelia had not agreed to her mother's selection of a dress on
Amazon, which had come as little surprise to Elspeth, but she
had agreed to going to the L'Arche store, The Hope Chest, to see
if there was anything suitable. Neither one of them had visited the
second-hand store beside the old arena before. They had heard of it
but they had never been sure about what it was. Now the desperate
need of a dress brought them through the gate. They had seen the
L'Arche community members at gatherings in the area for years, and
thought that it was interesting how people came from all over the
world to live and work beside those with developmental disabilities.
Elspeth knew as soon as they walked in the door, surrounded by
heaps of clothes and used books, that Cecelia was right. This would
be a fitting place to find her dress.

Cecelia approached a twenty-something girl with Down's Syndrome who was busy rearranging the DVDs about where she could find dresses.

The girl turned to her with a wide smile. "Do you like Patwick Swassie?" the girl asked. She was holding the *Dirty Dancing* DVD. "I love Patwick Swassie. He's so handsome!" She spoke with a slight lisp but her words were perfectly clear.

"He is very handsome. For sure," Cecelia replied. "But I think I like Tom Hanks more." She picked up a DVD of *Sleepless in Seattle*. "What do you think?"

"Huh! Naw, he's not as handsome as Patwick Swassie. He's old and boring." She put the movie Cecelia had picked back on the shelf. "You need to watch Patwick Swassie. That's who you need to watch." She put the *Dirty Dancing* DVD in Cecelia's hand. "My name is Tewesa. What's yows?"

"Theresa?"

The girl nodded.

"I'm Cecelia. I'm looking for a dress for the prom."

"Nice to meet you, Cecelia." She put out her hand and they shook. "Dwesses are this way." She led the way to the back of the store where some long dresses, looking brand new, hung suspended from the highest rack. "Pwoms are nice. I went to my pwom when I finished school. I danced with Mawk Wankin. He was so handsome. I love Mawk Wankin." She put her hand on Cecelia's arm. "But don't tell him I said that!"

"I won't say a word!" Cecelia looked through the dresses. But between the colours and the sizes, there was nothing that was going to do. Theresa had gone back to her work and Elspeth had starting looking through the used books section, giving her time to make up her own mind. Cecelia had the idea that her mother was worn down, about to give up entirely on the prom idea.

She walked over to her mom. "There's nothing here. I don't like any of the colours, even if a size was right for me. They are all so long." She looked down at her short legs. "I'd have to cut off about two feet and hem them and there's no time for that."

One of the L'Arche assistants with a European accent of some kind came over to talk to them. She was tall, with blonde hair, · model material, Cecelia thought. "I was in at the Ark Store in Iron Mines the other day and happened to look at their dresses. There was a wonderful royal blue dress there, shorter. It was gorgeous and I think it would fit you. You should try there."

Cecelia looked at her mother who nodded, resignedly. What else could she do? Cecelia said goodbye to Theresa and they drove the forty minutes to the other store. They had been making the trek from Sydney to Mabou for many years, but they had usually taken the highway route through Baddeck and then they'd scoot through Margaree, so they were surprised how much they felt like tourists in their own neighbourhood setting off that day. It had been a small shop, with the crafts at the front again, and another older man working, his glasses thick and crooked, slowly sweeping the floor. Cecelia asked right away, "What's your name?"

He pushed his glasses up with his thumb knuckle, and wiped his mouth with his hand on the way down. "My name is Trevor. What's your name?"

"My name is Cecelia. Do you work here, Trevor?"

He laughed, a shy smile coming to his face. "Yes, this is my work program. I shovel the walk, and I lift anything that's heavy, and I sweep. A lot. I sweep, a lot."

"Well, you're doing a good job, Trevor. The floor is very clean. I'm looking for a dress, a fancy dress. Do you know where I could find one?"

"What colour?"

"Blue. A fancy blue dress."

"Oh, I like the colour blue." He looked down at his blue dress shirt, and blue denim pants. "See, even my socks are blue." He pulled up the jeans a little and showed his bright blue socks. "And my shoes are blue too. But they're not suede, you know."

"So I don't have to stay off them," Cecelia responded.

He smiled. "Yes, if they were blue suede shoes, you'd have to stay off them!" He chortled a laugh, and Cecelia knew that this was a joke he used often. "I know where there's a pretty blue dress." He led Cecelia into the main part of the store, then into the back. From the rack on the side, he pulled out a blue dress, short but with lacy feathers of blue, iridescent, like peacock feathers. It looked magical.

"That looks perfect, Trevor," Cecelia said and smiled at him. "I'll take it." She hadn't even tried it on.

* * * * *

Cecelia insisted that she spend the day of the prom with Madonna in the hospital. She told her mother that everyone else was spending the entire day in hair and makeup so she had her drop her off at nine and told her to come back for her at the afternoon quiet time, two p.m. That would give her plenty of time to shower and put her hair up and get over to Amanda's for the four p.m. photo shoot, not that she really cared that much about it, but everyone else seemed to think the sky was going to fall if all the girls in grade twelve didn't get together for the photos before the Grand March.

Madonna had just finished getting washed by the nurse, who was packing away the toothpaste in a drawer, when Cecelia came around the curtain.

"I hope you don't mind if I spend some time with you, Madonna. I had Mom drop me off and she's going to come back after lunch."

Madonna couldn't suppress a smile of delight. "Oh, that would be wonderful, Cecelia! The hours are long in here and everything seems to be such a struggle. It takes all my strength to get a spoon to my mouth with all these contraptions."

The nurse had left, so Cecelia helped Madonna get herself in a more comfortable sitting position. "Well, I hope I can be of some help. Are they telling you much, Madonna?"

"Oh, the nice young woman doctor was around this morning. She says it looks like I had a mild heart attack and I may have some heart condition. May need a stint or something, but I'll have to go to Halifax or Sydney for that. They're still doing some tests."

Madonna waved her hand away. "I don't really want to think about it. What happens is God's will."

"God's will." Cecelia tried to strengthen herself for the conversation ahead. "I've been thinking a lot about God's will too, Madonna. Wondering if I have a part in it. The Church."

"What do you mean?"

"Well, there's a lot of young people joining up with an order called Mary's Maidens. It's a new order that's been set up out of Brazil. They are doing some good work, I think."

"Really? Mary's Maidens. I've never heard of them."

"Yes. Ah, they started out of Brazil, São Paolo, so that's a long way from here. It's not surprising that you wouldn't know about them. Not many people have around here. Anyway, they focus on getting youth involved in religious vocation, dedicating their life to helping people through working for the Lord. I guess it's sanctioned by the Pope and everything."

"Brazil?" Madonna seemed confused.

"Yes, in South America. It's a long way from here, I know, and it's got Mom pretty freaked out. I'm not saying for certain, but I'm really looking at joining. Being a nun. Like you. Did you always know that you wanted to be a nun, Madonna?" Cecelia sat in the chair in the corner, and felt the need to take notes as if she was in class but also felt that might be rude.

"In a way, yes. I did. There was always a part of me that was drawn to the Lord," Madonna said slowly. She was surprised, thinking about this young girl wanting to join an Order. It made a bit more sense now, to see why she was so interested in her, in the convent. She wanted to help her, but she didn't know if she could express herself well enough. She remembered those quiet memories, the best ones, down in the intervals, with the clouds floating along above her, waiting for the rays of the divine to touch her. Her mind had kept the darkness away for so long that the cracks that were appearing in her memory still didn't make a lot of sense to her. "I don't know what I can tell you. I went into the service of the Lord so early, fifteen years old. I don't remember any other options for me."

Because of those moments, she did not hesitate when Father told her she should be a vessel for God and lie on the floor of the vestry. Because of those moments, she knew it was right when they told her God had found a home for His baby and wanted her to be a nun, a bride of God. She had felt the sun on her face and knew she was a part of God's plan.

Madonna gasped and looked over at Cecelia, wondering if she had said any of those thoughts out loud. What was happening to her? Was she going crazy?

She had done what they wanted, following blindly as they pointed and prayed, prodded and pulled, since she had left home at Father's side. He'd taken her in the dark, when the little ones were in bed and the brothers hiding in the parlour. Not a place they would usually go, foreign ground really, but no one wanted to be watching her as she left the house. Da had come out and held her tightly by the shoulders for a minute, looking into her face. He hadn't said anything, but his fingers gripped her as if they had a mind of their own and didn't want to let her go.

"We have to go, Gussie. They are waiting for us at the convent and it's getting late." Father passed Madonna her coat, which no longer went around her and had to hang open, offering no protection at all against the gusts and gales of the weather, or people's knowing glances.

One more squeeze and Da turned away, and Madonna knew he was crying but didn't quite understand why. She was going to do God's work, and she had felt the life of the Holy Spirit growing and moving within her, and like Bernadette, she had wanted to be strong as she left her home.

For four months, she walked the halls of the convent, her belly cleverly hidden within the folds of a novice's habit, and she knelt and prayed and lived her life in a solitary room. At night, she would spend hours on her knees, saying the rosary again and again, until her knees were raw, her belly making it hard to get close to the bed, not that she'd rest her elbows on it or her head. She kept her back straight, like the Mother Superior had told her.

She had been a vessel for God, and then, suddenly, she was empty again. Her body was empty again. She knew there was a baby in the basket. It was making noise, whimpering a little, and the young nurse, older than she was but not by much, was cooing and marvelling at the baby saying, "Aren't you the prettiest girl? With your red hair. Aren't you the prettiest girl?"

She'd started praying, looking for strength and guidance, knowing that her life did not include a baby, that was not her path. The baby was on another path, and Madonna prayed for her life, that it would be a good one. Already she felt a distance and as they carried the baby out of the room, she felt the cord between them snap, with a pain that hit her harder than any labour pain, but she kept praying.

She'd wanted to be worthy of her path in life. She would work hard every day to be worthy. Like Bernadette would do.

Madonna became aware of the heart monitor beeping loudly. Cecelia jumped and ran to the nurse's station. The nurse came back and gave Madonna a shot and told her to relax. She could feel the warmth of the drug slipping through her veins and her muscles loosening. "Maybe I'll just have a little rest, Cecelia. Would you mind sitting with me? I don't really want to be alone … Not now."

"You rest. I brought a book with me. You rest and I'll sit right here."

* * * * *

It was an hour later and Cecelia was wondering if Madonna was going to die. It would be so sad if she died now, while she was there. She's the same age as Dad, and if she can die, well, he could definitely die. Men usually die first, right, especially with heart stuff. She had been saying her prayers and trying to come up with words that were special, not the same old ones. She didn't feel that she was getting to the heart of what she wanted to say.

The sound of the monitors became a backbeat to her thoughts. She had been emailing and texting with Bridget and Diane with questions and doing her research online. She had been impressed with the excerpts of the Maidens' personal stories on the website, how freeing it was to be preserving their virginity for the love of the Lord. Many of them expressed her own thoughts, her frustration with the vapid emptiness of the times and people right now. She felt that the girls were basically humiliating themselves, torturing their bodies and their souls, trying to reach some Hollywood-made image of perfection, rather than thinking about how they could get better as human beings. She closed the emails, feeling her anger flare and realizing that she would have to change her mindset if she was going to make it through the day ahead.

Finally, Madonna's eyes opened and they went immediately to Cecelia, to see if she was there or had been a part of her vivid dreams. "Thank you so much, my dear, for staying. I've come to realize that in my life, other than the Sisters, of course, I haven't had many people stay by me, look out for me." She caught herself. "I know there is always the Lord, but sometimes a person wants a live, breathing person to watch over them."

"I can't think of anything better to do," Cecelia said, meaning every word.

"Even though today is your prom?"

"Especially today. It's giving me a nice reason to miss all the hoopla. It's going to be a three-ring circus tonight."

"Well, I feel like an old dishcloth, good for nothing. I'm the youngest in the Convent, you know, and here I am, in a hospital bed. And your dad is my age, Cecelia? That's something."

"Dad's gone back to Scotland right now to spend some time with his mother. He goes about twice a year now, but this year, his mom took a fall, though she's ninety-five and usually fit as a fiddle, let me tell you. No flies on that old girl!"

Cecelia loved her grandmother. She had such a memory and loved to tell funny anecdotes, jokes. Her father would cringe at some of his mother's behaviour, but he knew he had inherited her sense of humour. She had insisted on Cecelia memorizing her favourite limericks when she was over to visit her last, felt that it was the best legacy she could give her.

"And your folks are pleased with their move? Not missing

Sydney?" Madonna shifted in the bed, realizing that she was stiffening up. She was afraid to move out of the bed, but she really should after Cecelia left.

"No, they are happy as pigs in ... Well, Mabou is perfect for them. It's like a little bit of Scotland for Dad, and home for Mom because her folks were from Glencoe. She went to high school here in Mabou. Dad did his time in Sydney, a penance he figures, to be able to be with the woman he loves. Or at least, that's what he says whenever he thinks he's done something to make Mom ticked off. It's so funny. Dad is always doing something, a course or researching a book, or practising his pipes, and he doesn't seem old probably because his mother is still alive, and yet Mom, who's a good fifteen years younger than Dad, well, I didn't even meet her folks, so she seems older in my mind. They died long before I was born. Do you think there's something in the water here? That people live longer in Scotland?" Cecelia suddenly felt a blush come over her, talking about dying to a woman in a hospital bed, tubes everywhere.

"I don't know. It seems like an awful lot of nuns make it past ninety as well." Madonna felt her shoulders relax, and the pain in her chest lessen. "I lost my mother so early. I've been trying, you know, to bring back her face or a memory of when she touched me, but I can't seem to bring anything to mind. I've been trying to think what it was like, to be young, like you, but I don't know. It gets confusing. There are so many emotions, and I can't figure out what's real and what's not."

Madonna paused before continuing, taking another deep breath as if all this talking was taking its toll. "I was cloistered, you know, for years and then I went overseas for years, to Honduras. When I came back, I think my family had just written me out of the picture. I never heard from them, and, well, the Sisters became my family." Madonna's crooked hands tightened on her lap. "But I'd like to remember them, and my mother, my father, before I ..." She stopped talking and looked out the window.

"Look, Madonna, my mother is a whiz at that sort of thing. You see, she'll come up with something. Those genealogical types, they're even better than detectives. Really! I've seen my mother have a chat with someone, say, here, at the Farmer's Market on a Sunday morning, and the person be wondering about how she is related to someone down the road, and before noon on Monday, my mother will be sending her a document with their lineage back seven generations to the boat from Scotland. I'm serious. She's amazing. I mean, my eyes start to glaze over when she and Dad start going on and on about it, but they do have skills, I'll give them that."

"It's too late, to be honest, I think, Cecelia. And if they had wanted to find me, it would not have been that hard to find a nun." Madonna wiped her eyes. "I'm feeling old and sentimental all of a sudden. Don't listen to me. Maybe I'm too old for mixing up things now, Cecelia. That's a young person's game. I've lived my life in one world, the religious world, and I'm not sure if my heart could stand getting a glimpse of the other side now. That time has passed."

"Well, tell me about Honduras. Do you remember much about that?" She could tell that Madonna was getting stressed, a line deepening in her forehead right between her eyes.

"Those memories are so strong. I was there for what? For thirty years? So much of my life."

"Oh, my God! Thirty years! That's forever." Cecelia could not comprehend that length of time. "That is so interesting! So you know Spanish?"

Madonna took a deep breath as another wave of memories filled her head. How was she going to deal with them? What did they mean now after so many years of keeping them in the shadows? She looked out the window again so her watery eyes would not be as upsetting to Cecelia.

"Why do I have to go to Honduras with all those French nuns?" Madonna had asked as she finished packing her suitcase. It was the one she took from home five years ago and she was struck by strange

sensations, smells, and quick, quivering glimpses of a past life she hadn't thought about in a long time. She saw the St. Christopher medal her father had insisted on pinning to the fabric on the inside. She touched it softly, before she started putting her few personal things in the case.

"I don't know. The word came from the Bishop himself that he wanted to send a young nun to help out with the missionary work down there and Father Landon recommended you to him." Sister Mary Patrick looked sceptical, but her face was hidden as she stripped the bedding off the small, metal frame bed. "I would have found it interesting myself, but it didn't seem to be open for application." There was no mirror in the room, but she knew her adventuring days were long past her now. She would spend the rest of her life within these convent walls.

"I've never been anywhere. I've been in Halifax for five years but I don't know the first thing about the city. I've just gone to church, served in the House here. That's it. I didn't even have visitors out in the common room. How am I supposed to go by myself to Honduras, wherever that is?" Madonna could feel the panic rising in her throat. She had been so settled in the routine of the Mother House, the daily mass, the cleaning in the kitchen, listening to the Sisters telling their stories. She had no wish to do missionary work, or to leave the security of her life.

"Well, the Bishop and Father Landon see it differently, so there you are. What did they say in the letter? Off 'to go and gather up the drops of Blood of Jesus' in Latin America. How's your Spanish, by the way?" She looked fondly at the young nun, and wanted to be helpful. She could only imagine the fear that must be overtaking her. She suspected but could never voice the suspicions that the dark side of the Church was controlling the girl's fate, but there was nothing she could do except to be kind.

"Don't make fun of me, Sister Mary Patrick! You know I don't have a word of Spanish, or French for that matter." Madonna slumped on the naked bed, her suitcase on her lap, weighing her down. She was going to be all alone. Again.

"I guess you will learn." Sister Mary Patrick's brown eyes showed her concern, looking at the almost childlike waif of a nun before her. She didn't look strong enough to carry that suitcase, let alone handle what life had suddenly placed on her shoulders. She sat beside her on the bed *for a minute, searching for the words to give her some assurance. "God will give you strength. Here, put the suitcase on the floor and we'll start a Novena together. That will give you nine days of us praying for your safe travel and finding your feet in a strange land."*

"You always know the right thing to say and do, Sister. I will miss you," Madonna said, her face clouding with sadness.

"Now, no need of that. The people in Honduras don't need a weeping nun adding to their problems. You are a helpful person, Sister, and you are always willing to listen, not like so many of the rest who only want to hear themselves talk. You will be fine. It will take a little time, and I will pray for you every day, much longer than the nine of the Novena."

Madonna remembered strong Sister Mary Patrick, who had been like a second mother to her, on her knees beside her as they faced the crucifix on the wall, taking out their rosaries and praying, "Hail Mary, full of grace, the Lord is with thee. Blessed art thou among women, and blessed is the fruit of thy womb, Jesus."

Blessed among women. Had she been blessed among women, or had she been cursed? She looked over at Cecelia and remembered that she was thinking of joining an Order. How did she feel about that, with all the memories she had in her head? She didn't know how to say anything that would make any sense of what she was thinking and feeling. She was concerned that she was having a stroke, but she wasn't going to admit that. She took a deep breath, a wave of loneliness washing over her before coming back to the point. Honduras. "Yes, I managed to become fluent enough to be understood in Spanish, and French too since all the other nuns there were from Quebec. I'm getting a bit rusty now, haven't been using them for twenty years."

"Honduras! Where is Honduras anyway? I feel that my education has been lacking in geography, that's all I can tell you."

"Central America, on the shores of the Gulf of Mexico. It's a beautiful country. Not too far from Brazil, and now you are thinking about Brazil. Isn't that interesting?" Madonna's voice was steady, considering the similarities. "Life is full of coincidences."

"Well, I'm sure it won't be as challenging as heading to Honduras fifty years ago. Technology and transportation make life a bit easier now than it was then. Translation apps and Google Maps should help, but you wouldn't have had anything of that. What did you do there? What was it like?" Cecelia asked eagerly. This was what she really wanted to know.

"I remember my time in Honduras as simple and straightforward, easy. It was all so different when I got back. Vatican II had happened, and we'd barely felt it. The world of the Sisterhood had been rocked from its foundation, and our identity of being a bride of Christ had been taken away from us." Madonna stroked the crucifix at her neck, and her eyes misted over. "It was like we had lost our identity, and some nuns, well, a whole lot of nuns, they left their orders. Walked out. We hadn't even felt that turmoil working every day, keeping on our white habits while so many tossed theirs away." She swallowed, fighting down a feeling of panic, thinking back to when she realized that she didn't have any other identity than being a nun. Nowhere to go. No family besides the Sisters and so many of them were fed up and leaving. "That was a long time ago. Now, we're just a few old women wandering the halls."

She sat silent for a few minutes before speaking again. Her voice tried to sound happier, though Cecelia could see the effort that was costing her physically and glanced over at the monitors. "Anyway, it's a good thing I'm not in Honduras now, working that hard. I had to do a lot of running around then, let me tell you. Teaching the little ones. That was what I was best suited for, and I loved it. They were sweet, the little ones. So willing to learn, and happy to have a place that gave some shelter and warm food. And once I got the basics in the languages, I was able to not feel so isolated. It took me years to truly have a conversation, a meaningful conversation with the Sisters, but the children were so easy to love. You didn't need so much language for the little ones."

The hot sun, and then the rain, the constant daily rain, from October to February. Everyone taking shelter where they could, listening to the pounding on the metal roof of the school. Shuffling paper from one side of the desk to the other as the rain dripped through the nail holes in the roof. She would lose her voice at least once every winter from trying to teach louder than that rain. She'd neaten up her classroom, and sit in the peace for a few minutes at the end of the day, enjoying the time by herself, day after day, praying that she was worthy for the Lord.

"Did you miss having your own kids, Madonna? Being a nun?"

Madonna's forehead wrinkled and her eyes squinted a bit. A pained, pinched look came to her mouth. "I didn't have a chance to miss a family." She stopped talking and looked out the window. "I wonder if they missed me."

"Would you like to see them, Madonna? You were from Cape Breton. Surely, it wouldn't be too hard to find them."

Madonna looked out the window for a minute. "I don't know. See them? I don't know. There's too much darkness there for me to think that's a good idea. I've lived my life and I had a lot of good people around me. Lots of laughs along the way. Some of the nuns, you know, they are very funny. No. If my family had wanted to get in touch, I was easy to find. You are a very thoughtful girl, you know, thinking about me so much."

"It's my pleasure, Madonna, and I'm being a little bit selfish here too. I'm trying to decide if I want to do what you did. Dedicate myself to others. I think I do, and I'm really excited about Bridget's cousin, Diane, and what she did."

"What did she do?"

"Well, she was the one I was talking to, you know, about Mary's Maidens. She was so brave, left university. She'd been going to McGill, and she just followed her heart, and went to Brazil. She seemed so calm and focused, you know. Like she knew that what she was doing was really making a difference." Cecelia could feel her own heart racing as she talked about the Order. "I mean, she's really doing it. The nun thing. She's living it every day. It scares me, but I think that's what I want too."

Madonna put her hand out for Cecelia to take. "You sound so excited, my dear, but there's a lot of loneliness on that path too."

"But you'd always have the Lord on your side, right there with you." Cecelia's bright eyes were wide with wonder. "I think it would mean so much to turn your back on all the shopping and the glitter and the waste, and really focus on what are the basically important things in life. Like educating the poor, like you did."

Madonna was trying to think of an appropriate response when Elspeth came to the door and they both let their hands slip away, as if they had been caught doing something wrong.

"You're looking better today, Madonna. I brought you a few treats and some fruit, and the *Oran*, of course." *The Inverness Oran* was the local paper and mandatory reading in every household.

"I told Madonna, Mom, about the Maidens. That I want to join them. Maybe." Cecelia seemed hesitant and shy in front of her mother.

"And what do you think, Madonna? Do you think it's a good plan?" Elspeth's voice rose a bit more than she would have liked. She was trying to stay calm about it all, but she wasn't able to restrain herself.

"I don't know. There haven't been many young people come our way in so long, I don't know how they would deal with a life of servitude. In my day, well, in my day, it was rather a relief, to make a plan and have someone tell you what to do, plan everything for you."

"But making the decisions is so hard. Maybe life is easier if someone tells you what to do," Cecelia said defiantly. "The choices out there are not worth the money."

"Cecelia! Women have fought for generations to have the right to decide for themselves what they want their lives to look like. Are you going to give all that away on a whim?" Elspeth responded with emotional conviction. She couldn't believe her daughter, in this day and age, would be willing to become a servant, with no say in her life. She wondered where she had gone wrong.

The lunch lady came for the tray just then, so all three of them went quiet. Madonna didn't know what to say, and was afraid that she was making matters worse.

"Mom. I didn't mean to give up my rights."

"Well, you might be. You might be giving up a hell of a lot more than you think you are. And you will be a continent away!"

"But what rights do women have around here? Look at the girls today. Take prom for example. All they are doing is shining themselves up like glorified dolls and will parade around tonight for what? To compete to see who has the best dress or who starved themselves enough that they can look like a clothes hanger with legs? I don't know where I fit into it all." Cecelia's anger was palpable.

"Well, you still have to go. We have the dress." Elspeth knew she sounded lame against her daughter's arguments. "I'm sorry, Madonna. You really don't need to hear all this."

"Don't worry about me. People may think that nuns don't see this side of things, but we do. Nuns are people too." She motioned for Elspeth to sit on the bed. "I am glad that Cecelia has been asking questions. She's got me thinking too, about my choices in life, or my lack of choices. They might have been the right ones for me, or maybe the only ones I had. I'm trying to clarify my thoughts. Would I do it the same way again? I don't know."

Madonna reached to her neck to caress the cross that hung there. Here she was, at the end of her life, and now she had to face the questions that she should have thought about decades ago. She didn't want to lose her faith, not now. Not now when she needed it the most. "Cecelia, I'm an old lady but I do know this. That if I had the chance to dress in a pretty dress and spend some time with my friends when I could move and dance and twirl around, I would. I would do it in a heartbeat."

Chapter 8

Shelter

Develop enough courage to stand up for yourself, and then stand up for someone else.

– Maya Angelou

Cecelia looked down at the dress, which had cost them all of fifteen dollars, and smiled. She had been posing for pictures for hours now, beside girls whose dresses cost ten times that, twenty times that, and she knew that she looked as good or better than most of them. She still enjoyed shocking them every time another girl or mother asked where she had found the perfect dress for her, but the word had gotten around now so the question had petered away.

Christie Ann's mother had put out a spread for the girls to nibble on. No one wanted to get anything on the dress, you know, but they had to eat something or they'd be in rough shape sooner than later. There was a selection of colourful cans in a bowl of ice, and Cecelia had to select carefully to get a carbonated water drink rather than a syrupy alcoholic tin that would taste like Kool-Aid with a kick. Some of the girls were guzzling them pretty fast though, and Cecelia wondered if there would be puke covering the front of some girls' dresses before the Grand March even started.

The sun was giving a soft, yellow glow to the evening and she stopped and admired the view from the deck, out over the water. All the parents had chipped in and hired a local professional photographer, even her folks, so there wasn't a barrage of cameras coming at them, just this dark-haired, crop-topped guy with a goatee floating around and coming at them from strange angles. Cecelia was surprised at how quickly they all became so comfortable with him snapping pictures constantly.

"Great dress," he had told her when it was her turn for personals.

"Thanks."

"Good hair too. Who did it?" He was snapping away as she was supposed to be looking out at the horizon.

She turned to look at him. "Me. In about five minutes."

He smiled and snapped a couple more photos. "Those should be good. You were easy." His glance showed that he hoped she was easy in more ways than one.

"Thanks. Who do you want next?" was her quick reply and then she went to find Sarah and told her to go see the creep.

She knew this must be what people feel like on the red carpet at the Oscars after she had gone through the Grand March. The flashes from the parents' cameras were constant and the gym was packed beyond any fire safety limit. This was the biggest social occasion of the year and parents, grandparents, neighbours, and friends had vied for the tickets to be in the auditorium. The heat was sweltering, and some menopausal women looked like they were coated in grease. Kids were seated on the floor on both ends of the gym, which was close to the bathrooms, the starting points for the grads to enter from, so Cecelia had to walk carefully over outstretched legs and she was once again glad that she was not in four-inch heels like so many of the girls.

Nathan was a good match, height wise, she'd give the girls in the class points for organizing that, until she realized that no one wanted to march with him. Not if they were going to be in four-inch heels. As she walked, she practically nodded her head as that hit her. He was dark and good-looking, but, yes, he was short.

Hence, the reason she got matched with him. Perfect sense.

"You looked amazing, Cece," her mother had whispered in her ear as they did the father-daughter dance.

"Thanks, Mom. It was a bit of a struggle, wasn't it, but getting this dress today was the icing on the cake for me. Local and used!"

"Are you sad about your dad not being here? Dancing with me?"

"Nooo, not at all. It's all good. I would have felt terrible thinking of him missing Gran's birthday to do one dance with me."

"Well, I was scoffing at the whole Grand March idea, but you all did look wonderful out there. It's nice to see everyone cleaned up, making an effort."

"I like my effort best that only cost max a hundred dollars between shoes and earrings. I can't imagine what the rest put out." Cecelia looked around at the range of colours, between the dresses and the makeup and the jewellery. "Can you imagine how much their weddings will be?"

"Oh, Cece. Just enjoy the evening, can't you? You didn't do any of those things and you are beautiful. Let yourself be young and a kid. For tonight?" Elspeth sighed. "You are only young once. Look, even Madonna said she'd like to dance. There's nothing wrong with enjoying what you have, where you are in life. You should live in the moment, not be so negative."

They both felt themselves tense and they finished the dance in silence.

Nathan's parents came over and insisted that they get a slew of pictures together. Amanda came too and then it seemed like Elspeth and Cecelia were standing in a bubble, mayhem all around them. Friends from grade primary, who had passed the thirteen years together, all dressed up in their finery, adults now. High school graduates. Many already had a good tilt on, especially the boys, though several of the girls were approaching the crying jag stage as well, hanging on each other's shoulders.

"So you'll call me when you want to be picked up?" Elspeth asked as it became so awkward she realized she had to get out of there.

"Yes. I'll call." Cecelia looked tense. Her eyes searched the crowd for Amanda. She needed a safe spot to go.

Elspeth looked at her daughter and knew that she was out of her element. She was doing this because she had to. It was expected of her, but she was like a girl going to battle, not to a celebration. She wished it were her going out, not that she wanted to be young again. God forbid! But because she felt that she would have enjoyed the evening, the dresses, the drinks, the stories. Cecelia didn't want any of it and she was going to be cranky the whole time.

"Okay then. I guess I'll head out. Call me. As soon as you want me to come, call me." Elspeth put a hand on Cecelia's shoulder, the bones sticking out, barely touching the dress strap, only a flash of colour over the girl's slender body. She couldn't help but feel how fragile her daughter was, and a second of fear passed through her as she thought of all the prom stories and rape stories and pregnancy stories. It was like they flicked through her mind in a parental nightmare before she calmed them. She wanted Cecelia to have fun ... but fun seemed scary all of a sudden.

"Yes, Mom. I will call you." But this time, even Cecelia could not conceal the panic in her voice and she looked at her mother with the threat of tears not far from the surface. "I don't think I'll stay long at the party. The bus is supposed to come for us here at 12:30, but look, Adele and Cassidy are already out of their dresses!" They both looked over at the two girls now wearing skinny jeans, their dresses a flash of colour slung over their shoulders, holding on to their boyfriends' hands and heading out the back doors of the gym. "Oh, my God, they paid a thousand bucks each for those dresses, Mom, and they aren't even going to stay for the dance!"

Amanda arrived over for a picture. "Hey, Cecelia, come on over with my folks. They want to take our picture. You want to come, Ms. MacKay. Elspeth?" she added awkwardly.

People were never sure what to call her, it seemed. She had kept her maiden name and most people found Elspeth kind of cumbersome. Elspeth rather liked the confusion and there was a part of her that watched how people dealt with it. "No, Amanda. I will leave you girls to your night. Have fun ... but not too much fun."

Amanda laughed while Cecelia glared at her mother. Elspeth was glad to get out of the school into the warm June night. She was once again wishing that Andrew had been here, so she wouldn't have had to deal with all that alone. He'd have been able to see the humour in the situation, while she, like Cecelia, could only see the horror.

* * * * *

It was one-thirty in the morning, and Amanda had finally given up and allowed Cecelia to call her mother. She had also been able to convince Cecelia that a few beers were absolutely needed to really enjoy the event, and Cecelia had gone along with that. The party tent was in the back yard of a house in Judique, and it would take her mother about half an hour to find the place, so Cecelia decided to drink one more of the six-pack she had brought and gave the rest to Amanda.

"See. Prom wasn't that bad," Amanda said, slumping down lower in the folding white plastic chair that had been rented for the event. She had changed out of her pale purple floor-length float-ing number that she said made her feel like a Disney Princess into a pair of jeans with carefully worn and strategically placed holes in them. She was wearing the Grad sweatshirt with the graduation year and everyone's signatures on them. Cecelia was wearing much the same outfit, but her jeans didn't have any holes. She had watched a David Suzuki documentary where he said those kind of people were the worst environmentally, so she was sure she wore second-hand clothing, ones with no holes.

"I just don't get it though. The whole thing. That beauty makes good people. I mean, look here. The stars out here are as beautiful as the gym was tonight. Did we have to spend all that money on the decorations and the photographer and the nails and the makeup? Couldn't we have just come here and enjoyed the beauty of nature instead?"

"Lighten up, girl. You gotta plan for things like this. It coulda been rainin', or foggy and cold. No, you gotta do it in the gym. And it's only fittin' since it's a school thing, and this was the last school thing we had to do. Well, I guess, other than walk across the stage in a couple of nights. Graduates. We're goddamn graduates, Cecelia. Do you believe that?"

"Yes. We are."

"I can't wait to get to St. FX. It's party central, they say. And us, all of us, we'll be changed. It'll never be the same, you know. All of us together like this, again. We'll be gone here, there, everywhere. Maybe runnin' into each other in the summer. Maybe." Amanda took another sip of her beer. "Life is gonna change."

Cecelia took a sip of her beer too before replying. "I'm going to go to Brazil. That's what I think I'll do. If I don't like it, well, I can quit. Come back."

"Mary's Maidens? You are really gonna do that? Ah, Cecelia, really?" Amanda turned quickly in her seat, some of the beer sloshed down her sweatshirt, and her hand smeared it quickly, drying it up in a half-assed way.

"Why not? I can't see myself at party central, that's for sure." As they were talking, a girl on the dance floor turned her back to her partner and started to twerk, her buttocks grinding into the tall, teenage boy who looked over at his friends with pride and excitement in his eyes. Cecelia was overcome with a feeling of shame for the girl and utmost disgust for the whole situation. "No. I am not cut out to be in party central." With that, she leaned over and gave her friend a hug. "I'm going to wait for Mom at the top of the driveway. Thanks for being such a good friend, Amanda. I hope your future is as bright as you are."

"You can't do it. It's a cult or something. That's what Mom says, 'A cult.' You'll get sucked into that and never come out of it. Someone's sex slave or somethin'!"

"Oh, get real, Amanda. It's a religious thing. Everyone sees everything on the Internet now. It's not a cult. It's just a religious order, like the Protestants or the Baptists, or whatever. A modern religious order, with young people in mind. That's got to be a good thing, I think."

"Oh, I don't know, Cecelia," Amanda said, shaking her head. "I don't think you should trust any of them."

"Don't tell your mom, okay? I haven't told my parents that I've made my mind up. They won't want me to do it."

"Can you blame them? You headin' off to Brazil to God only knows what? You can't do it, Cece. You can't. It's scary." She took another drink. "You'd be givin' up your whole life."

"And aren't you doing the same thing, only you're giving it up to student debt? Making the banks richer and richer? Taking years of university that might not even get you a job?" Cecelia could feel herself getting angry.

"Cece, just remember ... You can always come back home. Right? It could get weird there." Amanda was somber and serious, so unlike her normal self. "If you are going to do this, you can't be stubborn. Run away if you have to."

"I won't have to run away, Amanda. I'll be doing the right thing, for the right reasons. I'm sure of it."

"People who are too sure of anything are scary, Cece. There's always a dark zone, especially today." Amanda had grabbed Cecelia's hand. "And the brighter the light, the darker the shadows."

Cecelia was thinking about what her friend had said as she walked up the driveway from the shore, the stars glowing brightly against the dark night sky. Halfway up the road, Nathan caught up with her.

"Amanda says you're leaving. Already?" He wasn't even panting. It was a long driveway and steep. Cecelia couldn't help but feel somewhat impressed. "The party's just getting started."

"It's not really my thing. Parties."

"You looked really beautiful tonight, Cecelia. I wanted to say that. To tell you that, you know, say that without a million people around." He was nervous, she could tell, not his usual behaviour.

"Well, thanks. You looked good yourself." She wanted out of here. She turned to keep walking.

He walked with her. "I'll keep you company. Until your mom comes. That okay?"

She looked around at the dark woods. She nodded. Company would be good.

"You don't like boys, or what?" he asked, as if he was doing a survey or something. "I mean, it's okay, either way. Just want to know, that's all."

She looked at him with her eyebrows pinched together. How was she supposed to respond? "Yeah, I like boys, I guess. Theresa at L'Arche thinks Patrick Swayze is very handsome but I told her I was more of a Tom Hanks kind of girl."

He stepped back and looked at her. "I could see that. Are you sure you want to leave? We could do a little dancing. Walk down to the shore." He shifted in a bit and seemed prepared to make a move.

Cecelia felt her head bend backwards, her body following in retreat. This was more of the Nathan that she had expected. "I don't think so. Mom should be here any second."

"I think you're cool, Cecelia. Not like the other girls. I mean, I'm not going to be stupid or anything here. The year went by so fast with hockey, you know, and I work too. I meant to talk to you more, but it was September and then it was May. You know?" He seemed genuinely sad about it.

"Yes, the year went by quickly."

"Did it ever! I feel like I want to do it all over again, b'cause I really didn't get enough done. Not what I wanted to do, and now it's over. Life is going to really start. And then, when it starts, it's going to be over too, and we'll be old."

Cecelia was struck by the image of Madonna that came to her mind, lying in the hospital bed. The car lights of her mom's Subaru were clearly visible coming down the dirt road. She looked over at Nathan and leaned in for a quick kiss. Surprised, he did the same. "Thanks, Nathan. For keeping me company."

"Any time, Cecelia," he responded, waving slightly to Elspeth as Cecelia got into the car. Nathan tapped the roof twice and waved goodbye and she smiled at him. Then the darkness of the night descended on him once again as they drove away.

Cecelia wasn't sure if she had felt a pang of relief or regret. She looked over at her mother, who had a sly smile on her face. "Oh, Mom. Get a life. He was just keeping me company."

Chapter 9

Possibility

What a wonderful thought it is that some of the best days of our lives haven't even happened yet.

– Anne Frank

Elspeth spent the day after prom deep in thought as she drove to Halifax to pick Andrew up at the airport. He had called before he left his mother's home and the flight was on time. She had done the four-hour drive often enough that she knew every turn by heart. The drone of CBC talk radio filled the car, but her mind was racing between so many things that she was having a hard time concentrating on anything. She finally turned it off to give her own head noise full rein.

She felt excited about helping out Madonna, and thrilled to have a real life mystery to solve. She was so used to piecing together families from ships' logs from the 1800s that she was anxious to get on with this more modern quest. However, stirred in to the mind pot was the feeling that Cecelia should be thinking more about her future and less about Madonna, and Brazil, and the things in the world that were beyond her control. She had been pleased to see a boy waiting with her at the end of the road when she picked her up, but Cecelia hadn't wanted to discuss it and Elspeth didn't have the courage to pick a fight at that hour in the morning. Overall, she couldn't fight the feeling of dread she had, as if she was watching a movie and the music was getting weird and something was going to jump out at her very soon.

She waited down at the Tim's close to the airport until Andrew sent a message that he was at the Departures door so she could simply swing in and pick him up. She leaned over in the seat and they kissed in a haphazard, hurried manner as cars and vans pulled up and around them. *"An robh turas-adhair math agad?"*

"Not bad. Had a few red wine, watched a couple of horrible movies, and what do you know? I have you by my side again. *Mo bhean mhiorbhaileach! Bha mi gad ionndrainn!"* He reached out and stroked her thigh, which made her smile. He looked tired, and he was beginning to show his age a bit, but his gray hair was still dark and his eyes were young, full of fun and energy. "How was the prom?"

"I didn't get much out of her when I picked her up. Just that it was pretty much what she expected. She looked beautiful. We finally found the dress at the last minute. You'll never guess where." He shook his head and she knew he'd never guess. "The L'Arche store over in Iron Mines. Fifteen dollars and it was absolutely perfect. You can look at my pictures on the phone."

Andrew picked up the phone, punched in her code since they both used the same one, and scrolled through the photos. "It's all about the dress, or so they tell me. Oh, dear. She looks spectacular. Our little girl is something else, isn't she? And thrifty. I like that in a girl, especially my girl. She looks better than most of those girls in the pastel, puffy pillowcase look, that's for sure." He had been swiping through the pictures. Oh, that's a nice one," he said, angling the phone back towards Elspeth.

"I can't see anything, but I'll take your word for it." Elspeth could feel herself relax now that Andrew was with her. She had always felt that together they could conquer the world, and maybe it was because they had the same interests, were established in themselves when they got together, and were basically such good friends before they married that she felt this way, but she also knew well enough that she was lucky to feel this way at all. "How was your mom's party?"

"Oh, as good as you can get when you turn ninety-five. Mostly ancient old people looking frail, but there's some solid stock there, in that old village of Portree. Dougall MacAskill was at the party and he sang an old Gaelic song, all twenty verses of it, and he didn't miss a single word. Not one single word, and him, ninety-nine years old. I hope I'll be that good when I'm his age."

"That's what we all wish, my darling." Elspeth reached over and patted his hand. "I missed you. I felt like I really needed you this past month and for a time, I was really begrudging your mother. But now you're home and you can convince Cecelia that running off to a convent in Brazil is a really bad idea and that studying in university is, of course, a great idea for a young person with her talents." She looked over at her husband. "I've had no luck in that department, so it's going to have to be you. She doesn't want to hear from me on the subject anymore."

"She's still on that kick?"

"Afraid so, and she seems to be looking at everything that's happening in the world as another reason to go there, whether it be teen drinking, the environment, the price of dresses. I was up against it, let me tell you. Hoping she could not be so serious and just be young for the night. Even Madonna told her to go to the dance and have a good time."

"Madonna?" Andrew looked at Elspeth questioningly and then his left eye half winked in a concentrated piecing together of information. "Oh, the nun. The one in the hospital."

"Yes. Her. There's something about her, Andrew. I can see why Cecelia is drawn to her, but I don't want to have her saying that the convent was the best thing in her life or something and have our little girl go so far away from us. She spent all day in the hospital with her yesterday."

"Before the prom?"

"Yes. All day. I felt like I wanted to eavesdrop or something. Hear what they are talking about."

"Could you talk to the lady, you know, about what you are afraid of?"

"I don't want to insult her." Elspeth thought quietly for a few minutes. "Maybe. I did tell her that I'd do some research on her family for her. She seems to have lost track of them and after the heart attack, she's feeling that she should have some names or something. I bet she's thinking about her obituary if nothing else."

"Are you sure you want to go dredging up what could possibly be dirt in her past? Sometimes families have grown apart for a reason. It's not like something is written on paper, in a book. When people are still alive, it can get very messy," Andrew said, his hand coming to cover a yawn. "Don't know if I'd get involved."

Elspeth could see his point and took a few minutes to reply. "Well, I don't know. I said I'd do it and now Cecelia is pleased that I'm helping her out, and anything that will please Cecelia right now is my main concern. I feel like there's nothing I can do right around her."

Elspeth looked over and realized that Andrew's head had tilted back and his mouth had fallen open while she was thinking. She turned down the radio and hoped he'd get some rest before they got home so that they could have a nice dinner together before he crashed for the night. Jet lag was hitting him harder every year now, which was why she was always the one driving after a flight.

She thought how quickly a man Andrew's age could be gone and watched as closely as she could while keeping her eyes on the road for the rise and fall of his chest to show he was breathing. Then he started snoring and she relaxed. She didn't have a lot of experience with death, except her parents'. No aunts, no uncles, no cousins. It was a rare situation for a Cape Bretoner, but her parents were the youngest in their families and the rest had gone away and never returned. Died away, a priest, two nuns, and the rest of them with no children who survived. She couldn't help going back there, to the hospital, in her mind, sitting by them. Those last conversations. She looked at herself in the mirror as she checked the traffic behind her. She hadn't thought about that in years. She looked over again at Andrew and thought about how she had never talked to him much about it either, and now, well, it would be strange to try to analyze their last conversations. She supposed Madonna was in the same boat. Still waters running deep and undisturbed, but what happens when you stir them up, those still waters?

She shook her head, again looking over at Andrew who was now beginning to drool a bit. She knew he would not like that look so tilted his head without taking her eyes off the road. She remembered so clearly the day she had told him that they were going to have a baby.

"Andrew. Have a seat." Elspeth had cleared off the chair at the kitchen. Chairs, tables, counters. They all seemed to get cluttered up with papers and books between the both of them. Neither one wanted to blame the other because they couldn't be certain that they hadn't had them out for their own purposes. They had been so busy between Elspeth's marking and Andrew's research that housekeeping had been a second thought, even a tenth thought, for the past month or so.

"What? Did I do something? I want to apologize in advance if I did, because I really didn't mean it, and I'll never do it again. I promise." He put his hand over his heart as a pledge, his bulky knuckles seeming extra large in his narrow fingers.

"No. It's something we both did. And didn't do." Elspeth couldn't help but smile, but the panic in her heart stripped it from her face. She looked out the window at the foggy evening. She wasn't sure how she was going to get this out.

"Well, if it's that damn Ross guy who thinks I have to cite every source, and wants Chicago instead of MLA, well, he can go straight to hell. I'm sick and tired of jumping through every one of his stupid, mindless hoops trying to get published. I don't know who made him God Almighty at CBU Press, but I am fed up with the whole charade. They've only been at this, what, five, six years, and they don't know the first thing about publishing, if you ask me!" Andrew took a deep breath and looked as his wife. "That's not what this is about?"

"No. It's about us. Our lives." Elspeth could feel tears starting. "Our lives are going to change, Andrew, and I've been really stupid, and I don't know what to tell you."

"Now, Elsie. You're not stupid, not at all. You're the most intelligent, level-headed woman I know, and besides that, you're good in bed, can cook ... Put up with me ..." Elspeth burst out crying. Andrew hastened to add, "Great in bed! Is that better?" He got up and then knelt in front of her. "Elsie, you've got to tell me. You're scaring me now."

"I'm pregnant." She stopped for a minute. "We're pregnant."

"A Dhia Dhia!" Andrew stood up. "Gu h-onarch? You're pregnant? You're going to have a baby. Our baby. Right? I'm the father?"

"Ìos! Of course you're the father, you old fool!" Elspeth wiped the tears from her eyes, anger giving her some clarity. "And that's the problem. We're two old fools! We can't have a baby. We're getting ready to retire. The kid will be pushing us around in wheelchairs. We're too old for this! And the thing is I can't even end the pregnancy because I'm five months along and I didn't even clue in that I was pregnant. Ìos!"

"'Havin' my baby!'" Suddenly, Andrew started singing Paul Anka's classic tune. "'Havin' my baby! What a lovely way of sayin' how much you love me! Havin' my baby.'" He grabbed her arms and pulled her up to waltz with him.

"Look, old man, stop that right now or I'm going to deck you. This is not funny. It's embarrassing."

"Your mother had you when she was old. You'll be fine!" Andrew was thrilled, and the more the idea set in, the happier he was getting. "A baby! I never thought I'd get to be a father. This is amazing!"

"Stop that. This is serious." Elspeth could not share his jubilation. "I sat by my mother and my father and watched them die. I was only in my twenties when my parents died. My twenties! I don't want my child to have to go through that, by himself."

"Oh, come off it, Elspeth. My mother is seventy-six and she's kicking like a young horse, and I've got that longevity on both sides of my family. And your folks weren't that young going either. We can't think that way."

He had calmed her down and they had made it work, at least until now, when their precious baby was turning into an adult. An adult who wanted to be far away from them. That scared her more than pregnancy ever had.

* * * * *

"It's so sad, Mom. She's old, and alone, and I can tell that she would like to see her family again." Cecelia was peeling the cold potatoes for the potato salad on the deck overlooking the river. They had picked up a few lobsters at the wharf and were treating themselves to a nice dinner. "She's a sweet lady. I feel bad for her." Cecelia had biked to Inverness on the Great Trail. It was really the old train track, but it had been torn up and it made for a nice bike ride from Mabou to Inverness, not too steep and no traffic. The trellis bridge just before getting into Inverness was Cecelia's favourite spot to stop, to look down at the river and think about the forces of nature, so powerful, around her.

"There's not much you can do, Cecelia. She's a grown woman. If she had wanted to get in touch with her family, or them with her, it would have happened long before now." Elspeth put the big pot of water on the propane element part of the barbeque to boil. Lobsters were best cooked outside, and eaten outside, and Elspeth was enjoying having both the equipment and the space to do both. The new deck chairs and table, along with the new L-shaped outdoor sofa, still made Elspeth feel like she was house-sitting for someone else.

"She was a missionary in Honduras. Way back. When she was young."

Elspeth's eyes widened, and she realized yet again that Madonna's influence may not be good for her daughter. "Well, that would have been interesting. Latin America back in those days."

"She said she worked mainly with the kids, the young ones. Helping them with their English and reading and such, but she also worked with the families on hygiene and health things sometimes. It wasn't all God stuff, you know." Cecelia knew that she was sounding defensive. "She said that she felt that she had a good life. That she's done things that she's proud of … now that she's older and looks back. That's a good way to be, don't you think?"

Elspeth wished that Andrew would get out of the shower. "Of course that's a good way to think about your life. Of course it is." There was a quiet moment as they both kept setting the table. Finally, Elspeth put the nutcracker they used with the lobsters down with too much force on the glass table and the crack made both of them look twice to see if the table had been damaged. "So, does this mean that you are set? On the Brazil thing?"

"The Brazil thing? You mean Mary's Maidens? You can say those words, Mom. It won't kill you. You won't be stricken down by the Lord, you know." Cecelia's voice was rising.

"I've been doing some research, Cecelia. There's a lot of stuff about them on the Internet, and a lot of it doesn't reassure me. You think it's a thing with women in charge, but it looks like it's some type of a sect, a small part of something bigger, and that looks like every other Catholic-related men-dominated ..."

Cecelia put a hand up and stopped her. "Mom, of course you are going to look for the negative, and if you want to find the negative on the Internet, you can find it. Guaranteed. But there's also a lot of good articles there too. About how they are celibate and work with the youth of the world. And how they strive to bring beauty to the world. Not through makeup and artificial things, but through art, music, ideas that will save the world."

"They are under investigation all over the place." Elspeth looked up to see Andrew finally coming out on the deck. "Andrew, talk to her. Tell her not to just trust people blindly. She needs to know more before jumping into something."

Cecelia looked over at her parents. "You two don't know what it's like now. The world is in a bad place, and environmentally David Suzuki has said that we have to start thinking about human extinction. Human extinction! Don't you know that the people of the world are going to need to come together, somehow, some way, to face what's ahead? I want to be with a group of people who are trying to live simply, to give to the communities they live in, not just take, take, take!" Cecelia's eyes were welling up with tears.

"That sounds commendable, Cece. It really does, but we don't want you to go so far away. Okay, my girls, we're not going to settle this tonight and I'm barely in the door from two months away. I want to relax, have a glass of wine, some lobsters, and enjoy being with you two. Do you think we can do that?"

"But, Andrew, we need to discuss these things," Elspeth said, exasperated. She'd been waiting so long for him to be home, she wanted him to weigh right in.

"Yes, my dear. I know. We do. We have to talk about them, but I've been discussing the best places to get adult nappies and finding people's dentures since they all seem to take them out to eat at Mam's place. Must be something to do with her cooking, and the bloody dog had a habit of sneaking them off the table and hiding them, and, well," he paused, "this evening, I want to drink too much wine and enjoy my beautiful women and my beautiful home, if you don't mind."

Elspeth sighed and looked at her smiling daughter. She could wait, she thought. She could wait. "I think that dog just does it for laughs."

"I know he does. I darn well know he does." Andrew's laugh broke the tension, barking a blast that the neighbours would hear and know that he was home. Before long, there would be a few at the door and the evening would really get started.

Chapter 10

Discovery

The best way to find yourself is to lose yourself in the service of others.
— Mahatma Gandhi

The next morning, Cecelia and Elspeth were once more in Madonna's room. She was getting out and since Cecelia had insisted, she had told the Sisters at the Convent that she could get her own ride home. She had all her belongings in a Co-op bag at the end of the bed when they came in.

"I have to get the final word, if you don't mind waiting, before I can head out," she said. "The doctor was in this morning and said I have to be careful, and of course they gave me a prescription for more medication to take and I'll have to do a stress test or something in Sydney in a week or two, but I can get out of here today."

"That's good. No one rests that well in a hospital," Elspeth said as she sat in the chair. "I'm going to head to Sydney tomorrow, after graduation tonight, to start digging a bit for your family. Did anything else come back, Madonna, that you think would be helpful?"

The old lady looked away, realizing that she couldn't really distinguish any longer between the bad dreams and bad memories that had been flooding her head for some time now. She didn't want to say that out loud. She suddenly felt a wave of panic come over her. She had to stop Elspeth from doing any research. She didn't want to know. She'd be better off not knowing. "You don't have to do that, dear. Really. There's no need. An old nun like me doesn't really need to have those connections. I have my Sisters and the Lord. Those are the only roots I need to carry me to where I'm going."

Elspeth was surprised. "It's no problem. Honestly."

"She likes this kind of stuff, Madonna. Tell her about Honduras, and your time there. I was trying to get it across to her yesterday, about how cool I thought that was, but it wasn't the same as you telling me about it."

"Why did you end up in Honduras?" Elspeth was genuinely curious about that. Not many people had gone that far, especially at that time.

"I'm not quite sure myself, Elspeth. I went down with a contingent from Quebec. We had the nicest white habit, not so much black, probably because of the heat of the sun, so I thought we looked friendlier. And they were shorter, you could see our calves, you know. Wouldn't that have been scandalous around here? But it was so hot that I was pretty glad to have the shorter skirt. Didn't want us to smother, I suppose. It was a nice change for me, and the weather was lovely. There were such beautiful trees and flowers, and the birds. It was a paradise of sorts coming from a convent in Halifax."

"Cecelia seems quite drawn to missionary life," Elspeth said, partly choking out the last words. "What do you think of that?"

"Mom!"

"Cecelia, why don't you go and see if the doctor is around or get Madonna a drink of water." She passed her daughter a glass. "Just give us a minute. Okay?"

Cecelia wasn't pleased, but could tell that her mother was going to ask some questions whether she was in the room or not. She chose not to be in the room and took the glass.

Elspeth took a deep breath. "Sister Madonna. Madonna. I know you've never been a mother, but you must see why I feel so worried about her. I mean, the Church has been rife with abuse and scandals, and the world is full of con artists. What I see online does not make me feel any better. In your life, and your time in service, did you see a lot of that?"

Madonna's eyes glazed over and glistened, and Elspeth wondered if she had the beginnings of cataracts. The old lady blinked a few times and swallowed before speaking. "My faith and my belief in my Lord Jesus is my greatest possession, my dear Elspeth. Without it, I am nothing. I would be an empty vessel. Void. With no meaning. I would have nothing." Cecelia came back in the room with a glass of water and placed it on the table. "I enjoyed my life, and the women who I lived with, worked with, every day. It was a good life for me, Elspeth." Madonna stopped. "But when I think back, I don't remember clearly or I'm just old and confused, but I can't remember deciding to join the Order. You know, when I actually decided, having the conversation with myself or my family. I was just there, in the convent when my memory feels clear." She sat quietly, her short legs dangling over the side of the bed. "Choices. Those are things I never remember having. And the only choice I am left with now is to keep the faith, to keep my Lord Saviour in my mind's eye, to believe He is watching over me and will welcome me home when the time is right."

The doctor came in at that time to give Madonna a few words of advice prior to going home. Elspeth looked over at Cecelia and made up her mind that she was going to do research on Madonna whether she wanted her to or not.

* * * * *

"I can't believe you got me into this and now you're not going to even come with me to Sydney." Elspeth picked up the summer dress Cecelia had worn the night before from the floor of her bedroom, finding the prom dress underneath it. She found hangers in the closet, and hung them up, glad again that she hadn't paid a lot of money for them. Graduation had been a subdued affair after the mayhem of the Grand March and prom. Everyone had been on their best behaviour and although Cecelia had received a few community awards and placed in the top three in English, History, and Global Studies, she didn't receive any scholarships, mainly because she hadn't applied for any. Elspeth was feeling like one of those parents whose children become addicted to a drug, and she didn't know how to get through to her. She was hoping that a day together doing something for Madonna would be good for them.

"You'll be much faster without me, Mom. I'd only slow you down, and besides, I'm not going to get up at the crack of dawn to do it." Cecelia rolled over. "Go without me. I'll water the garden for you."

Elspeth left a goodbye note for Andrew, who had been up half the night unable to sleep, and then headed to Sydney, and for the whole hour and a half drive, while CBC radio talked about the latest political mess, her mind was racing thinking about where she could find what she needed the fastest. Recent information was sometimes harder to locate than the old stuff, with so much censored with the privacy issues today. Up to about the 1920s things were fair game, but now you needed to go through a lot more hoops to find information, and one was always wondering if the rumours about the folks at Ancestry.com, the Mormons, if they were really banking up people's information to put them down as Mormons in some book somewhere. She pulled in to the university, and felt a tinge of jealousy when she saw a car parked in her old spot. She'd have to pay for parking today. She thought there should be some retirement benefit package that included free parking.

Tracey jumped up from her desk for a big hug when Elspeth walked in to the office. "What are you doing here? Couldn't stay away, right? Retirement's too dull?"

Elspeth looked at her office. The door closed, the light off. It felt strange to be there, as if she didn't belong. "No, I'm enjoying myself."

"I bet you are cleaning up a storm." Tracey's arms were crossed, a smug smile on her face.

"Maybe. A bit. Anyway, I have a project."

"A project? Need some help?"

"No. It shouldn't take me too long. I'd love to go through the Catholic records for Dominion, say from 1935 to 1955 or so."

"Still can't do that. We tried to ask the bishop again for that access, but you still have to ask for permission on a case by case basis."

"I guess I'll start with the death notices through Vital Statistics. Maybe then I'll find an obituary, funeral home records."

"That would be a start. If you have to get into the microfiche, it will take the eyes clear out of you."

"It's for a good cause. An old nun that Cecelia has befriended who wants to find out what happened to her family. MacMillans, from Dominion."

"Well, that shouldn't be too hard. Did you try the phone book?"

"Not yet. I don't want to go door to door yet if I can avoid it. She's got her father's name but can't remember her mother's."

"Any siblings?"

"Four brothers and a couple of younger sisters, but she can only remember the boys' names."

"Interesting. Funny she can't remember her mother's name."

"I think there might be some dementia setting in. Mama is Mama to a kid, I suppose." Elspeth could see Tracey looking towards her computer. "Hey, I don't want to keep you. I'm just going to find a space to work and use your decent WiFi. We're having nothing but issues at home. I'll work through it and see what I can find out. If I have to, I'll head to Dominion and go through the cemeteries. I'm going to try to know for sure which one to head to first."

"We have a stupid working lunch thing that I'm supposed to have a report draft together for." Tracey nodded her head over towards Elspeth's old office. "He's got a bee in his bonnet about getting funding to track the occurrence of Dupuytren's Syndrome and track it back through the generations to Scotland."

"Dupuytren's? The Viking Disease? Where the hands go all crooked?"

"Yeah, that's the one."

"That'll be a challenge."

"I know." Tracey looked up at the clock. "I better get back at it. I wish I could skip the lunch meeting, but ..."

"No problem. We'll catch up another time. I'm going to see what I can get done here and then get on the road. It's a busy time at home."

"Oh, yes. Graduation, prom. I didn't even ask ..."

"We'll catch up. Soon." Elspeth waved and went back into the main room of the institute. She found a comfortable spot at a table where she could watch the door, in case there was someone who she hadn't seen for a while. She'd get a little chat in. She looked around the large main room with its old furniture and small displays, many of which she had actually put up. So many memories were here, for so many years, but now she felt foreign, as if she no longer belonged. How quickly the world changed, and she felt the slap of time making her feel old and unwanted all of a sudden.

She gave her head a shake and logged on to her laptop so she could record what she found out on the databases. It was easiest to see the deaths through the Nova Scotia Vital Statistics site, so she decided to start there. She knew that information before 1918 wasn't too difficult to find, but after that, it became more cumbersome. She thought about looking for Gussie's wedding, but without the wife's name, it wouldn't be easy or precise. Elspeth couldn't believe that she had committed to this task, just when she should be home with Cecelia. She should be spending time with her daughter rather than going through these websites. The thought of her heading off to Brazil grabbed her by the throat and she had to swallow hard to keep the panic down.

She'd spend a bit of time on this, but she wasn't going to let it consume her. She'd have to come up with something fast and get back to reality. She knew from long experience how quickly she could fall into a wormhole, searching for a piece of information that was burned in a church fire or was damaged in a basement flood. She checked her phone for the time and set the timer for two hours. If she didn't find something by then, she had to pull the plug.

She went to the Vital Statistics site and from there went on to the Nova Scotia genealogy site. She typed in Angus MacMillan, which she assumed was Gussie's real name, and clicked off the births and marriages options. If he had died after 1968, then she'd have to look elsewhere. The search came up with various Angus MacMillans but only three who had died in Dominion. One was in the '30s, another in the '40s, so it had to be the one who died in 1959. God, that would have left those little girls without a father or a mother at a very young age. Elspeth felt a wave of sadness pass over her and she could feel a flush mounting in her body, a wave of heat starting deep in her back, spreading. Damn menopause, she thought as she fought the tears coming.

Looking through Gussie's death certificate details, she came upon his wife's name. Hughena. With that, she was able to go back and find her death. She found her in 1951. Drowning, it said. Elspeth sat back in her chair, trying to picture this mother of seven drowning. Her brows furrowed and she checked again to make sure the cause of death. She pictured Gussie, his young wife dead, and all those children. Once again, she felt thrilled by the story written by the facts on the page. She had always been able to see the story, the humanity of people's lives, told by their deaths, their births, their marriages. She could so easily picture the rooms where those bodies lay, people sitting beside them, making sure they wouldn't wake up. Would the children have gathered around their mother? Stroked her hair as she lay in her coffin?

She decided to plug in the boys' names. Her eyes widened as

she saw Callum and David's deaths come up. Same date. They must have died together. A fire or maybe a car accident, she wondered, as she dug deeper into the site. Car accident injuries. That's sad too, she thought, and them only in their twenties. She put in Jerome's name, but nothing came up. Finally, she tried Angus. Yes, he was there. Self-inflicted injuries. Suicide. She pushed herself back from the desk, and closed the laptop. The two-hour alarm hadn't gone off yet, but she had had enough.

She walked over to the table in the corner of the room, and smiled at the picture of her old friend Sister St. Margaret of Scotland. She could feel the warmth of the woman coming back to her, thinking of how she would smile at Elspeth's first attempts at research. It was a prim, tight smile, precise like herself, with an intelligence that shone whenever she spoke. Her habit was back off her face so her gray, curly hair softened the curves of her crown. Elspeth couldn't resist picking up the picture and dusting it off with her sleeve. Sister Margaret would have been proud of what she was trying to do for Madonna. It was time to get out of there and she went back to get her laptop and notepad.

She was tired and hungry and decided that she had enough information to go out to the community. The girls, especially without their names, would be so much harder to find. She'd have more luck finding a MacMillan in Dominion and asking them a few questions than spending another chunk of her day torturing herself by going into the microfiche. No doubt, there might be something about the car accident in the newspapers, but it would take time to find it. People's memories were long enough for tragedies like that. Someone would remember something.

Elspeth couldn't help but think of Madonna, so young when her mother died. Hughena had died at only forty-one. That would have made Madonna about thirteen. How sad. She would have become the chief cook and bottle washer after that. Those four older brothers giving her orders. Poor Madonna. The convent would have been an easy choice, she imagined.

She decided to try Canada 411 and see if Jerome MacMillan still had an old-fashioned land line. The search came up with a whole whack of MacMillans, but only one in Dominion. J MacMillan. On Short Street. Well, if the name was correct, it would be easy to find.

Elspeth turned right on Grand Lake Road and then took the quick left towards Gardiner Mines. It had been years since she went down to Dominion. When she and Andrew were first dating, they would spend their evenings walking the length of the beach. She wondered if Madonna's dementia, because that must surely be what the problem was, would get much worse or would her heart be the thing to bring her down. Either way, she'd need an obituary and Elspeth felt a strange sense of contentment in helping provide her with some links to her past.

She turned into a short driveway in front of an old row house, the two sides of the houses falling in to one another. They have the same style in Inverness, though with the new golf course, most of the ones in Inverness look pretty upscale compared to these, she thought. There was no one home when she knocked on the door. It was a nice afternoon, so she decided to go through St. Eugene's cemetery, since it was right around the corner. It didn't take her long to find Angus and Hughena, and the boys, other than Jerome, were all buried close by. No sign of the girls. Hard to track women. They could have married, been buried anywhere, if they had passed away. It was a nice afternoon, the sun warm and the wind fresh. No flies yet. She sat on ground close to Madonna's parents and ate a sandwich she had picked up at Tim Hortons. She wasn't one to give up, so when she finished her sandwich, she tried again at Jerome's. The neighbour on the other side came out of his door.

"You won't find Jerry at home on a Thursday afternoon. Or a Friday either, I'm afraid." The elderly man was probably deaf, speaking loudly so others would do the same.

Elspeth followed his lead as she walked over to his door. "No? But Jerome MacMillan does live here?"

"Oh, yes. Yes, he does. No mistaking that. Do you know him?" The old guy pushed his thick black glasses up on his nose, his hands darkened by nicotine stains into a brownish yellow.

"I know his sister. Madonna."

The old guy looked startled. Shocked. "Well, there's a name I haven't heard in a dog's age. You don't mean one of the younger ones. You mean Madonna?"

"Yes. Madonna. She became a nun. A CND." Elspeth was surprised. Everyone always knew everything in a small place like this. "Did you grow up in Dominion?"

"All my life. Same age as Jerry there. Worked at the mine, got the retirement from Devco, and then worked on livin' ever since. Madonna. A nun. Well, isn't that something? Makes sense in an odd sort of way, I suppose. Are you sure you want to talk to Jerry? He'll have had a few by now and he's not the most pleasant conversationalist at the best of times." He took a cigarette out of an old Macdonald's cigarette package, the green box tattered and dirty.

"I didn't think they made cigarette packing like that anymore," Elspeth observed, surprised to see the colour on the box.

"Ah, the cigarettes don't taste as good coming out of those new-fangled boxes with people's lips and mouths all covered with sores. It's enough to turn ya right off."

"I think that's the point."

"Now, don't be gettin' all preachy with me, sister. I just take 'em out of that godawful wrappin' and I put them in my nice green Macdonald's box and they taste like heaven to me. And I'm too old to go changin' my ways now."

He was getting a bit testy, and Elspeth didn't want to aggravate him. She was a bit worried, and hesitant, but she had come this far so she might as well see it through. "Where would I find Jerome?"

"Oh, he'll be down at the pub. At the Shamrock. You can pretty much see it from here. He can walk, so he doesn't even have to pay for a cab." He pointed through the fresh green leaves of the short trees. "It's on the next street over. It's not much to look at, but we like it."

"Well, thanks for the information. Thanks. I'm Elspeth MacKay ... and your name is?"

He seemed to hesitate. "You're not from the press, are ya? I don't want my name splashed all over the place."

"No." She shook her head. He seemed a bit paranoid, she thought. "Nope. Not me. Just helping Madonna out a bit."

"I always liked Madonna. Nice girl. Quiet." He took a drag from his smoke and exhaled. "Elvin. My name's Elvin."

No last name. Interesting. "Well, thanks, Elvin. I appreciate your help." He nodded and turned to go back in his house. "There were other sisters, weren't there, Elvin? Younger ones?"

Elvin turned around, his face visibly angered by the question. "That's Jerry's family you're diggin' up dirt on, I can tell. Ya got questions, you ask Jerry. I'll not let him hear that you got anythin' from me." With that, he strode quickly around the corner.

Elspeth went back to her car. She thought she better drive in case things got heated at the Shamrock, if Elvin was any indication of what to expect from Jerome, and she needed a quick exit.

There were only a handful of people in the bar, and though she knew that smoking was prohibited in bars these days, she could smell a definite hint of cigarette smoke in the air. It was dark, and the panelling hadn't been changed since the '70s when they put it up. Maybe the cigarette smoke was still off-gassing after so many years. She went up to the bar.

"Could I have a Guinness?" she asked.

"Not enough of a market around here for Guinness, I'm afraid, miss. Just the basics. Oland's, Schooner. Keith's, of course ...," the blonde woman said behind the bar. She had the throaty voice of a smoker, and Elspeth wondered if she was the cause of the smoke smell. She'd probably stand by the back door behind the bar and smoke, pretending that she was blowing it out into the parking lot but all the time knowing it was really coming back inside.

"Keith's would be fine. And I'll buy one for Jerome MacMillan, if you can point him out to me." Elspeth turned to look at the few tables, with a lonely man at each.

"Jerome? He's a little old for you, now isn't he? Not family, are you? One of the girls? His brother Angus was in my father's grade.

He was the youngest of the boys. People said it was a shame, what happened to all of them." The blonde's skin was wrinkled and a dark brown, like the panelling, from many years in a tube top on the back deck, smoking.

Elspeth felt a little rattled after the confrontation with Elvin, and although she could tell the MacMillan family was a popular choice of conversation in the area, at least among themselves, she didn't feel comfortable venturing too deep without talking to Jerome first. "No, just want to talk to him, that's all." Elspeth paid for the beer and picked them up. She steeled herself a bit. "Which one is he?"

"The one at the furthest table. Looking out at the road. He hates television. Don't expect a friendly reception. He can be a contrary Christer when he wants to be." She rested her elbows on the bar. "Just say the word if you need anything else," she said, watching Elspeth walk away with the green cans of Keith's.

Elspeth knew she'd be the talk of the town for the evening.

"Jerome? Jerome MacMillan?" she asked, extending the beer as she spoke. As he took it, she sat in the orange plastic chair across from him.

"Who's asking? If you're from the newspapers, I don't know anything. Nothing. Never did and never will." He pulled the tab before she changed her mind and took the can back.

Again with the press? "The newspapers? Why would the newspapers be after you?" She was surprised, and took a drink of beer.

"Well, who are you then?" he asked her suspiciously.

Jerome reminded Elspeth of an elf, thin and spry, muscles still active on a wiry frame that has crept and crawled through small spaces all his life. His eyes practically vibrated with energy and suspicion when he looked at her. He took a drink, pushed his dead, empty beer can out of the way with a small swipe of the back of his hand. He did a quick sweep of the room with his eyes, self-conscious, feeling that everyone was looking at him and he hated that.

"My name is Elspeth MacKay. I used to work at the university there in Sydney, in the Celtic Studies department, but I retired last year and moved to Mabou."

"Well, good for you. Got the whole life story there, not that I was really askin'." He took another sip of beer. "That's got nothin' to do with me."

"Yeah, I suppose. Anyway, I'm doing some research for a friend. Well, more of a friend of my daughter's than mine. I only met her recently, but she's ill and she'd like some answers, I suppose, so I came down this way to see what I could find out for her."

"Are you going somewhere with this, because you are boring me to tears, to be honest. Don't need company, yours or anyone else's." Jerome looked over at the other tables of single men. They'd be thinking he was finally going to get some, at his age. Frig off the whole lot of you, he thought, but he knew not to say it out loud. He'd been thrown out too many times for picking fights.

"Well, I believe she's your sister. Madonna."

Jerome pushed his chair back. "That's enough. That's enough of that." He waved her off. "I don't want to hear any more. She ruined our lives, every goddamned one of us. I don't want to hear a word about her."

Everyone was openly looking at them now, and listening too. The blonde even picked up the remote from behind the bar and turned down the TV so she could hear them better.

"She's an old lady. A nun. And she's sick."

Jerome stood up and turned to leave. Elspeth stood up too, and since she was only slightly taller than him, she could look him in the eyes easily. His were wild, lost looking, like Madonna's had been, but with anger.

"Don't goddamn come near me. You hear? I don't know a thing about her. And I don't want to know a thing about her either." He stormed out of the bar, banging the door behind him.

Elspeth sat and drank her beer, confused about why anyone would be upset with having a nun as a sister. They were in every family in the day. A nun and a priest. Every Catholic mother's dream. She hadn't expected to orchestrate a warm family reunion, but she hadn't expected this. The blonde came from behind the bar and sat with her.

"You okay?" She leaned towards her. "Jerome's got an awful temper. Been in more than one fight in this room, let me tell ya."

Elspeth felt a little shaken, but the beer was helping to calm her nerves. "What's your name?" she asked the woman.

"Ramona."

"I'm Elspeth."

"Nice to meet you, Elspeth." She wiped the table where Jerome had spilt his beer. "Welcome to Dominion. Not like Jerome to leave a half-full beer on the table, let me tell ya."

They both laughed. "He's always like that?" Elspeth asked.

"Pretty much. Born angry, maybe. The whole crew of them. Did I hear you say Madonna? She was the older sister, the one who dropped out? Well, the first one to drop out of Dominion, and disappear. By the end of it, the MacMillan girls were an extinct breed in this town."

"She's a nun. She lives in the convent in Mabou, close to my house."

"You imagine! One of the MacMillans, a nun! Well, that's one for the books, that is." Ramona got up. "Want another one?"

"No. I should be going. I've got a long drive home." Suddenly she felt exhausted. Doing research had always given her a thrill, but it wasn't the same, looking someone in the eye and seeing the pain there, the hurt. Maybe the past was best left alone, until all the skeletons were safe to be uncovered. She felt like a gossip, an intruder, poking her nose into this family's dirty secrets.

"Jerome's neighbour there, Elvin Cummings. He's about Jerome's age. He might know more than me, if you dare go close to Short Street."

"I met him. He, um, he thought it best if I get information straight from Jerome."

Ramona nodded. "I believe that. If Jerome hears that you've been talking about his family, in any way, shape, or form, he takes it in the nose."

"I just thought it would be pretty simple, even getting the younger girls' names. I thought it would be simple."

Ramona looked around at the tables, all filled with men listening to their conversation. "I think Elvin is right. It's not my place either to be dishin' out the dirt on Jerome. He's not a bad guy, not deep down."

"I think it'll have to be another day. I've had enough for now." Elspeth stood and pushed in her chair. She felt shaky, vulnerable in this dark place. "Probably more than enough for one day." She wished it wasn't such a long drive back to Andrew.

Chapter 11

Shadows

Be comforted; the world is very old,
And generations pass, as they have passed,
A troop of shadows moving with the sun;

           – Henry Wadsworth Longfellow

"So, what did you find out, Mom?" Cecelia asked as soon as her mother came in the door, grabbing the bag of groceries from her and putting it on the island. She started to put the vegetables in the fridge and the fruit in the red Mexican three-legged bowl they kept on the counter.

"I don't know. Not much. I even talked to her brother. I think I need a glass of wine." She reached up and got a wine glass from the cupboard. Andrew was a big fan of pewter, so they had a lovely collection of heavy silver glasses in their house. Elspeth's favourite was a slimmer, more modern design, not quite so medieval as the ones that Andrew liked to drink from. "Let's sit on the deck, Cecelia. I've had enough of Sydney today. It made me realize why I was so eager to come to this side of the island!"

As they walked through the door outside, Cecelia said, "I called the Convent, but they said Madonna was sleeping so I didn't bother her. I'm glad I didn't tell her you had gone to Sydney."

Elspeth looked at her daughter and smiled. "Probably for the best. Her brother Jerome is a tough little guy. I don't know what to make of the whole thing."

Cecelia sat back in the new deck sofa. It was a wicker sectional, but it seemed that every time a person sat on it, the cushions wanted to come apart. "Oh, yeah? Makes being 'only lonelies' like us sound good?"

"Only lonelies?"

"Yeah, single children, no siblings. You get it, Mom." She shrugged her shoulders as if Elspeth was being thick. "Only lonelies."

"Nice. Basically, yes. God, what a piece of work he was. I thought he was going to hit me or something." Elspeth took a drink. "He said something strange. When I first came up to him, it was in this sleazy little bar, basically an old church hall, slash, pub. No atmosphere or decorations, and the first thing he said to me was, 'Are you from the newspapers?' I mean, why would someone from the newspapers want to talk to him? Do you think he's delusional or something?"

"Could be, I suppose. Everyone's got a mental health thing going on these days. We could all be diagnosed with something on a spectrum. The newspapers? Strange. Let me get the laptop. Google him." She crossed her legs, yoga style, and propped the laptop computer, which never seemed too far away from her, effortlessly across her knees. "Jerome MacMillan," she said as she typed. "Nothing. Mother? Father?"

"Hughena and Angus. I have their dates but I don't want to get up right now." Elspeth was tired. It had been an emotional day. She was glad to be sitting there doing something with her daughter, but she really needed to relax, to be honest.

"Nothing. Let me see, Dominion, Cape Breton. Lots of coal stuff, some history stuff between the Italians and the locals. Some nice pictures of the beach."

"It's pretty there. Low, be easy to bike around, and the beach stretches forever. It's nice, as the Sydney area goes, a softer area, without the cliffs of Glace Bay. Your father and I spent a lot of time there, when we were courting." She smiled as Cecelia rolled her eyes. She didn't lift her head up, though, focused on the tasks on the computer. "Nothing, eh?" Elspeth took another sip of wine. "Why the newspapers? I wonder if Madonna would know anything more. I didn't even think of Googling them. I guess that's the first thing your generation would do. Save a lot of time rather than digging through the databases for information."

Cecelia smiled absently at her mother's bland endorsement of her skills. "She doesn't seem to remember much of her childhood. One evening she was trying really hard, Mom, and she wanted to, I could tell, but she couldn't piece it together. Do you think she's losing it?"

"Oh, aren't we all? I don't think so though. I think there might be something there, well, something dark. Abuse, maybe? Family life was pretty tough in those days. That would make sense with a brother like Jerome, physical if not, well, mental anyway. But how do you bring that up to an old lady? *Do* you bring that up to an old lady? A nun, at that?" Elspeth looked at Cecelia, as if she would know the answers.

"There's nothing here that I can find. Would you want to know if you were in her shoes, Mom?"

"I don't know. Yes. Yes, I would." She took another minute to think about it. "I don't think I'd feel like I was being honest with myself if I ignored it. Pretended it didn't happen. I mean, she seems to want to understand her life in some way. But I just don't know if Madonna would feel the same, and want to know. She might be hoping for more of a happy ending than that. I'll walk up and see her tomorrow. Feel her out about it and I'll see how it goes."

* * * * *

Cecelia was starting her summer grant job at the An Drochaid museum on the main drag in Mabou, which was so close she could jump out of bed, brush her teeth, and be there in ten minutes. After she was gone to work, Elspeth sat with a second cup of tea and thought about what she should do. It was a glorious morning. Maybe the best thing was to do nothing. She would be very happy doing nothing today, drinking coffee and sitting on the deck and watching the world go by. That was what retirement was all about, wasn't it?

She had Madonna's parents' names now, and the boys, and that was almost all that Madonna wanted. There was no one to connect with anyway. Not with Jerome's attitude. She'd never let Madonna be subjected to that. She could say that she did the research and they were all gone, which was basically true. No need for her to tell about meeting Jerome.

But there was a part of her that wouldn't let it go, and she had been at the same crossroads a number of times in her professional career when her instincts told her that she should persevere, even if it was a bit awkward and painful, because the story would be worth it. She just couldn't think of this as an academic exercise though. She wasn't delving in to the long dead and buried. She was digging into much recent dirt. Dirt that still carried a lot of sorrow.

She decided to take the bull by the horns and walk up to the Convent. It was ten o'clock and the dew had long dried on the grass of the hill. Elspeth went in the door by the offices and it didn't take long for one of the Sisters to escort her up to Madonna's room. She looked frail in the bed, making only a slight lump in the middle, and she was awake, with her rosary beads in her hands, when Elspeth walked in.

"You look rested, Madonna," she said as she settled in the chair beside the bed.

"Yes, it feels good to be back in my own bed, let me tell you. It gets so noisy in the hospital with someone coming in or going out, checking on us at all hours of the night. I know it's their job, but it makes for an interrupted sleep, that's for sure."

"Graduation went smoothly. We're all glad to have all the prom and graduation events finished. Cecelia got a few awards, here and there, too, which was a nice surprise." Elspeth wasn't sure how much small talk she had in her, but thought a little was in order.

"Oh, I'm glad to hear that. She's such a smart girl. And so kind."

"Yes. She is kind. She could have done better, financially, but she didn't want to apply for any scholarships, and even though she's been accepted to a couple of universities, she says she's not going. Says it's a waste of time." Elspeth could feel her blood pressure going up and knew she'd have to give up on the dream of seeing Cecelia in the fall, excited with her term schedule in front her, making friends and broadening her horizons. That was her dream. It wasn't Cecelia's. She'd have to come to terms with that and not feel like someone had doused her with cold water every time it came up.

"She seems rather set on the Brazil experience. Mary's Maidens, I think she said?"

"Yes. I don't know what to make of it, really. I'm hoping that she'll lose interest if I don't show too much of a reaction." There was a moment of silence. Elspeth shook her head before continuing, "Anyway, we can talk about what her plans are another day. I'm here to say I went to Sydney yesterday, to do some research on your behalf."

Madonna looked at Elspeth and didn't say anything. It was as if she didn't want to hear what was coming. Elspeth waited, not wanting to go too far without a bit of feedback. She wanted to read between the lines and the only clues to this mystery could come from Madonna herself. It took a few minutes for the old lady to respond.

"I feel, well, I feel ... afraid, to tell you the truth. I've got these half memories, and some give me good feelings and some, well, some don't. I feel like my old mind is playing tricks on me, you know, and the past may be best left where it is ... in the past." Madonna's blue eyes were glassy, and there was a little pool of water under them as if the tears had leaked through the weak skin.

Elspeth reached for a tissue and passed it to her. "Your brother Jerome seems to feel the same way."

Madonna's head jerked up, her attention caught. "You met Jerome? My brother Jerome?"

Elspeth immediately knew that she was glad she had mentioned his name. It sounded to her like she had already given Madonna a gift, a link to her childhood. "Yes, he's got quite an attitude, Jerome."

"Oh, he always did, but he was a good big brother to me." She smiled, fond memories coming back. "He'd stick up for me on the playground, and when Callum and David, the big brothers, were picking on me, he'd say, 'Now, Madonna Mary doesn't deserve that, you big lugs.' Angus was too soft for that. He couldn't say anything to put those big guys in their place, but Jerome wasn't afraid of anything. That's what he'd say. 'Madonna Mary doesn't deserve that.'" Her gaze wandered to the window. "Jerome."

Elspeth was a bit taken aback, since Jerome's reaction when hearing his sister's name had been so different from Madonna's response. Could siblings really remember things so differently?

"Does he seem in good health?"

"Yes. He's got a youthful energy to him. Seemed in good shape. Though I think he spends a lot of time at the local pub. That's where I caught up with him. Seemed to be a regular hangout."

"Oh, that's too bad. But not overly surprising. His big brothers set him on that road long ago. Did you find out anything about them?"

Elspeth took a deep breath. "It seemed they all died quite young. None of them made it through the 1960s. Your dad died in 1959. Heart failure, it said."

"That's sad, isn't it? All of those fine boys, gone. And Da. He was a good man. I know he felt bad. The night I had to go. He felt bad, I could tell." Madonna fingered the rosary in her hands and went through a couple of beads, the prayers silently mouthed while she collected herself.

The night she had to go? Elspeth tried to figure out what that meant and knew it was important. Was it when she decided to join the convent? But again, wouldn't they have been happy to have one of their own joining the Order?

"What about the girls? There were two girls after me."

"I can't find any sign of them. It's harder if people move, and girls marry, change their surname, and to tell you the truth, I didn't push too hard. The few people I talked to feel that Jerome's business is Jerome's business. It will take me a bit more time to find them, probably. Gosh, your mother died young. You were only thirteen."

"Yes, I was young. And the girls were really little. I had to stay home after that. No more school for me. My life was full of washing clothes and making meals. Combing hair, the girls had long, beautiful hair. Mine was so dark black, but theirs was beautiful. Spun red gold in my hands." Madonna looked at the rosary beads sliding through her fingers and thought how the sensation was much the same, the hair sliding like silk between her fingers. "I took over Ma's duties at the church and the Glebe House too. Brought some money into the house."

"I couldn't see what your mother died of, Madonna. Do you remember?"

"It was sudden. It wasn't an illness. I'd have remembered her in the house sick, if that was the case, because it would have been me that would have to take care of her. I don't even remember a wake. It was fast. She was there, and then, she was gone." Madonna tried to think back, but it was like a black film was around her mother and her death.

"Do you think it was a heart issue too?"

"I don't know." Madonna's heart rhythm changed and she felt her face blush red.

"You don't look so well, now, Madonna. I think we should stop."

"Pass me one of those pills there, to put under my tongue. They told me to do that any time I felt that something was wrong."

Elspeth opened the bottle and passed her a pill. The old lady put it under her tongue and they both sat there quietly while it dissolved.

"You better rest, Madonna. I'll go and tell the Sisters what happened so they check on you. Okay? I'll go now so you can re-lax." Elspeth felt a guilty feeling that she had brought this on.

"Elspeth. Thank you. For all your time on this." Madonna reached out to grasp Elspeth's hand. Elspeth gave her hand a quick squeeze.

"Oh, don't thank me, Madonna. I'm glad to do it." She patted the old lady's bony legs on her way past the bed and wondered what she should do from here.

* * * * *

At lunch, Cecelia walked up to the Convent to visit Madonna. She was still in her bed, though she had told herself that tomorrow she would have to get up. She was going to get bedsores soon if she didn't move around, or pneumonia or something. She had rested enough, and if she wasn't going to just give up, she'd have to get up.

"I'm old. That's the root of my problem," Madonna had re-plied when Cecelia asked her how she was. "I'm laying here feeling sorry for myself, and I've got to stop that. How was your first day of work?"

"Boring. I had three visitors from Calgary who had long-lost relatives three generations back from the Mabou area and they all seemed rather disappointed when I said I wasn't even from here. Brought up in Sydney. I don't know if I'm the right person for the job or not. I did throw some Gaelic at them, which cheered them up a bit. Pretty strange, just sitting there by myself all day."

"I remember the first time I had to put on a habit. The full habit, not the novice one. I didn't know how to fold and iron and pin to get that pointed house look we all wore, the CND. It was quite a talent and you could tell the girls who just didn't have the knack of it. They'd have to get someone else to put it together for them. I felt like I was wearing a suit of armour, it was so heavy." She ran her hand down her body, remembering the sensation, and her hand went wide over her belly. Her eyes grew huge for a minute, surprised.

"Madonna?" Cecelia could see her crooked hand, suspended in mid-air above her belly. Hanging there. "Are you all right?"

Madonna dropped her hand quickly. "I just had the strangest feeling. I'm not sure what it was. I think it was a memory, but more of a body memory than a mind memory. Does that make any sense?" The old lady looked at Cecelia. "I think I'm going crazy." She shook her head.

Cecelia took a deep breath, watching Madonna, before saying, "Mom told me that she met your brother Jerome yesterday. In Dominion."

"She told me. He was such a good brother." Madonna motioned for Cecelia to help her up. "Help me sit in the chair for a while, Cecelia."

"Oh, yeah? He didn't sound very friendly now, it didn't seem to me. Mom couldn't get much out of him," Cecelia said while helping her to the chair by the window. "She did some research, and has the dates, you know, birth and death dates, for your parents and your other three brothers."

Madonna's face fell. "She told me. Your mother. She was here this morning. It's so sad. They're all dead, the other three."

Cecelia nodded in sympathy, then asked, "So Mom came up?"

"She couldn't find the girls, she said. I'm not even sure about their names." Madonna was tense. Her hands had clasped together, crookedly trying to give each other support.

"No sign of them, Mom says, but she thinks she could do more if she can talk to Jerome again. If you want her to, that is. She said Jerome said a weird thing when she first met him. She said he asked if she was from the newspapers. What do you think that's all about?"

Madonna looked puzzled. "The newspapers? I don't know." She shook her head. "I mean, my brothers were no angels, that's for sure. They were like the rest of them around there, if you ask me, fighting and drinking. That was normal." She sat for a second. "I mean, there were four of them, close in age, so they were a force to be reckoned with."

"Do you remember something?" Cecelia sounded hopeful.

"There's something there, coming back. The boys coming in. Angus had a black eye. I remember that. And Callum's arm was hanging way down. Pa had to push it back in the socket and he hollered bloody murder. And the girls were all crying. Something must have happened. Maybe that was what was in the news?" Madonna looked up at Cecelia, tired from trying to remember.

It had taken a few minutes, and Cecelia was trying to be patient, but she couldn't help looking at the clock on the wall. Bridget was supposed to be dropping by to look at possible plane tickets and she wanted to run home for a quick lunch and they didn't like the museum to have a closed sign up for long.

"I did a quick Google search, Madonna. Nobody in your family shows up in the news. That's for sure. I don't know what to tell you." Cecelia was wondering how she was going to get away.

"Oh, you tried, dear. And your mother. She's such a kind woman."

"Oh, I don't know if my mother is finished yet, Madonna. She's not one to give up that easily. I should be getting going. It's a big day." Cecelia stood up, and went over and bent down in front of Madonna. "Now, you rest, and you try to remember something more and we'll see you, maybe on Sunday. Would you like that?"

"You don't have to do that. Wasting your time on an old woman like me." Madonna smiled though, pleased that she would come back.

"I think you are many things, Miss Madonna, but never a waste of time!" Cecelia leaned over and gave her a little peck on the cheek and was out the door.

Madonna looked out the window and let her mind slip into thoughts about her brothers and that night, with the black eye and the arm hanging down. She could feel her heart rhythm change, but decided to not pop another pill. She was going to see this through.

"They are all talking about her, at the pub," Jerome yelled at his father. "Callum tried to tell them it wasn't true, but look at her, Da! There's something wrong there."

Jerome pulled Madonna by the arm to stand in front of her father. She felt as if she didn't have a stitch of clothing on her back. The boys had burst into the house and got her up, and she knew the girls would be out of their beds, standing at the top of the stairs, listening.

"They are only talking in the pub because the women are talking at home, and that means they are hearing it from their girls. I mean, she doesn't go out anywhere, but she's only a spit of a thing, and now she's a spit of a thing with a big Jesus belly!" Jerome jerked her arm as he pushed her in front of her father.

David growled, "Jerome. Simmer down. You're like a loud Jesus puppy yourself. The neighbours will be getting an earful as well, so calm down. Da, what do you think?"

Da looked at Madonna. "Turn around, girl." Madonna did as she was told. "Ah, she's such a good girl. You all know that. Sit down. Madonna, sit down." He put his head in his hands. "God, give me strength." He took a deep breath.

"So that's what we said, at the pub," Angus piped up. "She's a good girl. Quiet as a mouse. Never causes any harm."

"And that's when that goddamn Alfonso said, 'Well, she must be quiet when you're sticking it into her, in your own house, with your Da downstairs, 'cause she's got a bun in the oven, no mistaking that! Or maybe, it's your Da stickin' it into her ...'"

"And that's when all hell broke loose," Callum offered from the kitchen bench, where he was recovering from Da pushing his shoulder back into place.

Da jumped up. "They said that? They said that? That I'd do ... that? That you'd do that? Any of youse?" Da's fists were out as well.

Angus stopped him at the door. "That won't do any good, Da. It won't."

Da looked back at Madonna. "Maybe she's ill. Maybe she's got a tumour?"

"I don't know. They'll talk, even if it is a tumour. Madonna." Angus sat beside her on the chair. "Madonna. Do you think you might be havin' a ... havin' a baby?"

"Like Ma?"

"Like Ma ... Like Ethel next door, like Thelma down the road, like so many others. Were you with a boy, Madonna?" Angus talked quietly. Everyone else was listening.

"I wasn't with a boy. No." Her eyes shifted. She'd been with God, serving Father. She'd been doing her duty, saying her rosary. She was a vessel of God, Holy Mary Mother of God, please have mercy on me.

"One of the young guys in the neighbourhood, when we're all at work and the girls are at school? Or a salesman, forced his way in the house? Is that it?" Angus was getting riled up. It had to be someone.

"No, honest. No boy. I don't know what you're talking about. I want to go to bed." She stood up, her dress tight across her belly and her breasts. Tears were coming down her face as she walked across the kitchen and opened the door to the stairs. She raced up the narrow stairs, only part of her feet able to perch on each one, and she had the sensation that she'd fall, fall hard, before she reached the top and brushed by the two little heads gathered like chicks at the top.

Chapter 12

Coincidence

Coincidence is God's way of remaining anonymous.

— Théophile Gautier

.

Elspeth looked up from her purse where she'd been fishing out her sunglasses, getting ready to leave. She'd decided to make another trip to Sydney and Cecelia had come in from work, in a rush, but saying that Madonna had remembered something. "What did she say?"

"I brought up your meeting Jerome, and it morphed into this memory she had of her brothers coming home from a fight, or something. I told her that we did a quick search online and couldn't find anything about them, but it definitely seemed like something had happened, and I'd say it happened close to the time she went into the convent."

"Hmm. Interesting." Elspeth stopped for a minute, thinking.

"You sound like Dad." She stroked her own chin in imitation. "Interesting."

"Well, it is. Interesting. I think I may have to call on Jerome one more time. I was just going to talk to the neighbours, find out the basics, but maybe I'll have to tackle that guy again. See if

154 – Brenda MacLennan-Dunphy

he remembers that night." This felt so nice, being friendly, working with Cecelia on something. It was good to feel an ease in the conversation. It was a glimpse of a new relationship evolving.

"It could be nothing. She could just be confused."

"Yes, but I think there's something there that she doesn't want to face. Maybe there's more to her becoming a nun than simply devotion." Elspeth saw her daughter's face cloud over and kicked herself for saying the wrong thing. "I guess I'll have to bite the bullet. I'll start with the neighbour, Elvin. He might be a bit easier to talk to. I should be back for supper, but if not, you and Dad can organize something."

"Or we can head to the Red Shoe for sweet potato fries."

"Yes." Elspeth nodded in agreement. "Or get sweet potato fries." Cecelia laughed and rushed back out the door and back to work.

* * * * *

Elspeth pulled into Elvin Cummings' driveway, but before she had closed her car door, Jerome was outside.

"What are you doing back here?" he hollered from his side of the row house.

"I just have a few more questions. I thought your neighbour might know the story and be a bit more of a conversationalist than you, so I was going to start there." Elspeth leaned back in for her purse and her phone.

"Move your goddamned car out of Elvin's driveway so his grandson can come and get him. He's got a goddamned doctor's appointment in half an hour. Come over here. I'll talk to you, if you're that goddamned nosy." She heard him slam the door as he went back into his house.

Elspeth got back in the car and moved it over to his driveway. "What have you gotten yourself into this time, Elspeth? Is there really any reason for you to be putting yourself through this?" she asked herself aloud as she parked the Subaru. She had been known to go too far from time to time, researching a family story that ended up with skeletons a mile deep. Now she was deep into it, and she was starting to picture the skeletons reaching out for her. Too much meat on their bones to stay buried.

She opened the door Jerome had just slammed and walked through a small porch towards the back of the house. The kitchen floor had such a slant that she had to adjust her walk to make it steadily to the chair at the old Formica table. It felt like the house was falling into a pit, no supports under the middle where the two houses met. A good idea, a double house, but no foundation to support it. The room was clean, a good quantity of bleach products used over the years, by the look of the worn pattern on the table and the chairs.

"What are you back for?" Jerome asked, fidgeting with the pack of cards he had on the table. He shuffled and started dealing himself out a game of solitaire. "I told you, I don't know nothin'."

Elspeth watched him for a minute, trying to gauge the best way to go about this. "I wondered if something Madonna said would bring back some memories. She's ill, and she seems to want to understand her life a bit, I guess, before, ah, before it's over." She paused before adding, "She was pleased to hear that you looked well."

He looked up at her, matching up opposite suit cards. He didn't say anything for a few minutes. "She's dying, is she?"

"I'm no expert, and I haven't asked her, but, I'd say that yes, she could die." She looked over at him, at how dispassionate he was. "It seems to be her heart."

"Couldn't we all? Die? Didn't they all die, except me? Livin' for spite. Won't give any of those bastards the satisfaction of thinking that I ended it because I'm guilty of anything, because I'm not. Never was." He took a drink of tea from a cup dyed brown from use, and glared at her, fury in his eyes.

No Javex used there, Elspeth thought. She sat, keeping her mouth shut, hoping he'd be comfortable to talk, here in his own space, in his own time. She could wait.

"And she doesn't remember how she screwed us all over, every single last one of us with her simple stupidity? She doesn't remember that?" Jerome's voice was rising. "I could have had a woman. I would have had a family, a grandson like Elvin over there, but after her performance, we were all tainted with the same brush. Even the girls."

"I don't think Madonna would have meant to do –"

He interrupted her. "That was the thing! She was the simplest, quietest, little mouse of a girl you'd ever seen. That was the thing! If it had been anyone else, everyone would not have given it a second thought. Every girl, well, pretty much every girl, was caught in the same trap at one time or another, but her not sayin', not sayin' ... that just drove the Old Man to work himself into an early grave, and Callum and David, they just let the drink take them. Angus, well, poor Angus. He was always the softest, you know. Closest in age to Madonna and the girls. He hanged himself in the barn, couldn't deal with the looks and the wonderin'."

Elspeth listened, but he was talking so fast, so agitated, that it was hard to keep the facts from the emotions. Finally, when he finished and took a breath, started back on his game for a minute, she felt safe enough to begin again. "Are you saying that Madonna got pregnant?"

"Yes, she was Jesus pregnant, the whole community seeing. And the only places the girl ever went was home and church, so we got blamed for the goddamned mess." With each of the words, Jerome pounded the table with his cards.

"But no one came forward?" Elspeth asked tentatively.

"Look, you nosy busybody, none of us were involved, but it took ten years and me burying them all before it made any sense, and by that time, what good was it to anyone? The truth? Not one iota of good. Not to me, not to the girls. Not even to Madonna, or, well, not even to Mama." His eyes brimmed over and tears started coming down his face. "And there's no good going back through it, and there's no good talking about it, because it's over and done, and what's done is done."

He kept playing the solitaire, until he had lost. Both of them sat there, silent in their own thoughts.

Elspeth broke the quiet. "Could I make you some more tea, Jerome? I think I need some."

He looked up at her. She could tell that he had never talked about this before and it had been eating him up inside. He tilted his head towards the kettle as a way of agreeing. Elspeth got up and filled it and turned on the stove. She was trying to make some sense of it. She didn't even know what to ask at this point, and he was waiting, waiting for her to ask. If she didn't ask the right thing, he'd clam up.

"You really aren't here from the papers? I guess it's all old news now anyway." Jerome looked over at the calendar. There was a picture of a farm and the year was 1972. He liked the photo so he had kept the calendar on the wall where he could see it, the only picture in the place, some gas station's name, long out of business across the top with their phone number.

Elspeth sat back down, clasping her hands together on her lap to help her not fidget. She could not rush this, she knew that much. "No. I am only here for Madonna. She's having a hard time remembering her childhood. For good reason, from what I'm hearing from you. She does remember you and your brothers coming home from a bar and that you had been in a fight. It must have been important."

Jerome shuffled the cards, keeping his hands busy and his eyes down. "That night. That Madonna mentioned. The fight. I remember that night. The boys and I had been in the pub, and people had begun to notice. I mean, we hadn't noticed, but who really notices their little sister. It was girls in the neighbourhood who were talking about it, had seen her faint at church or something. Started watching her clothes, havin' the time to notice that they were gettin' tighter. We wouldn't have noticed that."

The kettle boiled, so Elspeth put the tea bags in the Pyrex teapot and put it back on the stove on low. She waited, her mind racing. Poor Madonna. No wonder she had blocked out so much.

"Everyone thought one of us was getting around her. One of her own! How disgusting is that? And the thing was, that even though it was staring her in the face, Madonna wouldn't say boo about who had done it. It was like it was a goddamned immaculate conception or something. She'd just say that she was a good girl, she did God's work. God's work, all right. She was so messed up, the poor kid." Jerome took a deep breath. "And she's dying, you say?"

"I don't know. She's not strong, that's for sure. She's back at the Convent now. She's stable." Elspeth opened the fridge, as stark and clean as the rest of the kitchen. "Milk?"

"Yes. Some milk and a bit of sugar." He looked out the window. "Heart. They can do a lot with hearts these days. Da's heart was poor too. Probably a good thing. Got him out of here." Jerome took the offered cup and set it on the table and reached over for a cigarette. He didn't ask if she minded him smoking and it was his house so Elspeth didn't say anything. "She was a good kid. A hard worker. After Mama died, she kept the house runnin', never sayin' a word of complaint. Da never got over it. When she left."

Elspeth paused, the cup halfway to her mouth, and she sat back down at the table. "She left? Your father didn't kick her out?"

"I don't think Da would ever have done that. No. It's just that Father Landon said that he knew of a place, and said that he could help. He took her." Jerome took a sip of his tea. "We should have known then. God, we were so simple. So stupid. So goddamn stupid." His hands clumsily jammed the cards together and he started shuffling with an angry jab, every time he cut into the deck.

"It was him? Father Landon? Who took her from home?" Elspeth felt her heart race. She'd heard that name before. Where had she heard the name before?

"Of course it was. He took her from home. He took her from us. He was the goddamn father, all right. And we should have put two and two together, shouldn't we? She was only here and there, at the church, cleaning for Saturday night and Sunday mass." He swallowed hard and stopped talking. The pounding of the cards on the table taking the brunt of his anger.

"Father Landon. He abused Madonna?"

"I guess that's the word for it nowadays. Abused. Shit. Abused. Used her like a puppet, a goddamn plastic sex toy, that's what she was to him. Until she got pregnant and there was no one to blame it on because God Almighty, if there had been an immaculate conception, it would have been Madonna's. Jesus, why did Mama have to call her Madonna? It's like we were all a joke, a goddamn bad joke, the MacMillans."

"So Madonna got pregnant?"

"Are you slow or something? Of course she was pregnant. Getting big as a barn when he hauled her out of here. That bastard ..." Tears were coming close but Jerome wasn't going to stop. He wasn't looking at Elspeth, concentrating hard on the cards held tightly in his hands. "That bastard screwed her up. And her mother before her." Two tears slipped out, but he didn't wipe them away.

"Are you saying that you think the priest abused your mother as well?" Oh, my God, Elspeth thought. This was the worst. What a mess.

"Chances are pretty goddamned good, now aren't they? Ma was a small slip of a woman too. Like Madonna. And he could screw her, *abuse* her," he said the word long and hard, "all he wanted since she was a married woman. No problem if she got knocked up. I guess it could have been worse. He could have gone for the altar boys, and then it would have been me and my brothers." He slammed the cards on the table. "The power. The power those men had. It's wicked. The whole lot of them should be put behind bars if you ask me."

"And when did this come out?" Elspeth took a sip of her tea, her hand shaking. This was more than she had anticipated, more than Madonna could handle, she was sure.

"About the priest? It was about ten, fifteen years later, like I said. Pa and my brothers were gone. I had tried my best to raise those girls, but what did I know about being a parent? I was only a little runt of a thing myself. Bernadette was smart, always had been. She saw the writing on the wall and took off. Took Faith with her. Then some young girl up Antigonish way came out and actually stood up for herself, and accused the old bastard, and word came our way, and then we finally started to get some goddamn answers to the riddle." Jerome drank his tea, his hand trembling slightly.

"And that's why you wanted to know if I was from the papers?"

"Exactly. It was hushed up pretty tight. It was only the late '60s then and the diocese still had a lot of pull. 'Cause, o' course, once they figured out he'd done it once, they went back through the parishes he'd worked at, and he'd been here a long time, and well, there's one girl, disappeared. People came by, asking questions. I didn't know what they had done with her after she was taken that night. And it was only after that, that I understood why Ma, well, why Ma went swimmin' one night with all those rocks in her pockets." His head came down on his hands and he sat there for a long while, sobs coming through his body. He pulled an old red and white handkerchief from his pocket. Blew his nose, and crumpled it back in his jeans.

Elspeth didn't say anything, just tried to keep breathing and wiping her eyes now and then. Finally, when he had recovered she said, "People commit suicide for a lot of different reasons. Maybe your mother ..." She stopped, unable to continue as she looked into Jerome's face.

"Don't you think I've been through enough? Who do you think you are, analyzing the past, *my* past, as if it was something for you to play with?" He was practically lifting himself out of his seat with his words.

"I have one more question, Jerome. And I'll leave you in peace."

Jerome looked up, seeming tired and worn out. His age settling deep into his eyes.

"When did all of this happen? When was Madonna taken away?" Elspeth held her breath.

"It was the fall of 1953. It was a rough Christmas that year, let me tell you. It was never the same again so I remember it well." Jerome picked up the cards and started shuffling them again.

She sat back in her chair, her teacup landing loudly on the table.

* * * * *

Elspeth didn't even remember the drive home. It was just a blur as she tried to piece together Madonna's story in her mind. She kept going through it, all the hardship and horror for the boys, for her mother, her father, and poor Madonna. She must have clung to the gospel as a way to make sense of it all, some reassurance in repetition, responses, and rituals. She imagined the priest putting ideas in the young girl's head, how she was going to be a vessel for God. Wasn't that what she had said? Did she remember or was she blocking it all out? Should she tell her or ignore it all and let her live in the peace and quiet of the Convent?

No wonder she was shipped off to Honduras. That must have been just when things were unravelling for Father Landon. Father Landon. Elspeth shook her head, wondering if that connection was what she remembered. She should have listened better. She should have been more compassionate, more understanding. Maybe she had been too young to understand. If she had been older, she would have made the connections.

Her parents. So devoted to each other, to her, to their faith, especially to their faith. Pa opening up the church every Sunday, up on the mountain, since they were the closest to it and always had lots of wood. He'd do the shovelling, well into his late seventies, eighties even. The rosary said every evening, without fail, after the supper dishes were done. They'd always only do it with the kerosene lamps on. Said it didn't feel the same with the electric lights on in the parlour. And they always said it in the parlour. Not the kitchen where it was warmer, and would have had some comfort for a little girl, but they said the sacrifice of the cold air would make her appreciate the warmth in the kitchen, which she did, so she didn't argue.

And she thought back to that fateful day, leaving for university, and what they said and didn't say that day. She went through it all, looking for clues, dying to get home to close herself in the library with the computer to look up more information on Father Landon.

When she got home, Cecelia was watching her father make supper. Andrew was cutting their roast beef sandwiches in half on the larch wood cutting board on the counter. "Want one?" he asked.

"No sweet potato fries?"

Cecelia shook her head. "Lineups too big."

"Sure. I didn't stop to eat." He gave her the one he had been making and started another one for himself.

"Any visitors at the museum today?" Elspeth asked between bites.

"Ah, it's still early in the season, and it's a sunny day. I had a couple of people walk down from the Shoe who were waiting for a table, but otherwise it's dead. There's a Gaelic session tomorrow afternoon so that should bring a few folks in. What did you find out in Sydney?"

Elspeth felt a strong reluctance to say anything. She was still trying to get through it herself. "I had another chat with Jerome."

Andrew piped in, "I hope he was a bit friendlier than he was the last time."

"Yes, he was. He's got good reason to be hostile though." Both of them looked up at Elspeth when she said that, but again, she didn't want to go any further. "I've got a bit more digging to do. I need to do some research before I go much further." The drone of her thoughts was like a mosquito circling her head. They were waiting for her to go on, but she looked out the window instead, collecting her thoughts. The river was quiet today, too late for the eagles to be hunting. They were probably feasting now on their day's finds, back in their huge nests around the bend. "I got a lot more than I expected. I think he was happy to talk, when he knew I'd listen. I think he'd like to see Madonna again too, deep down, but I didn't bring that up today."

Elspeth caught Andrew's eye so he'd know not to ask questions, unspoken signals from a long marriage enough to tell him to keep quiet. Cecelia finished her sandwich quickly and headed to her room. Andrew brought Elspeth in a cup of tea where she had settled in the library with the computer and her notes in front of her.

"So? What's going on?" Andrew asked, settling in the wing chair with his tea. "There's definitely something going on. You are definitely perplexed."

"I am. It seems that Madonna was pregnant. That's why it all came out and the family had a big fight, and then she was taken away. I thought she had been thrown out, you know, by her father, but no. She was taken away. By the priest."

"That happened. She wouldn't have been the first wayward girl who ended up having a baby in a convent setting."

"Wayward girl? Jesus, Andrew. You sound so judgemental! In this day and age, why is it still the girl getting the label?"

"Oh, Elsie. I'm sorry. You're right, you're right. Of course, you are right. I'm an old man stuck with my old habits, but that's no excuse and I know it. Anyway, the poor girl was stuck with the consequences, a story as old as time itself."

"Exactly. Madonna was stuck with the consequences, and I'm not sure if she even remembers or recognizes what those consequences did to her family. She had been such a good girl, a real homebody, that when she got pregnant, you can guess who got blamed." Elspeth looked knowingly at her husband.

"Her father? Her brothers?"

"Exactly." Elspeth sat back and crossed her arms. "The whole community had them tried and convicted and it just ate them up. It's so sad. Heart attacks, alcoholics, and suicide. Three brothers and her father dead before the truth really came out."

"And the truth?" Andrew asked intensely. "What was the truth?"

"Seems it was the parish priest, but I didn't want to mention that with Cecelia in the room. She might go off with her holier than thou attitude that I was just digging things up so she won't go to the convent herself."

"Oh, wow. The priest. Of course, the priest." Andrew nodded his head.

"Jerome was honest enough to say that he was glad that it wasn't him ... That the priest picked on his sister, and, well, I might as well tell you what he said, his mother, instead. It took them so long, blaming each other, pitting them against each other. No one suspecting the goddamned priest!" Elspeth yanked the computer open.

"He let the family disintegrate, blame each other, become social outcasts in the community, and he played the saviour. Taking away the problem, taking away Madonna, before she could talk, tell anyone what had really happened. It sounds like she was a simple, quiet little girl. She didn't say anything about the priest." Andrew thought out loud, summing up the situation.

"Exactly! Oh, the poor thing! Maybe that's why she doesn't remember it at all. Maybe that's why she's got such a blank. And Jerome, he's angry at Madonna because she didn't say anything, point the blame."

"Madonna has a lot of demons to deal with. No wonder she's blanked out so much. Did Jerome say much about the younger ones?"

"It's so hard. He's so angry and when I ask a clarifying question he pushes back, and I can't blame him. Can you? Looks at me like I have two heads or I'm just plain stunned or something."

"In his defence, it's got to be painful to discuss all this," Andrew said, crossing his long legs and resting his elbow on his knee. "You've got to give the man some credit for even letting you in the door."

"Yes, you're right. Of course, you're right. He gives me little taste of things and then I'm left guessing at something that maybe is pure speculation. Real Gael mentality, deep in there. He certainly insinuated that he felt the priest had abused his mother as well as Madonna."

"Oh, that's an awful story."

"Yes. Now, I can't prove it, but I think he thinks the younger two girls, well, that they might have been the priest's daughters. They left before it all came out. I'm going to see what I can find now." Elspeth slumped back on the computer chair. "But now I'm stuck with the dilemma. Do I tell her? Madonna?"

"I can't answer that question for you, my dear. I can't answer that question." With that, Andrew patted Elspeth on the shoulder and took his tea to the deck and left her alone.

She opened the computer and put the name Father Landon in the search engine. Of course, a dozen possibilities or more popped up and she tried to hone down what she was really searching for. She found the church records for the Catholic church in Dominion and unearthed some obscure news articles that mentioned his name in connection with the parish, but there was enough of a cover-up in place that his name was not associated with much. Maybe she could elicit some help from Andrew, get him to try to dig in the actual diocese records, head to Antigonish or back to the Beaton Institute.

She looked at the room, the office as they called it, surrounded by books and papers, records and documents. She had hung some of the photos of her parents and herself as a baby in the room and she looked over at them, the couple in the black and white photo looking more like grandparents than parents. She could see the date on the bottom of them all, in the white border, 1954. There would have been a lot of babies born that year, not only her and Madonna's baby.

It had been a hard winter, she knew the story well. Priests had been rare up on the mountain, but that winter a priest did come, and he stayed with her parents. The weather had been wicked and people had said the rosary in their homes, waiting for masses to resume some type of schedule in the spring.

It had been such a miracle to have a priest in the house to do her baptism. There had been no one else there as witnesses. She had been told the story so many times, it was almost by rote, the words. Almost a piece of mythology. She had the document in the box with the rest of the baby pictures. Her mother had never applied for her birth certificate. She had to do it herself when she went to university. She pulled down the full plastic box of old photos, the ones she had taken off the walls of the old house. There had been so many of them taken that winter. Her as a baby in her father's arms. Her mother's arms. None with the priest. At the bottom of the box, she found her baptism certificate. It was well worn since she had used it for identification for so many years. The priest's name was Father James Landon.

Chapter 13

Power

I took my power in my hand
And went against the world;
'Twas not as much as David had,
But I was twice as bold.

– Emily Dickinson

Elspeth sat there looking at the paper with Father Landon's name on it. She sat back in the chair by the computer, frozen for a minute. Trying to piece it all together. What was Father Landon doing up in Glencoe? Madonna was taken in the fall of 1953. Months along pregnant. Visibly pregnant. He would have been panicking. Madonna's mother had been safe to have sex with. A married woman. She could get pregnant without real concern, but a teenage girl who never went out of the house except to church? Both of them had to get out of the community and he must have asked for a temporary assignment. Off the grid. And did he take his new daughter there too? Could she ...?

She looked at the paper again. She could be Madonna's daughter, if the priest had brought her up the mountain to hide her.

It had always seemed so strange. Her mother being forty-six having her. Even if she had been a menopause baby, like Cecelia, why was there no one there to help her mother – no woman skilled as a midwife, no doctor, or anyone else to tell the story? Surely one of the neighbours would have once said to me that they were there, but all they ever said was what a miracle it had been, my birth. Like I came out of nowhere. Ma would have said something to someone, been worried about the situation, pregnant in the winter up there, but it was only Ma and Pa in the house, in the story. She thought of it now as a myth. It had never seemed to really ring true when she thought about it.

Her mother, as she died, had tried to tell her something, but it had been so convoluted that it had never made much sense to her before. She remembered she had been sitting beside her mother in the Inverness Hospital.

Agnes had bruises on her arms and legs from the needles, and Elspeth was wrapping a hot water bottle in a soft towel to see if it would help ease the aches in her mother's back. She looked so pitiful on the bed, her glasses off and her teeth out. She was fighting off tears, not wanting her mother to see in her face how far gone she was.

"You were always our little girl, and you'll always be our girl. No matter if anyone ever tells you anything different."

Why would they tell her any different? Who would tell her any different?

"You know why we chose your name? Elspeth? Because it means chosen by God, and that's what you were to us. Chosen by God." Agnes got a little choked up, and her hands grasped the blanket tighter, trying to get a hold of the world which seemed to be slipping away. "I feel awful that you are missing your studies, Elspeth. You should go back to Sydney. Dòmhnall can help me."

"Pa has got the animals to care for, and you know, he'd be useless around a hospital. It's better if he stays where he is, I think, Ma. I'm glad to have the time with you. The books in the library can wait, and so can my studies. They'll be there next term. What's the rush?" Elspeth put the bottle behind her mother's back, noticing the bruises there as

well as the johnny shirt fell open. Where's the dignity in old age? "That feel better?"

"Tha, mo nighean. That feels much better. And it's nice to have you here, speaking the Gaelic with me. There's not many girls working the floor who seem to have much of the language left. You're a comfort to me, gu cinnteach." Agnes's eyes closed for a minute, enjoying the heat on her back, a bit of relief.

Elsepth had looked in the mirror, her red hair heavy from lack of care. She splashed some water on her face and grabbed a comb. She needed to get some sleep herself. She was lying to herself as much as her mother, saying that the books could wait. Her marks would suffer and she'd lose her scholarship at this rate, and since Sister Beaton's death, she had been so busy helping to organize the Cape Bretoniana resources in the library. Elspeth had a good grasp of both written and spoken Gaelic, and so many of the old, important Cape Breton works were in Gaelic. Sister Beaton had depended on her to deal with them. It was so sad. All these beautiful, old, Gaelic souls leaving the world. There was no one who could replace them.

She rubbed her eyes with her hands and stretched her head back and forth, trying to work out her own kinks. Sleeping on the hard chair by her mother's bed for the last three nights was taking its toll.

"Elspeth!" Agnes was sitting up, eyes wide and staring.

"What, Ma?" Elspeth's heart was racing. "Do you need the nurse?"

"I just had the worst feeling, Elsie. The worst feeling." The old lady's eyes were streaming. "God is calling. I'm hearing him, girl."

"Should I get Pa? I can call over to MacDonald's and they can run for him, even if he's in the barn." Elspeth tried to get her mother to lie back in the bed, but her mother was having none of it. "You have to save your energy, Ma!"

"Father Landon. He said never to say a word, you know. Not even to each other. Never let it pass our lips, about you. He made us swear over your head as he sprinkled on the holy water. He said we'd be doing a good thing, that we were good people. He baptized you, you know, with the two of us there. No one need ever know the difference. At the time, people talked. I know they did, but you were there. Our baby in our arms. Living proof if there ever was."

Elspeth felt that her mother was confused. What was she talking about? Never know the difference? Of course Ma and Pa were good people. Of course they were.

"I was so old when you arrived. We had no mid-wife, no doctor. People didn't know what to make of it, but we got on our knees, you know we did, and we thanked God for you every day, and it all seemed to work out fine." Agnes was getting tired. Her eyes closed, and her breath became a bit shallower.

"You're not angry at us, at me, are you, Elspeth?" she asked quietly.

"No, Ma. I could never be angry at you," Elspeth replied, tears filling her eyes, not quite understanding why her mother would think that she should be angry with her. Especially now.

"And we could never be angry at you, my girl. You were such a good girl. Still are. Don't tell your father I said anything. Please." Agnes pulled Elspeth's hand to her chest, hard and wheezing. Elspeth would never forget that moment, and her mother wouldn't let go until she said the words. "We had sworn an oath, on your little head."

"I promise. I won't tell Pa you said a word."

Her mother released her hand, exhausted from the effort, and Elspeth watched as her eyes closed and she relaxed in the bed. Elspeth then sat, the sensation of her mother's grasp still on her own hands, looking out the window over the fall colours blazing with their splendour. She breathed in and out, her quick mind trying to piece together bits of a puzzle that didn't make sense, but she could tell were important.

Her mother had told her. She had told her all those years ago, but she just hadn't understood.

* * * *

Father Landon. He was the key to the puzzle, Elspeth knew it now, but did it even really matter? If he was still alive, would she really come out and ask for a DNA sample? Would that help her, or Madonna, or Cecelia?

Andrew walked back into the library. "You're in a complete daze, my girl. I've never seen you like this. To tell you the truth, I'm a little worried. I figured I was going to be the one hit with Alzheimer's."

"Andrew, I need some help. I need someone to bounce this off, and I don't want to come off as crazy." Elspeth didn't know where to start. "Just sit down. No. Close the door and then sit down. No, pour me a glass of wine, then close the door and sit down."

"You really are scaring me now," he said but came back in the room shortly with two glasses of red wine, closed the door, passed her a glass, and sat down. "What's going on?"

"You really are wonderful. I need to tell you that before I begin." She took a big drink. "Okay. I had a bad feeling, you know, ever since Jerome told me about when all of this happened, and I've been trying to piece it together, Madonna's story and my own."

"Piece it together? Why would your story have anything to do with Madonna's story?"

"Father Landon. That's who abused Madonna in the first place. I think he might have been my father."

"What!" Andrew, caught in mid-drink, coughed on the wine so it took him a minute to get his breath again. "Why in the hell would you think that?"

"His name is on my baptism certificate."

"There could be another Father Landon, you know. I mean, it's not as popular a name as a Father MacDonald or a Father MacLean, but it's possible. He signed it to make it legal, being the presiding priest."

"Of course, of course, that's why his name is there. I'm not saying that, but if it is the same Father Landon who left with Madonna from Dominion, who was pregnant, very pregnant, in the fall of 1953, then it is pretty suspicious for him to be taking shelter on the top of Glencoe Mountain, presiding over a baptism for a couple who no one seemed to even know was expecting a baby." Elspeth took a deep breath. "Don't make me feel stupid here, Andrew. I'm just trying to piece it together because it's not making a lot of sense."

Andrew took another look at the baptismal certificate. "Okay, let's go through the facts that you know. What makes you jump to the conclusion he may be your father? That's pretty wild."

"I know, I know, but I've been thinking. Ma insinuated some things, when she was dying, and I think she was trying to tell me, in that good old Scottish way of not telling something out plain, making you guess, that I wasn't theirs. That he had brought me to them. That they were never to say anything to anyone about it. He made them swear on my head, that's what she said. Made them swear not to tell anyone, about me. I mean, she was forty-six having me. And she did it alone, apparently, no one up there on the mountain but them. It never quite made sense. I know Catherine Ann or Flora – they were good neighbours, those women – would have stayed with her for days, even weeks, if they had known she was going to have a baby, but there was no one there."

"It could happen, Elspeth. It could happen." He could see that she was looking for him to follow her on this, but he didn't want to jump to unsubstantiated conclusions. "Okay. So you have his name on the baptismal certificate. What else do you have?"

"Madonna was taken away from her family in the fall of 1953. I was 'born' according to my baptism certificate – I never had a birth certificate – in January 1954. The only ones at the baptism were my parents and the priest."

"Because of the weather, right? It was a hard old winter or something, right?"

"Yes. We both know the story well. It was told to me over and over and the house was full of baby pictures of me as an infant. It was almost like they were building up the evidence." Elspeth took a drink.

"I wish I had met them," he said. "I mean, my family, my mother especially, are such a big part of my life. Too much, maybe."

"You think?" Elspeth laughed.

"Maybe that's why I found it so easy to move twenty-five hundred miles from them," he said, while toasting her glass. "But your parents, they were all you had."

Elspeth couldn't get an image out of her head. "Think of it. They could have just told me that a special stork brought me. A black stork, with a white collar." She cringed at the thought and wondered how she was going to deal with this now.

"But you don't have any proof, my dear. You have no proof."

"No, you're right. And with Madonna's heart the way it is, I think that maybe I should simply ignore the whole thing."

"Can you ignore the whole thing? Really?"

"Probably not." Elspeth knew she'd need to know one way or the other.

Andrew smiled at her. "Probably not." He got up and patted her shoulder. "I think it's going to be a long night for you. Where are you going to start?" He hesitated, then asked, "Do you want me to help?"

Elspeth looked at him and smiled. "We know that never ends well. You'd drive me crazy with your questions and your little notes everywhere. Let me plug away at it first. I'll start with the Diocese records, I guess. Maybe find some record of what Jerome was talking about, the girl from Antigonish who came forward. Any ideas come to mind?"

"Yes. That all makes sense. You could look through the local papers. Maybe *The Chronicle Herald* had something. Might have to head in to look at the microfiche records. It'd be big."

"And it might not be enough anyway."

"No, but you might find something. Be sure to call me if you need anything, and, my dear, don't let it go around and around in your head. It's good to talk it through, so remember, I'm just a shout away, and I have a bottle of red opened whenever you need more. I'll leave you to it." He left the room and closed the door behind him.

Elspeth looked at the window and contemplated her reflection looking back at her. She rubbed her forehead and then let her head rest in her hand. This was so much to take in, and maybe she was jumping to conclusions rather that looking at it objectively. She turned to the computer and typed Father Landon, Antigonish Diocese in the search engine. It was going to be a long night.

* * * * *

Over the next few days, Elspeth started to delve in to the Internet, looking for signs of Father Landon, and reading peer-reviewed articles about sexual abuse of girls and women by the clergy. As she read on and on, all she could do was worry more and more about Cecelia thinking of entering this world, her eyes lit with the power, and the naivety, of youth.

Over and over again, the reach of the Church struck her. How it could inspire such loyalty and devotion, while ripping and tearing away at the fabric of people's souls. She could feel her worries mount and she wondered if she got Madonna on her side about what happened to her, would that change Cecelia's mind about it all? At the same time, with Madonna's heart condition, she shouldn't put too much on her shoulders. It might be too much for her. Could she do that to her? Especially knowing the possibility that she could be her own mother? The thought felt foreign, like something lodged in her throat. She pushed it back and focused as if she was doing a regular genealogical exercise.

Elspeth tried to look for hard evidence that she was, in fact, Madonna's daughter. She took down a box of pictures of when she was young, and there were many but only in the photos at university did colour photos really show up to highlight her hair colour. She got up and went to the bathroom, taking a university grad photo with her. It had been a splurge paying for the professional photo, but one only had a few good photos at the time, and graduations were important. She saw the same eyes and face looking back, but the auburn hair, so similar to Cecelia's, popped out of the photo, and her gray hair, not as long, not as thick, was the biggest change. She thought of her mom and dad, who were gray as long as she could remember them, and knew that there was no one left to ask if they had been redheads or not. She had no brothers or sisters, no cousins, to ask. Everyone was long gone.

She did have sisters. Or she might have sisters. Madonna's sisters. They could possibly be sisters and aunts, technically. What a mess. Elspeth went back to the computer and sat down. Her coffee cup was empty again. She was going to get the shakes if she kept living on coffee and wine.

"I'm heading up to visit Madonna, Andrew," she shouted from the hall to the deck. "I'll be back for supper."

"You're going up? Really? I'm surprised." He came into the kitchen, looking concerned. "Are you ready for that?"

"No. I'm not. Cecelia has dropped in to see her, but I've been so deep into this stuff that I'm not dealing with the reality. If she is my mother, I should show some compassion, shouldn't I? I suppose I should show some compassion to an old lady even if she's not my mother."

"Do you want me to go with you?"

"No, not today. Maybe the next time. My mind is still sunk in this stuff, so I just want to spend a little time getting to know her and then I need to get back at it before I lose my train of thought."

"See, that's where little yellow Post-it Notes come in handy." He nodded at her knowingly. "You laugh at my system, but it works for me."

"Look, could you help me out? Search through what I've got there so far with fresh eyes. Give me your two cents. I may get you to search too, about Father Landon, see if you can make any sense of the scandal around him. There's about a million emotions and details to deal with and I'm too involved with the dynamics of it all. I need some help."

"Of course. Of course. I've got some skills. Many skills. In many departments."

She smiled at his usual sexual innuendos. "Yes, you do, but today I need your research skills. I'll be back before supper. It's just a salad and burgers so that won't take much to put together."

It was a warm afternoon, and it felt sleepy and deserted when Elspeth walked into the main hallway of the Convent. Her steps seemed to echo and she wondered if everyone was napping. She made her way to Madonna's room without seeing another soul. Madonna was awake when she opened the door slowly, the creaking noise echoing in the hall.

"Come in, come in, Elspeth. Don't worry about the rest. They sleep like the dead in the afternoon." Madonna looked rested and more energetic than the last time Elspeth was there.

"You look much better."

"I'm feeling stronger, been walking around a bit. Just got back into bed actually."

"Maybe you wanted to nap?"

"No, no. It's a good pastime, sleeping. Better if I can talk to someone though."

"I went down to see Jerome again a few days ago, Madonna. He was much more talkative. He talked about you, and when you left." She paused for a minute, trying to gauge the reaction. "You know, the night you left with Father Landon."

Madonna didn't say anything for a few minutes. "Father Landon. Huh. I've been trying to figure out what's true and what's not true in my memories. Some of my memories, if they are true, they aren't nice. Not nice at all."

"I believe that, Madonna. I think you had some bad things happen to you. And I think you had to do what you had to do to be able to deal with them." Elspeth leaned towards the woman in the bed. "I want you to know that I understand, and I only want you to talk about what you want to talk about. You don't have to talk about the rest."

"I always loved our church, you know, when I was young. It was like my home. I loved the smell of the incense and the glisten of well-worn pews. I loved the clunk when the kneelers hit the floor. One of my strongest memories was cleaning the church, first with Mama, and then by myself, when we had the church all to ourselves. After we'd finish, Mama would have us kneel at the altar and look up at the crucifix and she'd say, 'We all have to suffer, Madonna. That's life. Suffering. Especially for women.'"

"Suffering can be good but some suffering can be avoided. And sometimes, the suffering just gets to be too much. Too much for anyone to handle. Your mom, Madonna. Jerome said it was suicide. She went swimming with rocks in her pockets." Elspeth took the old lady's hand and stroked it. "I'm so sorry."

Madonna's face went blank. She drew a curtain over her eyes and sank back into memory.

She was drawn back to the kitchen table, and she could smell the roast that her mother had put in the wood stove. There was no juice left in the pot. It was dry and burning. Why was Mama leaving it in the stove for so long?

The girls needed their Saturday night bath, but Mama hadn't brought the tub down from the back room, so Madonna went and got it. She put it on the floor and started filling it with warm water from the stove. She had peeled the potatoes and the carrots, but she didn't know how to do the gravy, so had been waiting for Mama. She took the meat out of the oven. She hoped Mama would be here before Da got home.

She got the girls in the tub, one at a time, Bernadette with her wiry curls and Faith with her straight, fine hair. Washed them up and then dressed them for Saturday night dinner. Everyone else would need the tub later to get ready for Sunday church, so it was good to get the girls finished early.

Ma still hadn't come home when Pa arrived. "Where's your mother at?"

"I don't know, Da. She went to the Glebe House earlier and was going to give the church one more going over before tomorrow's mass. I guess I can try the gravy. I've never done it but I guess I can try." Madonna was nervous. Everyone always complimented Mama on her gravy. She was very particular about it.

Da looked in the roast pan. "No drippin's left anyway. That roast's so dry we're gonna choke on it. For Pete's sake, mash the potatoes and get the girls ready for supper. The rest will be in when they're finished in the barn."

Just then there was a knock on the door. It was Father Landon and young Ralph Myers from the Shore. Da told them to come in and sit down.

"No. Not now, Gussie. Why don't you tell Madonna and the girls to go upstairs?"

"Go upstairs? Why in the world do they need to go upstairs?"

"They should, Gussie. For everyone's sake, send them upstairs. It's bad news."

Madonna picked up Faith and put her on her hip, and took Bernadette by the hand. She took them up the stairs and put them in their room and then she lay down on the floor so she could look down through the grate into the kitchen.

"Young Ralph here found her. Down along the Shore. It was shallow. I don't even know how she did it really." Father Landon sat. He put his face in his hands.

Young Ralph nodded, holding his cap in his hands, strangely important all of a sudden.

"He came to me first, and I've told him that no one, not a soul, needs to know the details. Right, young Ralph? If you tell a single person that it was anything but a drowning, your soul will rot in hell, right, son? And is hell a good place, Ralph?"

"No, Father. Hell is a place of eternal damnation, where hellfire and pestilence never ends." Ralph had studied his catechism well.

"And you promise me, and Mr. MacMillan here, and the Lord God Almighty who watches everything we do, every day, every minute of the day, that you will never say but that Mrs. MacMillan accidentally drowned?"

"I promise. I promise, God Almighty, I promise." Ralph was shaking in his boots.

"You go now, boy. Your duty is done." Father Landon dismissed him with a wave of his hand and Ralph ran out. "I took the rocks out of her pockets, Gussie. And I threw them. I threw them as far as I *could. But she was gone. Gone to the Lord, Gussie, but we'll bury her in the cemetery. We will. She drowned, no doubt about it, and it must have been an accident. A tragic accident."*

Madonna's eyes refocused and looked at Elspeth with sorrow shining through them. "I guess I might have known that, some time ago, but I wasn't sure if it happened that way or not." Madonna seemed to shrink in the bed, pulled the cover up as if she was cold. "I'm sending you on wild goose chases to answer questions that I already know, deep down, or maybe are best left unanswered."

"That's okay. I think I'm finding some answers. Maybe I won't have them all today, but I have some answers. Did that bring anything else to mind? Anything that would help?"

"The girls' names. The girls' names were Bernadette and Faith."

Of course they were, Elspeth thought. Bernadette and Faith. Of course.

Chapter 14

Courage

I learned that courage was not the absence of fear, but the triumph over it. The brave man is not he who does not feel afraid, but he who conquers the fear.

— Nelson Mandela

Cecelia was glad that her mother was distracted. It had been an adjustment, when she retired and they moved to Mabou, an adjustment for them all. Cecelia had been used to her own space, her privacy, her own thoughts, but now her mother seemed to be there all the time, hovering over her, asking her what she wanted, suggesting solutions. She now realized she missed the old mom, with her head in some project that kept her absentmindedly jotting notes at the table, or running to the computer to look something up. She used to find it annoying, but now, now that the whole focus was on her all the time, she found it hard to take all the attention.

Diane and Bridget had been visiting her every morning at the museum. It was a quiet space so it was nice to have the company. She'd make them tea and they'd talk about what life would be like in Brazil. Diane said the weather was amazing, always warm and sunny. It would be nice to not have to deal with the snow and the cold. They wore simple white habits, kind of like Madonna had described about when she went to Honduras, with a simple kerchief over her head and a white dress with a red cross with a rose on it. They went out in the villages to do the Lord's work, even helping to dig wells and make concrete to build schools, or into the poor areas, the favelas, in the city. Every day seemed to be filled with something worthwhile, according to Diane. They helped at a hospital or with the children at the preschool, and every morning and evening, you had a prayer session focusing on how you could improve something about yourself.

"The aim is always to be a better you," said Diane. "You can't help anyone unless you feel good about yourself, so we spend a lot of time thinking about how we can aim to rid ourselves of the things that bring girls down, you know. Like shame, and guilt, and not feeling sure about yourself."

"That sounds wonderful," said Bridget. "I'm always looking at Facebook and comparing my face, my thighs, my ideas. Everyone else seems to be smarter, and happier, than I can ever be. I like the idea that I can just focus on what I need to improve on and we all wear the same thing, work towards the same goals."

Cecelia had nodded with agreement. She felt like she was finally having conversations that made sense to her and looking forward to something that could really make a difference in her life. Today, Bridget was bringing her mother, so Cecelia put another chair out before looking down the road. The summer traffic was picking up on Route 19. The Red Shoe Pub next door caused a bit of chaos every day. It seemed like tourists were willing to be run over in the busy road to get the perfect selfie with the place in the back. Cecelia had already heard brakes screeching a couple of times and went out to watch a local screaming at a tourist to get off the road. It was going to be a long summer, but she knew she would probably be gone long before the summer was over.

She looked at all the displays in shelves around the room, the old pictures hung high and the old piano used occasionally in the corner. She knew this was one of her mother's favourite spots in the entire world, with the Gaelic part of every board and nail. Her mother would spend hours here looking through song lyrics and old Gaelic poetry, commenting on who wrote it and how they had lived, who they had married. She knew the history of the foundations of buildings and could tell a story about how they brought the rocks from so far away to some remote place to make the building strong, back in the days before backhoes and bulldozers. It really was a wealth of knowledge that she possessed. Cecelia figured the Board must have been trying to make her mom happy, giving her the grant job.

She sighed and sat down, feeling once again that sense of not being connected, not understanding, not even really caring about the history around her. What did all that mean if people were not going to be living beyond a generation or two more? If people were going to be struggling for survival, who would have time to spend on academic exercises of tracing back family trees to the boat they came from Scotland on? People were going to need to have skills to survive, and hope in something bigger than history. History was only showing the mistakes people made, over and over and over. There needed to be a focus on simple living, farming, not running around trying to pretend something is important when it's not.

Bridget, her mother Jessica, and Diane were walking up the sidewalk, and Cecelia looked towards her own house, hoping her mother had really gone to Sydney to meet with Jerome again. That had been her plan at breakfast. She didn't want her landing here with a sandwich or something for lunch for her.

"It's been years since I was here," Jessica said coming in. "The place hasn't changed much though."

"I guess that's the point," Bridget said to her mother. "It is a museum."

"I know. I know, Bridget. Beautiful morning, Cecelia. Have you had any visitors?" Jessica asked.

"No, you folks are the first ones in the door, other than myself. It's been pretty quiet so far." She pointed over towards the guest book sitting open by the door. "Still on the first page of the guest book, but things will pick up, so they tell me."

Diane sat down first and primly crossed her hands on her

knees. "Let's start with a simple prayer, shall we, before we lose our focus."

The other three looked at each other as if they had done something wrong and then sat down, their chairs forming a small circle in the open space of the room. Cecelia felt a bit self-conscious about people walking by on the street and them seeing her praying. She tried to fight that down. She would need to put that on her list of self-improvements that would need to be tackled when she got to Brazil.

"Oh, our dear and precious Lord, and his blessed mother Mary, we beseech your help today. Holy Mother Mary, our Madonna, we as women strive every day to become more and more like you, sacrificing our own comfort and happiness for the good of others. As decisions need to be made, and directions confirmed, we need you to help guide us to pick the right path, the meaningful path, for this day and for all the days ahead. Amen," Diane concluded and raised her eyes, unlinking her hands from prayer.

"Amen," they all responded. Everyone's eyes coming up and all three looked to Diane, deferring to her to set the tone for the rest of the conversation.

"It's an exciting day for me, and I am so happy to be here with you today as I pass from being a Contemplative Novice of the Order of Mary's Maidens and become a Professed Promised Sister! I will be part of a large ceremony when I get back to São Paolo, and all the girls who started with me two years ago who have kept the faith will receive the red head scarf and the red belt to wear on our habits." Diane's excitement was contagious.

Bridget reached over and touched her arm. "That's wonderful, Diane!"

"Yes, it's been hard work, but every day I've been learning more about how my spiritual practice can fulfill my life and help others around me so I can't believe it's been two years already. I've learned so much, so much more than I ever could have in a university."

"Can you give me some examples of that, Diane? I'm going to have a very hard time convincing my parents that this is a good idea." Cecelia knew it was going to be a hard sell and she wanted to have as much ammunition as possible. "Do you mind if I take some notes? I'll go blank, I know I will, when the time comes."

"Well, the visa application is in the works and the plane ticket is going to be set soon. You are going to have to tell them that you are going." Diane looked at her, surprised that she still hadn't told them.

"I'm sure they will be fine with the idea," Jessica chimed in. "I only wish I could go myself, but with the two young ones at home ... I will have to live spiritually through Bridget here!"

"You can serve the Lord wherever you are, Jessica," Diane smiled at her. "Besides, we really are focusing on the youth right now."

Cecelia could see that Jessica was a bit put out by that comment, and she was glad her mother had not been there because she would have gone down Diane's throat, but Jessica just shrugged it off and replied, "I missed my chance, I guess, but I'm so glad that Bridget will have the chance to offer her life up to the Lord."

"Well, Cecelia, let me put it this way, it's like you get a whole background in not only spirituality, but the history of the Church through the centuries and what was happening in society all the time that impacted humanity. And there's psychology, lots of psychology, because we do a lot of grief counselling when we get to the Professed Promised level, along with working with the sick and addicts. We do a lot of behaviour intervention training too, so we can deal with children with special needs or maybe work in jails, that sort of thing."

"Wow. That's a broad bit of knowledge." Cecelia was scribbling down as much as she could on the back of an envelope she had found. "I need some more paper. Can you give me a minute?" She dug through a pile of papers on a table in the corner and found an old agenda from a Board meeting, blank on the back. "So who teaches you all this?"

"Oh, we have people come in who work in those fields and who we will be working with, and the Perpetual Devoteds have a lot of knowledge, on-the-ground knowledge, you know, of how spirituality can help in a whole bunch of situations. It's kind of like going to university but with a purpose. We want to minister to those who need our help, and we have to have the skills to do that correctly, with a focus that keeps their spiritual health foremost in our minds." Diane stopped for breath and to let Cecelia catch up. "I'm sorry. I can get pretty excited about it all, and I haven't even started on how we get trained to help out in environmental disasters, or the time we spend on community cleanups or sustainable agricultural teaching. There's so much that needs to be done!"

"And once you are trained, you work mainly around São Paolo?"

"Oh, no. We're going all over the globe, Cecelia. We're taking the message of what youth can do by being part of Mary's Maidens and Gideon's Guardians worldwide now, but the base, the starting point, will always be Brazil. It's important though – spreading the message, working for the good of the planet, and the Lord too, of course. It's an amazing thing to be a part of, and it starts with you, and me, and Bridget, here. It's up to the youth to change the mess of the world that we've inherited." Diane looked at Cecelia, assuring her that she meant every word.

"That all sounds wonderful, Diane, but how is it done? How can Mary's Maidens afford to send people all over the world? That takes money, some type of support system in place." Cecelia felt awkward asking about the money. She hated talking about money, but she knew that would be the first question, the major flaw that her mother, and her father who was Scotch cheap to the bone, would ask.

"It's in our vows, Cecelia. We vow to live simply, so we're not staying at expensive five-star hotels. We stay with supporters, believers. They give us donations to help us with our work. You have to embrace getting charity, and you have to embrace giving to charity. What you have, you share. We live as a community, a world community, and between us all, we have enough to make it happen."

"I've cashed in all of Bridget's Registered Education Savings Plans. She's not going to need them," Jessica said. "Signed and deposited the cheque yesterday, and I know it will be money well spent."

"Donated," Diane corrected her. "Money well donated."

"Yes, donated. To a great cause. To Bridget's salvation and the salvation of the world. What better cause can there be?" Jessica asked.

Cecelia looked at Bridget, who had been very quiet, she thought. Bridget saw her questioning glance. "I get to go to Brazil, Cecelia. Brazil! That ticket itself is expensive. And I'll be learning and living there for free. It would have been a waste if I just spent it on university because there was nothing I wanted to do. I'm afraid I'd go there and party like the rest of them. Get someone to write my papers, or scam them from the Internet. Write tests about whatever, and then forget it the next day. That's for sure a waste of my time and Mom's money. I'll be getting so much more out of the money this way, and giving back too."

"Yes, you are expected as a novice to put something in the pot, I guess you'd say. There's a lot of money that will go into your room and board, plane tickets, training, and equipment. Your habits, the furniture in your room, it all does cost money. If you were going to university in the fall, your folks would have been paying for all that anyway, right?" Diane asked.

"Yes. I guess so," Cecelia responded.

"But now, they'll know that you won't just come out of it without a job, without a future. You will not only have a future, you will have a vocation. Do you know what that means, Cecelia?" Diane leaned towards her. "You will have a mission. A purpose. A life full of spiritually where you live in an intentional community, one not driven by consumerism or popularity or power. You will be living a life with a direction of sustained social action. Doesn't that sound good to you?"

"Yes. It does." Cecelia nodded her head. It did sound good, and she looked at her notes. "Could you say that last bit again? I think I will need every word to convince my mom."

"Cecelia. You are your own person. You don't need to convince your mom of anything." Diane sat back and crossed her arms. "If you are ready to do this, then they will support you. But you have to be sure. Are you sure?"

Jessica, Bridget, and Diane looked at her intently.

Bridget jumped in. "C'mon, Cecelia! If you really don't like it, you can always come home."

"Can I? Can I come back home?" Cecelia asked.

"Of course you can, but they do expect novices to give it a try. They recommend that you don't come back for at least two years, so you can get a full taste of the training and get some skills under your belt. All communities want to ensure that people don't simply give up. It's easy to quit something, especially in the beginning. I mean, look at university. Most people have changed their minds, quit, or switched programs, well, at least fifty percent, by December of the first year. As a Contemplative Novice, you need to practise your vows of chastity, simplicity, and obedience for the two years. And then, if you don't like it after that, well, then you can come home."

"Two years in Brazil doesn't sound too shabby, does it, Cecelia?" Bridget's eyes were shining.

"No. I guess it beats two years of kinesiology at St. FX." Cecelia's smile lit up the room. "Okay. I will convince them. I know I can."

"Great. Your visa should be ready for next Wednesday. After that, your passport will be back and we can work on getting your ticket organized. Your donation will be due then too. Always remember that vow of sharing what you have. Soon, you will have few possessions, just like the rest of us, but for now, you need to think of your donation as the first step on the path to becoming part of the bigger community." Diane came over and gave Cecelia a big hug. "You will never feel alone again. We will all be sisters. Sisters you never had."

* * * * *

It was barely ten o'clock when Elspeth once again pulled into Jerome's driveway. There didn't seem to be any action at either his place or Elvin's, and Elspeth was struck again by how poor the place was. Neither side had seen a lick of paint since long before the war. The first one, that is. Someone had tried to put siding on Elvin's place, looked like it had been left over from another project or something, but they only had enough for the top half of the house. Luckily, Elvin and Jerome had agreed on a colour, since both sides had been white, with black trim, way back when. Now, it was a scraggly-looking gray, what was left on the shingles. Elspeth looked down the road at the other row houses, which reminded her of the Two-Face character in Batman comics, the two sides such different, contrasting colours.

She had stopped at Tim's and bought some muffins and biscuits, figuring Jerome would have to like one or the other. She picked up the box off the passenger seat and walked timidly to the back door. She wasn't really surprised to already see him there, waiting, a cigarette in his hand. She wasn't sure if that meant she was welcome or she was barred from entry.

"You're here again? The neighbours are going to talk," Jerome grunted at her. He hesitated a minute, and then he swung the door open so she could come in. He turned his back to her and walked into the kitchen.

"I brought you some biscuits. And some muffins." Elspeth put the box on the table. "Wasn't sure which you'd like, so I got a few of both."

"I suppose you'll want some tea," he said as he sat down. He opened the box.

"Sure," she said, thinking this is more of a welcome than she expected.

"Well, you can make it yourself. Kettle's by the stove." Jerome took a biscuit out of the box and slapped some margarine on it from the yellow plastic container on the table.

Elspeth filled the kettle and put it on to boil. She took a mug from the hanging rack that was on the counter with two other mugs, each of them orange, both brown in the middle from tea stains. She made the tea and put it on the stove to boil. It was evident that Jerome liked his tea boiled, and hot, and often.

"How's Madonna doing?"

"She's back in the Convent. Resting well. She's going to make it, I think. You want some tea?"

He motioned toward his mug, enough to say, Of course, stupid, and she picked it up and filled the cup. She put the milk on the table. He could do that much himself.

"So, what do you want? Some big, jeezly family reunion or something? I can't see that being good for anyone." Jerome spit out the words, obviously thinking Elspeth wanted to orchestrate some wonderful moment with them breakin' down cryin', sayin' everything was going to be all right.

"No. Probably not. She showed a glimmer of recognition about the priest, Father Landon. I don't know if she remembers having a baby or not. I mentioned your mother's suicide and she thought she recalled it. She says that some things feel more like a dream, a bad dream, than a memory. She did remember her sisters' names, Bernadette and Faith. I didn't tell her, and she remembered their names."

"Well, she should. She was more of a mother to them than Mama ever was, poor little things. Of course, I understood why when it all came out, slapped me in the face with something I should have figured out long before that." He stopped talking suddenly to get himself together. "Them being such red-headed girls and us all so black. Them with their strange greenish eyes, and us all blue-eyed."

"You mean, the priest, right? You think they were the priest's daughters?" Elspeth wanted to be clear about the details, but she knew she was playing with fire.

"Of course they were the goddamned priest's daughters! Jesus! Isn't that what we're talking about here? And poor Da, first the wife goin' off and killin' herself, and then the daughter, Madonna, who didn't leave the house, up the stump with no one to blame for it but the men in the house. Everyone looking at everyone else as if they were guilty, because they good and damn well knew it wasn't them. The house wasn't fit to live in. If I could get my hands around that Christer's neck, by Jesus ..." Jerome's voice cracked and then he stopped, taking a drag of his cigarette with enough force that the end almost flared into flame.

"What happened to him? Father Landon?"

"Oh, he was well hidden after the Antigonish crowd got their hooks in him. There was a bit of a story there, in the late '60s, and the Bishop even came to town, visited all his old stomping grounds, buying our souls off with some extra prayers and contrition. They said he was sent to a monastery and would never harm anyone again. Though they never came clear out and said that. It was all in codes and prayers and bullshit. Wouldn't get away with it now, but the folks around here, they knew the score. He's bound to be dead by now. Hopefully, burning in hell."

"So Madonna, before she left, she took care of the girls?"

"Of course she did! She always had from the beginning. She was the girl and Mama had her own things to do. She'd make sure they had their baths, stuff like that. After she went, Angus took over, since he was the youngest and by that time, the girls were in school, getting big enough to look after themselves. By the time Angus had had enough of the sideways glances and the guilt, the girls were in their teens. I had them here for a couple of years, after I got rid of the farm. No one was left by that time so the three of us came to town. Bernadette was a hard worker though, and she said enough was enough. Everyone treating them like they had the plague or something. She got them on the train and headed for Halifax. She found a way, and look, it was the best thing that could have happened for Faith. The best thing."

"Do you ever see them? Faith and Bernadette?"

"Sometimes they send a card. Christmas. Once in a while on my birthday. They don't come down anymore. What's there to talk about? It's all dead and gone. Besides, we're all getting older too now. No need to be digging up the past." He patted his pocket for his matches and shook another cigarette out of the pack.

Elspeth waiting quietly while he drew a few breaths to get the cigarette lit. "I think I'd like to meet them."

"Faith and Bernadette? Why in the hell would you want to meet them? And why in the hell would they want to meet you? An even better question, I suppose."

Elspeth was silenced. What could she say? She had no reason why they would want or need to meet her and she wasn't sure if it was even a good idea. Why did she want to do this, open this can of worms any further? Was there really any point in any of it?

Jerome looked at her as she considered her answer. "Well, at least you're not trying to pretend to be anything other than nosy."

"Okay, Jerome. I understand what you're saying. It's not all about Madonna, or your family. I've got a personal stake in this too. Here's my reality right now. My daughter, she's eighteen, has it in her head that she wants to be a nun."

His eyebrows lifted in surprise. "No one becomes a nun these days."

"That's what I thought too. Anyway, my daughter befriended your sister Madonna and brought me into the picture since she's become ill. I've got a background in genealogical research, so that's where I fit in." Elspeth hesitated. She wasn't going to go on about half-baked hunches. "The more I learn about your story, the more worried I am for my daughter."

"So you're not doing this for some news story or angle that's going to have my family's name plastered all over *The Chronicle Herald*, not that many read it these days anyway." The thin copy of today's paper lay on the table. "Takes about five minutes to get through the thing now, but I still don't want to go back to the days when I was afraid my name was going to be there."

"No. This is only for Madonna ... and for my daughter. So I guess that makes it personal, for me." Elspeth looked at the man, who could be her uncle. She had never had an uncle or a cousin, let alone a sister. She searched his face, looking for a resemblance, but couldn't see anything striking. Of course, she barely recognized herself in the mirror these days, still shocked by her gray hair and wrinkles. She realized how personal this story really could be, that this could be her story. The most important research she had ever done in her life. She waited, realizing that she was holding her breath, wondering how he would reply. She felt she couldn't come clean about her suspicions, because that was all they were, and not very substantiated suspicions at that. Jerome would not take them well, she was sure.

He ground out his cigarette in the large, brown ashtray overflowing with butts on the table. His hands went instinctively for the cards and shuffled them. "What's your daughter's name?"

"Cecelia."

"Like the song?"

"Yes," Elspeth said, smiling. "Exactly like the song."

He took another cigarette out of the package and lit it. He took a couple of drags before slowly getting out of the chair and going to an old desk under the window on the opposite side of the room. He pulled out a drawer, stuffed with old newspapers and receipts. He put the cigarette on the edge of the desk, its lit end dangling out, and all Elspeth could think of was what a fire hazard this whole place was, her eyes fixated on the cigarette until he picked it up again. He came back with a well-worn envelope with a Christmas card inside.

"Faith doesn't send one every year, and, well, Bernadette gave it up about ten years ago since I never so much as called in response, but Faith, well, Faith keeps up the faith, I guess. That was last year's. You can get the address off it. That's the best I can do for you." He placed the card on the table.

Elspeth took her phone out and took a picture, but decided she should write it down as well, so jotted the name and address on her notebook. "Thanks, Jerome. I appreciate this. I do. I know all this must be awful for you. To have to go back and remember all this."

Jerome looked at her. "I spent so many years blaming Madonna, to tell you the truth. Blaming her for being weak, for not speaking up about who had knocked her up. It had to be someone, you know? But then, when it came out, that it was that bastard Landon, well, then, all I could do was blame myself and Da and everyone else for not seeing what was right in front of our noses. What's the good of all that now? Blame. Guilt. I don't know." He took another drag of the smoke, looked down at his yellowed fingers, another quick drag and snuffed out another dead soldier. His hands almost reached for the pack again, but instead pushed it away.

"I guess, as we get older, we realize that answers aren't that simple. Life was so black and white when we were younger." Elspeth felt that she didn't know what to say. It was easier to think about the dynamics of a situation when people were dead and long gone than when you were sitting across from them.

"Black and white. They certainly were black and white." Jerome went back to the desk, pulled open another drawer. "I have a photo here, of Madonna's confirmation. It was taken before she left. She was ten, maybe going on eleven. There's Mama, not much bigger than Madonna, was she? And that bastard Landon. Mama was pregnant at the time, with Faith. Not sure where Bernadette was. Da must have took it."

Elspeth looked down at the black and white photo, September 1948 scrawled on the back. A young Madonna with jet black hair, seemingly darker by the white dress and little veil framing her face, dwarfed by Father Landon on one side, her mother, only slightly taller than her on the other. A little bulge in the dress the only evidence of Faith to come. "Do you mind if I take a picture of this? Show it to Madonna?"

Jerome hesitated. "Take it with ya. It's been sittin' in the drawer for years and I don't want to see that Jesus man's face again as long as I live. It's hard enough to live with his face in my head. Take it with ya." He shoved his hand, motioning as if he could rid the house and his memories so easily of things he didn't want to face.

Elspeth could see that he also wanted to send a message to Madonna, a kindness, a forgiveness or a request for forgiveness. She wasn't sure exactly what the message was, but there was something there. She'd take it as a gift. And she'd show it as a gift.

Chapter 15

Action

Do not be like the cat who wanted a fish but was afraid to get his paws wet.

– William Shakespeare

"I think I have to go to Halifax," Elspeth announced at supper that night.

They were eating on the deck and passing the salad around. Andrew looked up from picking up his portion. "Halifax? What now?"

"I'm going to see if I can talk to Madonna's sisters. They were pretty young when she went, but it would be nice to talk to them. What do you think, Cecelia?" Elspeth looked over at her daughter, whose head was bent, texting. "What happened to our 'no phones at the table' policy?"

"There's a group going to the square dance tonight. I thought you'd like it if I went to a dance in Glencoe. I'm just trying to make plans," Cecelia replied defensively.

"Glencoe? Sounds good. Want to go, Andrew?"

"Ah, my hip's not feeling up to that tonight. Next week for sure. You could go, Elsie."

Elspeth looked at her daughter, who didn't usually socialize that much so she could easily read her signals. "No, I won't cramp your style, Cece. You go ahead. How was the museum today?"

"A few in. Not many, but a few." She was relieved that her mother wasn't coming. She had planned to meet up with Bridget and Diane at the dance and although she'd get a couple of square sets in, they were really going to hang out and talk about Brazil all night. She was hoping to build up a bit more ammunition before she tackled her parents early next week. She'd be ready by then and she'd need to get the donation and she'd be on the plane by Friday. She knew she had enough in her savings to probably cover enough of a donation to be accepted, but she wasn't sure. She'd have to talk to the folks anyway. She couldn't just run away. That wouldn't be fair to them.

Elspeth had shown the picture of young Madonna when she got home. She knew she was looking at it with her new eyes, seeing Father Landon as he was, a pedophile, seeing her possible mother and grandmother at their most vulnerable. But she didn't want to bring that up yet, in case it set Cecelia justifying the Church again. She could see in her daughter's eyes though that she was looking at the idea, being a bride of Christ, young Madonna in her white dress and veil, and was still enamoured with the idea. How was she going to get through to her?

"I think I'll do a fast up and down trip tomorrow. To Halifax." Elspeth felt a sense of urgency coming over her. "See if I can track Faith down. It's only a tank of gas."

"Or two. And lunch. And shopping, if you stop at Winners," Andrew interjected.

"I'll bring a sandwich, and I'll be home before supper. Maybe," Elspeth replied.

* * * * *

"You've been avoiding me," Amanda said, grabbing Cecelia by the arm and pulling her towards the bathrooms at the back of the hall. "What are you doing coming out here with Bridget and that Diane one? I'm not good enough for you these days?"

Cecelia looked back in the hall and could tell that Diane was a bit concerned. She wondered if she was intimidated by the dance. She said she'd never been to a square dance before and that she shouldn't leave her alone. There was no place to sit in the hall so she was standing a bit off to the side, by the canteen, alone since Bridget had been taken by one of the old men who were always popular at the dances, since they were often some of the best dancers.

"No, of course not. I've been busy is all. With work." Cecelia avoided Amanda's eyes, knowing that she really didn't want to talk to her because she knew she'd have to admit the plan and she wasn't sure how her friend would take it.

"Be quiet! There's nothing going on at An Drochaid and you know it. What's going on with you and Bridget and Diane? Mom told me that Bridget's mother told my aunt Jane that Bridget is going to Brazil with her next week. To be a nun in that Mary's Maidens. What's going on, Cecelia? You aren't really thinking of heading there, are you?"

Amanda had her pinned in the hallway, blocking the entrance to the hall. Cecelia could see Diane watching them intently. "I'm thinking of it. You know I don't have any desire to head to university, and I don't see a lot of options. A trip to South America sounds like a good adventure, a good gap year."

"Bridget's mom thinks it's the best thing since sliced bread, Bridget heading down to serve the Lord, but Mom thinks it's a bunch of hogwash. That Bridget's mother should get her head examined, allowing her, almost pushing her daughter, in to that shit show down there. Does your mother know? I can't see her being too happy about it."

Cecelia felt a moment of panic. "Amanda, you can't tell them! I know that they won't see my side of things. They are so set in their ways, so old. They can't see that the world is changing and that we will all need to make some tough decisions soon enough."

"Oh, don't give me that whole end of the world crap, Cecelia. You're just running away because you don't know what you want to do, and you can't make up your mind and this is the best and most interesting option you've seen so far." Amanda's arms were crossed, and she wasn't about to let Cecelia go without saying her piece.

"There's more to it than that. I want to do something good for the world. You wouldn't understand." Cecelia felt guilty, being so hard on Amanda. She had been the only girl who had gone out of her way to be a friend to her since she had arrived. Amanda had lots of friends but Cecelia had felt a connection, one she hadn't had often in her life.

Diane appeared behind Amanda. "Everything okay, Cecelia?"

Amanda turned around. "You've got her convinced that Brazil is a good idea, eh? Goin' to serve the Lord? Right. She'll be servin' somethin' and somebody, but I doubt if it will be the Lord."

"I've been there two years now, and I have enjoyed every day. It's been a great experience. Maybe you should think about learning more about something before you condemn it." Diane reached towards Cecelia but Amanda pushed her hand away.

"Control. That's what I think. You people like to control the ones you have under your power."

Diane stood tall. "I saw you out in the parking lot, guzzling beer with those boys. Maybe if you practised a little control yourself, you'd feel a bit of power too. C'mon, Cecelia. It's time we were heading home anyway."

Cecelia dropped her eyes and she slid past Amanda.

"Cecelia, think about what you're doing."

But Cecelia didn't turn back to say anything. She kept Diane's ponytail in sight and followed her through the crowd.

* * * * *

"And you're sure you don't want me to go? For company on the drive, or to be an objective observer? Check out for any resemblance, that sort of thing?" Andrew said as he followed Elspeth out to the car before she went to Halifax.

Elspeth hesitated since that wasn't such a bad idea, but there was a part of her that wanted to be alone, not just for the meeting, but to prepare for the possible meeting with her possible sisters. "No pun intended, but since I am on this journey to find my Faith, I feel that I should do it alone."

"Finding your Faith, good one, Elspeth. Good luck with that." Andrew smiled at her. "You are one tough chick, did I ever tell you that?"

"Ha. I don't feel that tough today, Andrew. I feel like I am on a precipice. Not sure if I'm going to jump or fall flat on my face with this, or maybe I back away and forget the whole thing before I even get there. I'm going to see if the drive will give me an idea of the direction to take."

She shut the car door and waved at him as she pulled away. She didn't even turn on the radio. Her mind was racing in so many directions that she knew she'd be too deep in thought to hear it anyway. She tried to think of how she was going to approach this woman, if she found her home. She tried to think about why she wanted to even go down this road, but every time she seemed to be getting to the root of the issue, her heart would start palpitating and she would almost turn back.

Where was the proof in any of this? A priest's name on a baptismal certificate. That's all she really had. And a couple of half-remembered strange conversations with her parents. Her parents. Her mom being forty-six when she was born. That had always seemed a bit far-fetched, until it had happened to her too. Far-fetched, but when that was the only option to believe, you believe it, don't you? How else would a baby appear on a secluded mountain in the middle of nowhere in the winter?

Elspeth also thought long and hard about Madonna, if her heart could even take all this news. A possible baby? How would she deal with the guilt and shame, if she hasn't dealt with it up to now? A life she was robbed of by the religion that she trusts so deeply. Elspeth knew she'd be angry, if it had happened to her. No wonder she couldn't face the facts. She was told to bury them, the memory of a baby, her family, so deep. Would she be able to deal with the idea that her mother had also been used, abused, discarded, buried in the same way? As she stood looking down on the valley of death, would she fear no evil, if she really knew the evil that had been done to her? Could Elspeth be the one to take away that faith?

* * * * *

Cecelia was glad to see Diane and Bridget arriving alone at the museum. She poured them all a cup of tea after they had held hands for a short prayer. They were in such a routine and Cecelia felt very comfortable, sharing the adrenaline of the upcoming adventure that they were planning.

"It's going to be so great, when we are in São Paolo, working in the favelas, with the poor," Bridget said. "It will feel like we have a purpose. Something meaningful, don't you think?"

"The favelas, where most of the poor people live, are so colourful, but they're basically shacks. It's hard to call them houses, all of them stacked on top of each other. It's really easy to get lost when you head in there, except you know that if you head downward, you will finally reach the street and get out. It took me a long time to feel comfortable finding the school where I was going to be working without someone guiding me in every day."

Diane's voice always seemed so animated and excited when she talked about her work. It was contagious. Cecelia looked around at the museum and how she struggled to stay awake all day, the hum of the electricity in the afternoon lulling her to sleep. She felt a pang of guilt, knowing that they'd be left without a student for the summer with her leaving, but there were enough volunteers with the museum that they'd fill in, or find a slack student who hadn't applied for a job yet this summer to fill her position.

"So, have you told your parents, Cecelia?" Diane asked.

"No, I think they'll try to stop me, so I want to wait. I mean, I love them dearly, and they are the best parents a person could ever wish for, but it's going to be hard on them, me moving so far away, at least until I'm there, and settled and happy."

"What about your donation?"

"I have a lot in my own bank account, about seven thousand dollars. I've been saving up since I was in grade six for post-second-ary and I'm not a big spender, so it's there."

Diane took a second to consider, and she knew the Devoteds usually like to get the parents' buy-in because that made for more long-term support, but she had also been told to fulfill her commit-ment to the cause. She had to come back with a certain number of Contemplatives. Seven thousand dollars was a substantial donation, and she would be able to book the tickets without worrying about parental interference.

"That sounds good. We can book the tickets, say, Wednesday of next week? Be on the way maybe on Friday? What do you think, Bridget?"

Bridget smiled and reached over for Cecelia's hand. "I'm so glad you are going to be going with me, Cecelia. I'll feel so much better with you there too."

"I'm nervous. I'll tell you that, but I think it would be stupid if a person wasn't nervous. I think it's a sign that it's important to me." Cecelia took a deep breath. "Mom and Dad will be fine, once they see how happy I am there."

"I agree, Cecelia. My parents are so proud of what I am do-ing, and look at Bridget's mom. She knows that what we are doing is just one piece of the puzzle to help out in the world today. Let's say a prayer of thanksgiving." Diane took a hand of each of the girls, tugging them down to their knees.

Cecelia took a quick glance toward the street, but she didn't have time to check. It would be inappropriate now. Her head bowed in silence, she listened intently to Diane.

"Mother Mary, please look down on your daughters here, on bended knee, asking for you to watch over us and help us on this journey. We look forward to doing your work in Brazil, putting the needs of others before our own, working in a community with the intention of bringing faith and inspiration to those with little light in their lives. Look down on your newest Mary's Maidens, Bridget and Cecelia, with your pure heart, and help them deal with the people who may try to divert them from the path you have shown them. May they be strong in their ability to stay focused and committed, and may we all travel safely to do the Lord God's work. Amen."

* * * * *

It had reached eleven o'clock when Elspeth pulled into the driveway of the address in Halifax that Jerome had given her. It was a split-entry suburban house with a neatly kept lawn and a curving sidewalk with nice perennials making a colourful path to the front door. In Cape Breton, everyone would automatically head to the back door, but this felt a lot more formal than that, Elspeth thought, as she steeled herself to push the doorbell.

A teenage girl, slight, with short hair cut in a pixie style, opened the door with a big smile. "Hi, but Granma said to say that we don't need anything today."

"I'm not selling anything," Elspeth replied. "I'm looking for someone."

"Who is it, Trena?" a voice called from upstairs.

Elspeth could see up the stairs into the kitchen area, the railing to the living room above her head as she now stood on the landing. The girl had waved her in and had turned to go back up the stairs.

"She says she's looking for someone, Granma. You better come and talk to her yourself." She retreated up the stairs and stood at the top, leaving a space for her grandmother to come down.

Elspeth could feel her heart beating and wasn't sure what she was waiting for. It seemed to take a long time for the woman to finish whatever she was doing in the kitchen and Elspeth and the teenager were left awkwardly looking at each other, neither one of them ready to venture into a conversation.

The woman who finally appeared at the top of the stairs was young-looking for a grandmother, slight and agile, with dyed red hair. Elspeth searched for some resemblance to Jerome, or to Madonna, and even to herself, but there was nothing that jumped out and said, "Yes. You are my long-lost sister." She wished there had been. At the same time, there was a similarity in build, in the face. It was like trying to grab fog, this feeling of going into the unknown, looking for ghosts.

"Well? Do you have a name? Of the person you're looking for?" she asked, and her brusque manner certainly reminded her of Jerome.

"I was given this address by Jerome MacMillan. I'm looking for Faith MacMillan, his sister."

"Yes, Jerome is my brother. Come in, then. Come in. No good having a conversation like this." She gestured for Elspeth to come up. "Come in to the kitchen."

Elspeth bent down and took off her shoes, with each motion wondering what the next move should be. She felt that she was walking in water with uneven footing, trying to judge what would be the best step without slipping and drowning, hitting her head on a rock. She went up and sat at the table, both Faith and her granddaughter sitting across from her. Elspeth didn't know where to begin so there was an uncomfortable silence until finally Faith decided to ask the first question.

"How is Jerome? I haven't been down to see him in years now, and he's not one to write or call. I suppose I'm not the best sister, but he's not always the easiest brother either, to tell you the truth. Did he look well?"

"Yes. He seemed to be doing okay."

"Still smokin'? Drinkin'?" she asked, concern evident along with a share of self-preservation, after years of trying to change something that wasn't going to change.

"Yes, I'd say, but he's holding his own. His house is neat. He has food in the fridge, tea in the pot." Elspeth smiled. "He's a bit of a character, that's for sure."

"That's a nice way of putting it. Funny he'd even let you in his house, let alone in his fridge." Faith was curious. "You must have said something pretty important for him to let you in the door."

"It's your sister, Madonna. She got me in the door."

"Madonna? My sister, Madonna? I thought she was dead." Faith looked at her granddaughter. "Trena, why don't you go and do your homework now? I'd like to have this conversation in private. Can you do that?" Elspeth could see where the creases of time had etched themselves on Faith's face, even if her dye job and the haircut kept her youthful from a distance. "Madonna. Funny Jerome even let you in the door, if you brought her up."

"It wasn't easy. It took a couple of times going to Dominion to see him. He's an angry man."

"Poor Jerome. He's a fighter. Had to be, I guess. Bern and I left him to his own devices as soon as we could." She looked over at Elspeth as if she was seeing her for the first time. "I'm sorry; I haven't even asked you your name."

"I'm Elspeth MacKay. I live in Mabou, and my daughter befriended Madonna when she was up at the Convent there one weekend."

"Convent? She's in a convent?" Faith seemed genuinely shocked.

"Yes. She's a nun. She joined the Order shortly after she left your family home."

"A nun. She's a nun? It was all such a mystery to us. I remember her more than I remember Mama, but it's still all of a blur. It's not like I could have talked about it to any of them anyway, really. Too small, I suppose. And you just didn't do that, back then, did you? Growing up in Cape Breton? You didn't talk about things like that. Dig up the dirt. And Jerome. It lights a fire, sets him off, if we would even try to get any answers. It wasn't worth it." Faith's eyes were darting back and forth. "Do you mind if I call my sister

Bernadette? I suppose you know about her too? She's only a couple of years older than me but she's been mother and father to me all my life, poor Bern. She lives in an apartment not too far away. It won't take her long to come over. Are you in a rush?"

Elspeth shook her head. "No. I came here today just to do this, to talk to you. I can wait for Bernadette."

"I'll put the kettle on after I give her a call." Faith left the table in a rush, grabbing her cell phone and leaving the room. It wasn't long before she was back in, putting water in the kettle and turning it on.

Elspeth could see that it was as if she didn't want to go any further before her sister came. "So, Trena is your granddaughter?"

"Yes, she's sixteen going on nineteen, if you know what I mean. Her mother gets all riled up about her sometimes, so she spends a lot of time with me."

"I have a daughter who's eighteen, so I know exactly what you mean."

"Eighteen?" Faith's eyebrows rose in surprise, taking in Elspeth's gray hair.

"Yes, she was a bit of a shocker to me too. But hey, she made our lives interesting. Still does. In fact, she's why we got so involved with Madonna since she's flirting with the idea of being a nun."

"A nun? They still do that?" Faith put the tea bags in the teapot and put it on the stove.

"Some people do. Not many. The worst of it is that it sounds a bit more like a cult than a convent to me."

"Maybe it always was."

The women looked at each other, surprised and aware of how apt the comment fit the situation. There was a commotion around the glass doors heading out to the deck and Bernadette let herself in. She was a bit wider than her sister, and her hair was gray, cut short and severe. Elspeth steeled herself for what was to come. She felt that talking to Faith alone might have been the easier option.

"Bernadette. This is Elspeth. Elspeth MacKay. She knows our sister."

"Madonna? You've been talking to Madonna?" Bernadette slumped into the chair closest to her. "That's just plain shocking, isn't it, Faith? Like something out of a movie or something."

"She's been in a convent, Bern. A convent in Mabou." Faith shook her head, still reeling with the impact of it all.

"She hasn't been in Mabou all this time. Only the past fifteen years or so, maybe twenty, I think. She was sent as a missionary to Honduras, I'd say maybe when she was twenty or so." Elspeth looked at the two sisters, and felt a strange importance in being such a messenger, bringing these women a gift of a sister ... possibly two if she had the guts to bring it up. But she wasn't sure how much the women knew of the past, even of their mother's situation. Who their father possibly, probably was. "She's not well. A heart issue."

"That's what Da died of. Heart, wasn't it, Bern?" Faith asked, turning to her older sister again.

"I believe so. I remember the wake and being at the gravesite. I think he worked himself into the grave, that's what I think. People were so hushed around us. We weren't told the whole story, and we had to guess at why the boys were such a mess. It was like if we were sat down and given the truth, we would have gone off the wheels like the rest of them." Bernadette looked deep into Elspeth's eyes, looking for answers.

Elspeth was suddenly struck by the sensation of looking into her own face, the darkness under the eyes, the same wrinkle in the middle of her forehead. She had to shake it off to respond. "It was a tough situation, from what I understand from Jerome. He was quite hostile the first time we met. Thought I might be from the newspapers. I couldn't understand why he felt I'd be from the newspapers."

Bernadette and Faith looked at each other, feeling like they couldn't contribute a lot. "All we ever got was bits and pieces of info. Nothing concrete. I think they kept a lot from us. Being girls. Being so young," Faith finally said. "We didn't have a lot of friends either. We thought it was because of the boys, I mean, with Angus's suicide and the other two drinking themselves into early graves. I mean, sure it was a car accident that took the two of them, but they were always loaded, as much as I recall."

"Yes. The police were always at the farm, looking for them. They'd be fighting or up on charges for drinking and driving. No one was surprised by them passing away. The heaviest burdens ended up on Jerome's shoulders, all those deaths and funerals in such a short time. He turned plain bitter and didn't want much to do with us. I made the decision as soon as I was sixteen that we were out of there, and we were." Bernadette's determination was evident, even after all those years. She was a survivor, a fighter, but she had to be. "Came up to Halifax and started on Gottingen Street at the Woolworth's store, then moved on to Woolco when it came around. Ended my career at the Walmart."

"Bernadette gave everything up for me. Let me stay in school, supported me through university. She never once let me give up on trying to make something of myself." Faith fought back the tears, trying to say a thank you that was not often spoken.

"Well, you're helping me out now. Paying my rent every month." Bernadette swallowed hard. "It's hard to make a go of it on just the pensions I get every month, but Faith insists that she and Sam, that's her husband, have good teachers' pensions coming in and so they pay my rent."

"It's the least I can do, Bern, so don't talk about it. I wouldn't have that pension if it wasn't for you and you know it. I would have been right there at Walmart with you."

There was a moment where it felt that they had forgotten that Elspeth was in the room and they had lost the track of the conversation. Faith got up and put a plate of cinnamon rolls on the table and everyone took one, having a drink of tea and a bite in silence, before they came back to Elspeth once again.

"So. Does Madonna know what went on? Or did Jerome share more with you than he is willing to talk to us about? We rarely see him. We send cards and make the drive once in a while, but it's almost as if he's embarrassed when we're there." She looked over at Bernadette. "We stuck together like glue, the two of us. We were sisters, friends, and family. All of it."

Bernadette jumped in. "It was like we had the plague or something. No one would invite us to birthday parties. We never had someone stay over at our house. It was like we didn't really exist until we left the community and came to Halifax where no one knew us. Then we became people."

"That's right, Bern. It's like we weren't real or something when we were there. We could never figure it out."

Both women had turned to Elspeth now, ready for some answers. "I'm not sure where to start." She looked at the women, patiently waiting. She took another drink of her tea. "Well, this is what I understand, and it's more from what I pieced together from Jerome than what Madonna told me. She seems to have a bit of dementia or she's blocked all this out. It took a long time for her to even come up with names and she's not sure if what she remembers is real or just a bad dream." She paused again, trying to choose the right words. "Okay. So, as far as I can tell, Madonna was abused by the parish priest."

"Shit!" Bernadette responded. "And now she's a nun?"

"She doesn't seem to really remember it all, or if she does, she's not saying. Anyway, when she left, she was pregnant. At about fifteen or so, I'd say. She was pregnant and unwilling to give the name of the father."

Faith started to fill in the blanks. "She was unwilling to give the name of the father, because the goddamn Father had put the scare of the Lord into her."

"Probably. And she hadn't been one to leave the house. She hadn't even been going to school since your mother died a couple of years earlier. She was home or she was in church, didn't socialize with friends or go to school, so when she started showing ..."

"The rest of them thought it was one of the boys!" exclaimed Faith.

"Or Da himself. Who had knocked her up." Bernadette sat back in her chair. "No wonder no one would stay at our house."

"No wonder the boys were so angry and didn't want anything to do with us." Faith looked at Bernadette. "That explains so much. Why the whole world seemed to be against us when we were little."

"About ten years later, probably just after you headed to Halifax, someone in Antigonish finally came forward. A girl. Saying that the priest had abused her. And there was a bit of an investigation and news got back to Dominion because they were asking Jerome about it. Told him that Madonna was probably one of the victims." Elspeth took a breath. It was intense, this conversation, and she felt that she was shaking slightly. She had thought they would know some of this.

"Oh, the poor girl. And she had been whisked out of the country by that time. Right? Didn't you say she was working in Honduras?" Bernadette asked.

"Exactly. She was out of sight and out of mind." There was a moment of silence, before Elspeth spoke again. "But Jerome believes there was another victim in the house." She paused. "Now, there's no real proof, but he thinks that the priest may have also abused your mother. To him, that explains her suicide."

"Mama committed suicide too?" Bernadette had obviously not known that. "I thought she drowned."

"Jerome said she went swimming with rocks in her pockets. She drowned, but she drowned on purpose." Elspeth was exhausted. She knew she could not add anything more to this. She couldn't bring up her own part of the story until she had more proof. These women had too much to deal with as it was.

"Why would she do that? With all those kids at home?" Faith stopped, then it started to really sink in. It was so much to hear and understand. "The priest. He was getting at Ma first."

"Possibly for years." She looked around the table, not sure how to say this. "Hair colour seems to have been his main evidence so there's not much else to go on."

"Hair colour?" Faith asked.

"We were redheads, Faith. Gingers. Everyone else in the family was dark, black or brown. We were redheads." Bernadette looked at her sister with her dyed red hair. "You are still, but we all know that's from a bottle."

They all laughed, trying to ease the tension in the room. Faith looked at Elspeth. "Was the priest a redhead?"

"That's what Jerome thinks. I don't have any proof of that. I think he believed that you could have been Father Landon's daughters."

There was a long silence in the room. The pings from Trena's video game down the stairs in the TV room were clearly heard for a time. A car going by. Faith got up and went to look into the back yard. Bernadette played with her cup, and Elspeth wondered if she'd been a smoker in the past. Her fingers seemed to have a hard time resting still, reminding her of Jerome.

Finally, Elspeth spoke. "I don't know. Maybe I shouldn't have come. All of this was probably a mistake. You didn't need to know all this, but I just, well, I just sometimes get carried away with families and their stories and I always think that people would want to know. But maybe I'm wrong. Maybe it's better not to know some things."

Faith turned and looked at Bernadette, giving her a slight nod to indicate that she could speak first. "No. It makes sense. All of it. It explains so much and fills in so many blanks."

"Same for me. I mean, there's no need to go spreading it from the mountaintops or heading to the papers. I hope that's not your intention?" Faith asked.

"No. No. Of course not. This is purely personal, this interest."

"Why?" Bernadette asked. "Why is it personal?"

"I have a daughter, Cecelia, who wants to run off to Brazil to join a religious sect of some kind. She started talking to Madonna about what it was like to be a nun and I guess I'm looking for a reason for her to give up on that idea. Then Madonna had the heart attack and the poor woman couldn't even think of who she'd put in the obituary. All she could really remember was that her father was Gussie MacMillan. I started from there, which led me to Jerome, and I followed up on it." Elspeth felt she had to explain. "I retired last June from a career in Celtic Studies, and genealogy was my area of expertise. But I was usually dealing with ancient history, the Highland Clearances, that sort of thing. My husband is an expert there as well." She finished weakly, knowing that the women weren't really listening anymore. "It was my career to be nosy."

The women smiled, and Elspeth relaxed a little. "What do you see coming next?" she asked.

The sisters looked at each other. "A road trip to Cape Breton to see our long-lost sister Madonna seems like the thing to do, right, Faith? The poor thing. Used and abused and carted off all over the world. And poor Mama. It just puts a whole new slant on my life." Bernadette fought back tears. "Holy shit, women had it rough, didn't they?"

Faith nodded. "Gentle Madonna. I missed her so terribly when she left. I remember how kind she was, always brushing my hair. And now she's old, and we're all old. But she's alone. We can't let any more time slip away."

Chapter 16

Answers

They shall mount up with wings as eagles, they shall run and not be weary, and they shall walk and not faint.

– Isaiah 40:31

It was Sunday, and Cecelia was lying in her bed, looking at the ceiling and a wave of panic was passing through her body. It had been a strange discussion last night after Mom got home from Halifax. Her father asking questions, trying to piece it all together, and her mother revealing that she had found out that Madonna had been pregnant as a teenager. That's how she had ended up in the convent. She wasn't sure what to think of it. Surely, the world was a different place now. People were more aware. She knew all the safe touch stuff. It had been talked about over and over again in school. Girls weren't so stupid now, she was sure.

She sat up. She didn't feel any sense of loss, thinking about leaving this room. The carefully chosen dresser and bed, so new and fresh, like everything in her room, in the house, did not fill her with any sense of home or belonging. The room could have been from a picture in a magazine, and probably was. Though her mother had asked her for her opinion on everything, Cecelia had simply agreed to the suggestion, letting very little of her own needs for colour or comfort enter into the conversation. Now, she wondered if she had already known how little time she would be spending within the walls of this room, this house.

Whenever a darkness of doubt entered her mind, she was warding it off with a prayer and putting in her mind the image of her helping poor children. She tried to imagine their faces as she got them clean drinking water, as she showed them ways to keep germs from infecting them, killing them. She had only been able to get five hundred dollars out of the bank machine yesterday. Only five hundred. And when she asked Bridget about it, who asked her mother, she had found out that it was because she had a student account and that was the daily limit for withdrawals. She'd never be able to get the seven thousand for Diane by Tuesday at that rate. Holy Mary Mother of God, have mercy.

A knock on the door shocked her back to reality. "What do you want?" she asked, bluntly, not wanting to have her mother and father at her right now.

Elspeth's face peeked around the door. "Can I come in? I just want to talk to you. I need your help."

Cecelia sat up, loosening the blankets that she had been subconsciously winding around her. "Okay. What do you need help with? Is it the DVD player, Mom? You really need to know how to learn how to use that remote. You're not stupid."

"It's complicated, Cece, and I didn't want to bother you yesterday, you looked so upset yourself, but I think we need to come up with a plan. For Madonna. For all that I've found out. Especially with Faith and Bernadette arriving later today. How much should we tell Madonna? I'm worried about her heart, and her head, if she's blocked this stuff out for so long."

Cecelia was still sitting on her bed, as if she was frozen. She felt that if she started talking to her mom, it was all going to come out, and maybe it should all come out. Maybe it would be best if it did, but at the same time, she had committed to Diane and Bridget and there was no turning back. She'd have to get the money, go to the bank on Monday.

"What's wrong, Cece? You really haven't been yourself lately. Are you okay?" Elspeth sat on the side of the bed. "Maybe I've been too wound up in Madonna's problems. Am I missing something here?"

"No. I'm all right, Mom. Really." She looked her mother in her eyes to reassure her. It seemed to work.

"Well, you know it was quite a meeting I had with Faith and Bernadette. Finding out how little they knew about the situation, and the whole bit." Cecelia nodded, so Elspeth continued. "Do you think Madonna is going to be able to deal with all this? Her sisters? Discussing the abuse and her mother's death, well, suicide?"

"You said Madonna kind of admitted that she understood her mother committed suicide. I don't think you should bring that up again, Mom. Maybe just see how she responds to Faith and Bernadette."

"I want you to come up to the Convent with us when they get here. You started all this and I think it's important that you be there to support Madonna, and be a friendly face in the middle of this chaos. You up for that?" Elspeth had been glad that Cecelia hadn't overreacted about the abuse, the priest. She hadn't taken it personally or acted defensively and Elspeth had been sure to keep looking at Andrew and not bring the Brazil group up at all. At the same time, she was wishing that Cecelia would put two and two together and come up with four, and realize how powerless she could be if she decided to go there.

"Yeah. That makes sense. I did start this whole thing. I should go." Cecelia and her mother both turned to the window as they heard a car pull into the driveway.

"Well. That sounds like they're here. Let's go and do this. My God, I feel like I'm heading into a boxing ring or something. I'm not ready."

"You'll be fine, Mom. I'll be there too."

"I'm glad of that, Cecelia. I think it's an important thing we'll be doing today, and I'm glad you'll be with me." She smiled, then patted Cecelia's leg. "Off we go. Ready or not."

* * * * *

Madonna was in the chair in the library when Cecelia and Elspeth walked in. They had decided that it was too much for them to all walk in at once, that Cecelia and Elspeth should break the ice. The old woman was glad to see them and waved them to sit in the chairs across from her.

"How are you feeling, Madonna?" Cecelia asked.

"I'm feeling much better, thank you, dear. The reports have come back and there was a slight blockage on one side, and some strange arrhythmia issue, but they think with one of those balloon things they can open it up. I don't know. It doesn't make a lot of sense to me, no matter how many times they try to explain it to me. At least, I don't feel that I'm going to die any minute, which was kind of what I felt like for a while there."

"That's good," Elspeth said, "because you are going to need a strong heart today."

"Oh, dear. That sounds troublesome. Did you go to see Jerome again?"

"Yes, I did and he gave me an address. I found your sisters, Faith and Bernadette."

Madonna sat quietly, looking from Elspeth to Cecelia and back again, not quite clear about what was happening. "You found them?"

"Yes, I went to Halifax and I met with them. They are lovely women, Madonna. They worked hard all their lives to help each other out, and they had no idea about what happened to you, or why the family was so dysfunctional. They found their way, but it was based on their own strength, no parents to guide them. You've got to give them credit." Elspeth looked at Cecelia and nodded.

"And they're here, Madonna, if you want to meet them. If you feel it wouldn't be too much for you. Would you like to meet them?" Cecelia asked.

"The girls? They're here?" Her eyes widened and her hands tightened on the arms of her chair.

Elspeth and Cecelia nodded. Madonna looked through the window, unable to speak.

The girls. Faith and Bernadette. Faith had been so tiny, perched on her hip, all the time, chattering away. She always had to be careful that she didn't pull something off the stove or off the table. Bernadette so serious, except when she was alone with Faith. Then Madonna would hear their laughter through the wall, an ache growing in her heart. As she had packed her suitcase, knowing she would never be back, she had taken her dolls, the two that she had, and put them at the end of the girls' bed, one on either side. She had always felt more like a mother to the little ones, too old, too big, to be a sister. Them with their little hands, their big eyes and silken hair, so soft, so fragile compared to her. And when she washed their hair, she'd always have them bend over the washtub for one final rinse, their hair a curtain over their faces and at the base of their skulls, where only she would notice, on each of their necks, was a little cherry-coloured birthmark. A little red stamp on their heads. Marking them as special.

"They're really here?" Madonna's voice reflected both hope and fear.

"Yes," Elspeth responded. "They drove from Halifax today, but they weren't sure if you would want to see them."

"Yes. I'd like to see them. I'd like to see them very much," she replied quietly.

Elspeth turned and left the room, leaving Cecelia alone with Madonna. There was a moment of silence before Cecelia asked, "How do you feel, Madonna? Are you going to be okay with all this?"

The old lady's eyes were watery, washed-out orbs looking at the young girl. "I've been thinking so much lately, laid up, looking at the ceiling and looking back at my life. Trying to piece it all together. You once asked me why I became a nun, and, Cecelia, I still don't really know what the real answer is. I think something bad happened to me, and I'm afraid those girls know it. Know the truth. I don't know if my dreams, my nightmares, were the truth. I mean, what is the truth anyway after seventy-eight years of living?"

Cecelia didn't know what to say so she went to the window where she could look down into the parking lot. She could see her mother taking a minute to talk to the women, then step back as they started getting out of the car, smoothing their hair and their clothes. Bernadette snapped a couple of hairs off her shoulder and one off Faith's back as they walked across the parking lot. "Do you think you're strong enough for all this?" she finally asked.

"Oh, yes, my dear. I am strong enough for this. I have to be. This is a gift I never expected." She shook her head. "Family is family. I felt dead to my family, as if I had never existed. For a long time. Dead. Now, I feel something I haven't felt in a long time. Those memories, the good ones and the bad ones, connecting me to something I didn't even know I was missing."

"They seem like nice women, Madonna. They're easy to talk to, Mom says," Cecelia added.

"That's good. I'm sure they are, dear," she replied and they could hear the footsteps in the hall, coming closer. "Sit in this chair next to me, okay, Cecelia? Just stay close."

"No problem." Cecelia smiled and quickly sat in the chair closest to the old lady. She felt a surge of protectiveness as she looked at Madonna, so frail and afraid before her. She tried to imagine what she was thinking, as she had when she was with her watching the movie. The delicate gradations of fate that had changed her life had now come full circle. She was struck with the feeling of being an adult, not wanting her child to be afraid, but knowing that she'd have to face what was coming. She reached over and took her hand, and Madonna responded with a strong squeeze, glad of the support.

Elspeth ushered Faith and Bernadette into the room. Bernadette looked at Faith, who urged her forward with a slight tilt of her head.

"Madonna? It's me. Bernadette." She hesitated again, not sure what she was dealing with, Alzheimer's, dementia. "Your sister? Do you remember me?"

Madonna sat in wonder, not saying a word.

Bernadette pressed on, bringing Faith forward. "And this is Faith. She's the youngest. She was only four or so when you left." It was so quiet, everyone looking expectantly at Madonna. "I was six." She stopped talking.

Elspeth brought over two more chairs and they all sat down. Madonna was still, looking at the women. Finally, she spoke. "You are so old." Her voice was quiet and sad.

Elspeth tried to lighten the moment. "Aren't we all! Well, except Cecelia, I guess."

Madonna's eyes filled with tears. "You were so beautiful, the both of you. I thought you were little angels, with your red hair and soft, clear skin. It was the best joy I had, dressing you, doing your hair." She choked up, unable to go on speaking.

Cecelia reached and grabbed a couple of tissues from the box on the small table in front of them and passed them to Madonna. Then she looked and realized all of them needed some, even her mother, so she passed the box around. Everyone waited patiently for Madonna to speak again after she finished blowing her nose and taking a deep breath.

"I guess I shouldn't be so shocked that you are old. You couldn't stay children. I know that. I'm not crazy." She smiled a bit and shook her head. "Not yet, anyway. It's so nice that you are real. But my life has passed by, and only now I am seeing you."

"Are you all right, Madonna? Do you want to have some quiet time to adjust? You don't want to overstress the heart." Elspeth was concerned. Madonna's face had lost all colour, and her lips had taken on a bluish tinge.

"No. I'm going to be fine. Really. Faith, could I ask you a strange favour?"

"Sure, anything, Madonna."

"Could I look at the back of your neck? At the hairline?" Madonna seemed embarrassed, but insistent.

"My neck?"

"Yes, if you don't mind."

Faith came over and slowly knelt beside Madonna's chair. She bent forward and Madonna swept the hair up at the base of her hairline. Everyone heard Madonna take in an audible breath. "It's there." She traced something with her thumb, and Cecelia, overcome by curiousity, came to look at what Madonna was seeing.

Elspeth asked, "What is it?"

"It's like a birthmark, a red patch. Just within the hair at the base of the neck," Cecelia explained.

Madonna caressed it one more time. "I used to always watch for it. Every time I washed their hair, their heads over the sink in the kitchen. That little stamp of red on their neck."

Bernadette asked, "I have it too?"

Faith got up. "Let me see."

"Yes, you have it too, Bernadette. It's a birthmark of some type, I suppose. But it brings me back, seeing it again. To the kitchen, dealing with the pair of you, getting you washed up."

"I remember that too, Madonna. I do." Bernadette let everyone look at the base of her neck, and then, once again, the rest checked out Faith's neck as well.

"That's interesting," Elspeth said, sitting back down. "I've heard of moles being in the same spot for one family for five generations. But family birthmarks are not that common. Interesting."

"I thought so too," Madonna said. "That they both had a mark." She got quiet again, and everyone sat, wondering if she was going to bring anything up about her mother, or Father Landon. She looked out the window, the heat of the summer afternoon creeping in with the sunshine.

The sunshine on her face as she walked through the field to the church. The swaying grasses waiting to have the first cut, whenever Da could borrow the harvester. The feeling of serenity as she left the house, the girls waving from the doorway, knowing that she'd be home after she finished at the Glebe House and sweeping the church. She let herself fall in to that feeling of peace, of serenity, of serving the Lord, with every step she took. Her mind becoming a prayer, filled with the joy of the world and her place in it. She was a vessel for the Lord and that had to be a good thing. Father said so.

"Madonna?" Bernadette's voice was concerned.

"I never really went back, in my mind, you know, until Cecelia here came and made me think about my family." She reached out for Cecelia's hand. "And now we know, don't we, why my mother would have picked the name Bernadette?"

Cecelia smiled, "Of course. Because of the movie, *A Song for Bernadette*."

"A movie? I was named after a movie?" Bernadette asked with surprise. "I was sure it was just another saint or something."

"Oh, she was a saint too," Cecelia said. "I watched the movie with Madonna a couple of weeks ago."

"It must be an old movie, if our mother watched it." Faith sat back and crossed her legs. "I don't ever remember going to a movie when we lived in Sydney."

"It was a special evening. You and Bernadette weren't even born yet, Faith," Madonna said. "Just me, and Mama and Da went. It was something for me to watch it again." She could feel the tears coming again. "Bernadette and Faith. Holy Mary Mother of God."

Normally, afterward, he would motion for her to get on her knees and he would place a hand on her forehead and pray, "Dear Lord, please look down on us believers on earth who you try to tempt into depravity and sin. Look down here on your vessel, Madonna, and cleanse her of her impurities and her womanly weaknesses that bring her into the darkness of temptation. Madonna, are you ready to make your confession?"

She would bow her head and repeat the words she had learned through her catechism: "I confess to Almighty God, and you, Father Landon, that I have greatly sinned, in my thoughts and in my words, in what I have done and in what I have failed to do, through my fault, my most grievous fault, so I ask Blessed Mary ever-Virgin, and all the angels and saints, and you, Father Landon, to pray for me to the Lord our God."

"You are a daughter of Eve, full of evil and temptation, but the Lord God forgives you, Madonna, because He knows you work constantly to serve him. May God have mercy on you, and forgive you your sins, and bring you to everlasting life."

With that, she would feel his hand lift from her head, but she would keep her eyes on the floor, feeling more than seeing his black cassock whoosh out the door, closing it, and leaving her with her penance and her cleaning duties.

Elspeth was getting more and more concerned. Madonna had not said anything for quite some time. "Madonna? Maybe we'll leave now? Let you have a quiet time?" Still no response. "Cecelia, why don't you stay here and we'll go down to the house for a bit? We can come back up in an hour or so? Give her a chance to rest. If she wants to sleep, you can just walk home."

The three women left the room. Cecelia stayed sitting beside Madonna, whose eyes stared blankly into the space ahead of her.

Chapter 17

Family

When we imagine we have finished our story fate has a trick of turning the page and showing us yet another chapter.

— Lucy Maud Montgomery

"I'm sure she just needed a bit of a rest, a little time," Elspeth said, passing a cup of tea to Bernadette. "It must have been a huge shock. Seeing the both of you after so many years."

"Yes. I can't imagine what's going through her mind." Faith took the tea and sat back in her chair with the cup. "I remember her, but barely, like a watercolour painting. A flash and a sensation. That's about it."

"Oh, I remember her very strongly, and I know how hard it was on Pa when she went away. We were too young to do much, and it was Angus who got the brunt of the work. He was softer than the rest, poor Angus, and he wasn't fully equipped to take care of us, two little girls. Those poor men. When you think of it, they'd probably be watching each other. Who would really want to be seen bathing their little sisters after all that was being said about them? It's so clear to me now why we were left to ourselves, to be clean or not. It was really up to ourselves, so bathing became much more of a rare occasion." Bernadette shook her head. "We were probably the only kids who asked for the bath to be filled once in a while, but we were locked in the room by ourselves. No one was allowed to come in until we were fully dressed. I simply took it for normal."

"Do you remember any conversations, as the years passed?" Elspeth asked. "Words between your father and your brothers about Madonna?"

"No. She was never spoken of, not in the house that I could remember. I mean, in school, as I grew older, girls would ask about my older sister. They'd ask if we ever heard from her, that sort of thing. I just figured she'd run away." Bernadette looked out the window, noticing an eagle perched on a spruce tree at the edge of the river. "I'm trying to imagine what she's thinking about, but it's hard to piece it all together."

"How different her life must have been, especially when she was taken to Honduras. She must have been so scared." Faith shook her head. "I can't even fathom what the young girl went through, especially with no one to talk to, after the abuse."

"And the baby," Elspeth spoke up, looking at the women in her living room. "We can't forget about the baby."

"Do you know anything?" Faith asked. "In your research, did you find anything?"

Elspeth took a breath, then shook her head. "Nothing for sure. Only what Jerome said. That she left the house pregnant."

"The boys and Da looking at each other, wondering who was guilty." Faith looked at Bernadette. "Thank goodness for Bernadette, getting me out of there before it all blew up."

Bernadette replied, "I'm not so sure. Maybe if we had stayed until word got back to us about the rumours following that priest, maybe we could have done something. Tracked Madonna down, maybe. If I hadn't been so selfish." She fought back tears. "I really couldn't deal with it anymore. You know? The tension. All of them, so wrapped up in guilt and accusations. Da. Funeral after funeral. We were all just plain lost."

"You did what you had to do, and that wasn't easy as a

sixteen-year-old. To pack up her little sister and head off on your own." Faith went over and put her arms around her sister. "You had no choice."

"When I look back, it's like none of us had a choice. None of us." Bernadette could not stop the tears.

"I guess it made a nun of one of us," Faith smiled, looking Bernadette in the eyes, forcing a smile out of her. Bernadette shook her head at the sad pun.

* * * * *

I hope she isn't having a stroke, was all that Cecelia kept thinking while she waited for Madonna to come out of her reverie. She felt that this was all her fault, bringing all this on the old lady, pushing her mother to do the research, making her face her past. She tried to tell herself that she had simply been trying to do the right thing, but that was hard to accept looking at Madonna's pale face. She had closed her eyes now, and seemed to be sleeping in the chair.

She thought about her father, and his crazy laugh and his energy, and how shocking it was to see the difference between him and Madonna, who looked so frail but who was the same age. Could she really leave him and Mom and go so far away? What if he got sick and she wouldn't be here to help? She didn't want to think about it, but she knew the revelations of the day had shaken her rosy picture of the religious life. Was there something else she could do to make her feel the same way she did about Mary's Maidens? Useful. Helpful. In a community of people doing good things. But Diane and Bridget were depending on her. She'd given her word. She didn't want to be one of those people who are always quitting on their dreams, their ideals. But was that enough to go to Brazil?

After twenty minutes passed, Cecelia received a text from her mother asking how things were going. Madonna, hearing the ding from the phone, finally opened her eyes.

"How are you feeling, Madonna?"

"I feel brittle. That's how I feel, brittle."

"Like, your bones? Like you're going to break?"

"No. My spirit. That's what feels brittle, Cecelia. When I was young, young like you, I was pliable. That's what I was. I was pliable, like one of those dolls you could stretch and change and turn into whatever shape you wanted it to be. And now, now, I am brittle. My mind wants to accept things, but I'm afraid I'm going to crack, trying to change even a little."

"Is it because of your sisters? Was that too much, meeting them?"

Madonna looked at the young girl in front of her, and, while looking into that innocent face, she tried hard to piece together images and memories of her two sisters, those women, old women now. She had been innocent and young, like Cecelia, and so had they, once. "It was a shock. A huge shock. I am trying to get my head and heart to accept it all. That I have my own family. People who grew up in the same house. Who have stories about my brothers, my father, my poor mother. It's amazing." She stopped for a minute, catching her breath. "Cecelia, I gave away too much. I did. You have to think about your life. Don't become too pliable."

"What do you mean?"

"Don't let them change who you are." Madonna leaned towards the girl and took her hand, squeezing it fiercely.

"Who?"

"The ones. The ones who are going to make you a nun. Don't let them change who you are. Don't let them take you away from your family until they are old." She was squeezing Cecelia's hand.

"But I want to be special, Madonna. I want to do something different, something that will help the world, the poor." Cecelia was feeling a bit afraid, wanting to pull her hand out of Madonna's clutches, but not sure how to do it. "Besides, my family is already old." She smiled, hoping that Madonna would smile too. "Dad's your age, remember?"

"Cecelia. Something bad happened to me. Something really bad." Madonna looked up, her pale eyes searching and intense. "Does your mother know? What happened to me?"

Cecelia was uncertain what to do. She wished her mother hadn't left her alone to deal with this situation. Should she tell her what she knew? She nodded.

"She found out from Jerome? About when I was taken away? Do the sisters know?"

Cecelia nodded again. Madonna released her hand and sat back, almost relieved. "Good. I don't think I could talk about it. I'm an old lady. An old nun. May God forgive me my sins, and bring me to life ever-lasting." She crossed herself and didn't say anything. "Such shame. I can still feel it. In my bones. I can feel it."

"I don't think you need to consider them your sins, Madonna. There was a lot of darkness in the Church at that time. People know better now than to put up with that. You were only a young girl."

"They do, do they, Cecelia? You think about that long and hard, my dear. Please. Think about that long and hard before you commit to Brazil."

"But you still have your faith, Madonna. I can see that you do."

"I have my faith, yes. I have to keep that. My mind, my soul, where it would be without my prayers and my belief that God is waiting for me? But did I really have my life?" Madonna looked at Cecelia, who looked away, not sure how to respond.

"They want me to give them my savings," Cecelia blurted out.

"The Brazil people? They want your money?" Madonna's eyebrows lifted.

"And my parents' too. Said it's like university tuition and I'll learn so much." Cecelia could tell she was slipping, losing the steam to keep going. She felt like a little girl finding out about the tooth fairy, Santa Claus, where babies come from. She felt embarrassed and knew that her fear of telling her parents was probably rooted in her unwillingness to face the reality of the situation, her uncertainty of what she wanted to do in life. She could see the romance of it all dimming against the harsh light of Madonna's experience.

"Don't be a pushover, Cecelia. Don't be like me." She shook her head and wiped the tears from her eyes. They sat in silence, listening for the women to return.

* * * * *

Elspeth looked at her phone when she heard the notification. "Cece says that she's talking again. She'll meet us at the door. Are we ready for round two?" She looked over at the women on the sofa, her sofa, in her new home. She could see the three of them in the mirror, and she was struck by the resemblance between them, the shade of gray so similar between her and Bernadette, Faith's hairline the same as her own. But she had no proof.

Before they were able to leave the house, Andrew came back from the grocery store. He had picked up some things for a nice meal later. "I'm glad I caught you, Elsie. You don't mind if I steal her for a few minutes, do you?" He gave Elspeth a knowing glance.

"Excuse me, I won't be but a minute. I know you want to get back up there. Make yourselves at home. Check out the view on the deck. It's lovely." She followed Andrew into the office. Within a few minutes, she was back in the living room saying that she was ready to go, looking back at Andrew, who gave her the thumbs-up sign in support.

Cecelia was waiting in the parking lot for them. "I'm so glad you're here, Mom." She hugged her mother, with a sense of urgency that Elspeth hadn't felt for some time.

"What happened? Is Madonna okay?"

"Yes. She's doing remarkably well, I think, though she's pretty shook up. She's remembered that something awful happened. That she left home in shame. I think that she knows she was pregnant, but she's not saying it straight out. She asked me if you knew, Mom, what had happened to her and I said yes, and she doesn't seem to want to discuss it. Not out loud. It's pretty intense and I'm not sure if I'm the one to help her through it."

Elspeth pushed the hair back on her daughter's forehead, again recognizing the hairline, the cowlick making the hair curl up and away off her face. She smiled at her, glad to see her connecting again. "You are the perfect person to help Madonna through this."

Bernadette started walking towards the door, pulling them all towards the building with her motion. "Did she say anything else?"

"About the past? Just that she felt that she had been 'pliable.' That was her word."

"In other words, she knows she was used. Used, abused, and discarded." Faith sounded angry, and her footsteps going up the stairs were heavy with determination. "How do you deal with that? At her age?"

"Shush, Faith. We want to support her. Not make it harder," Bernadette responded.

"Yes. She says she feels brittle. Like she could break." Cecelia looked up at her mom. "She doesn't know how to deal with what she's remembering."

"Who would, my darling? Who would?" Elspeth had everyone stop a few feet from the room. "I brought the photo that Jerome gave me." She showed the photo of Madonna, with her mother and the priest. "I'm not sure if I should show it to her or not, but I think she's open to it now."

Bernadette looked at the photo. "Jerome never showed that to us."

Faith looked at the photo. "That was Mama? Gosh, she looks like a girl herself."

"She was pregnant with you there, Faith. That's what Jerome said." Elspeth took the photo back.

Faith looked up at Elspeth before responding. "I think she's tougher than we think. I think we should start being honest, opening it up. Get it over with."

Elspeth looked over at Bernadette, who nodded. "Okay. Cecelia, you stay close to her."

They went into the room and all sat down again. Madonna's hands were busy saying the rosary, her eyes closed, her lips not moving. They waited until she opened her eyes. She smiled at them and slipped the rosary into her right hand, her arthritic fingers covering it, protecting it.

"It's been a big day for you, Madonna," Elspeth started. "And we all know that going back to those days, when you left home, are hard ones to think back on. Cecelia says that you talked to her and know that something sad, shameful happened at that time, and I think you also know that the priest was involved. Father Landon. Am I right?"

Madonna nodded her head. She didn't say anything, just the little nod to signify as much. Her sisters brought their chairs closer, and Cecelia knelt by her chair. Her eyes began to fill, but she leaned over and took a tissue on her own. She nodded again, looking at Elspeth to continue.

"Jerome told me that the family had a terrible time after that, because people in the community ... Well, the people in the community weren't looking at the priest. They didn't consider that angle, Madonna, so your brothers, your father ... They got the brunt of the blame."

A short intake of breath was all that Elspeth could distinguish to show that she was following the sad narrative. Madonna reached out for Cecelia's hand.

"They couldn't deal with it. The boys, Callum and David, they turned to drink to drown their anger and frustration and died young in a car accident. Angus, who had taken on a lot of your responsibilities in the house, well, he committed suicide, and all of it was too much for your Da. His heart gave out. I'm not sure when you girls headed to Halifax." Elspeth looked at Bernadette.

"We left in the spring of '63. Jerome had sold the farm a couple of years earlier, and we moved into town with him for a little while." Bernadette's voice was calm and quiet, showing little emotion.

"Until the endless tension drove us away," Faith interjected. "But, I guess, looking back, we should give Jerome a bit of a break. He probably did the best he could."

"It was only after the mess of those fifteen years or so that something came from the Diocese in Antigonish, and in the late

'60s, a preliminary inquiry into Father Landon came about after some complaints. A girl came forward in Antigonish. A girl whose family was a bit better connected. But it didn't go far. Father Landon was defrocked, but from what Andrew found out," Elspeth took a paper out of her purse, "he was defrocked, but 'not excommunicated and remained in communion with the Church as a baptized brother in Christ.' No charges were laid. He stayed a priest. The case was closed and he went to a monastery to live his life in penance and prayer, supported by the Church. He died in 1982."

Madonna took a deep breath. Her whole body relaxed as Elspeth spoke of Father Landon's death. Faith and Bernadette were listening intently.

Cecelia looked at her mother, calmly dealing with the situation with such quiet compassion. She felt like an adult, a grown woman in the grown women's circle. She looked around at the faces, and imagined the years fade away, as they were all brought back to when Madonna was a girl, all of them young, dealing with so much. She could not remember feeling so intrinsically a part of something, like a heart beating. It was a feeling that she would remember for her whole life, a moment ingrained on her soul.

"Madonna, Jerome gave me a photo. Of you, and your mother, and Father Landon." Elspeth passed Madonna the picture and she let the rosary slip onto her lap as she held the photo between her two hands.

She looked at her mother's face, the small bump under the tight dress. Her face had always been a blur to her, and she avoided looking at Father Landon. She wanted to see her mother's face, the face she had dreamed of for so long.

"So much of this is your mother's fault, her sin of being unable to accept being the Lord's vessel, accepting his seed. First John 3:9 states 'No one born of God makes a practice of sinning, for God's seed abides in him.' Or her. God's seed abided in her, and she was a chosen vessel unto me, and she grew large and strong with God's seed, but then," he stopped and his finger traced down the side of her face in a rare moment of recognition, "she rejected the idea of being His vessel the third

time. She rejected it by doing what she did. Do you see the error of her ways? She was not a pure vessel, willing to fulfill the sacrifice demanded of her by God. You, Madonna Mary, you are a pure vessel, so pure in fact, that now that you have accepted the seed, you must go."

Madonna stayed still, thinking of her mother, her mother going through this. For years. A pure vessel filled twice. She looked up at Father Landon with his faded red hair and dark brown eyes. She could feel the colour more vibrant, strong, passing through her fingers as she washed Bernadette's hair. She felt like her tongue had been removed from her mouth. She was speechless, speared straight through the heart with the agony of her mother.

"Yes, Madonna Mary, you must fulfill your destiny and become a cloistered nun, and serve the Lord as you were meant to do. Kneel, Madonna, and I will hear your confession and absolve you of all your sins, and prepare you for the life of servitude ahead."

The tears crept down Madonna's face, crawling over the creases of the wrinkles and down into the hollows of her neck. They were silent tears, no sobbing, or catching of breath, just little trickles of sadness leaking out and pooling in the folds of age. She passed Cecelia the photo and put her hands out to her sisters.

"Poor Mama," was all she could say before the dam burst and they all had to take a breath and cry. "I should have done something. I should have been stronger. For you, Bernadette, and you, little Faith. I should have been a woman who could speak, who could say something, but I'd never been a talker. I didn't know how to do it."

The women all hushed and made small soothing sounds as Madonna cried. They rubbed her back, tried to draw away her pain. "You were so young, Madonna. So young. It's not your fault. None of it is your fault," Bernadette kept saying.

Elspeth came closer to the group, huddled around Madonna's chair. "And you had the baby, a girl."

Madonna nodded, looking up at her, almost surprised to hear the story continue.

"Do you know what happened to the baby?" Bernadette

asked, surprised. Faith's and Madonna's eyes were fixated on Elspeth. Cecelia couldn't believe all that her mother had figured out in such a short time.

"I think I do. I had Andrew confirm something while we were at the house." She stopped. "I think we all need to sit back down for this." Everyone but Madonna was up, no longer sitting in a chair. After everyone was comfortable, Elspeth started again. "It was a strange coincidence, I guess, starting with Cecelia here, even meeting Madonna and striking up a friendship. But some of the dates seemed to be too coincidental. When I started doing research, it started lining up, the dates. Fall of 1953, winter of 1954. My birth date being one of those times, and me never having a birth certificate, and it all lining up around the same time as Madonna was taken from home."

Cecelia was shocked. Was her mother losing her mind?

"And I started thinking back to a few cryptic conversations I had with my own parents, one of them in the hospital in Inverness. I could get my hands on my baptismal certificate fairly easily, and can you guess who baptized me?"

"Father Landon!" Cecelia exclaimed, her hand coming up to her mouth in shock.

"Exactly." Elspeth smiled. "Exactly."

"You've got to be kidding," Bernadette responded.

"So I had Andrew do a bit more digging, and Father Landon was at the parish up in Glencoe, just for a few months, during that 1953-54 time frame, in the winter, and then he was moved further down the province, to get him out of sight, no doubt." Elspeth paused. "Now, none of this is proven, right? It's a bit of a coincidence, and there's no definite proof, but Madonna gave us another piece of the puzzle today." Elspeth walked over and kneeled beside Madonna's chair. "Can you check the back of my neck, Madonna? See what you can see?" She tilted her head forward.

Madonna looked at her sisters, and slowly lifted up the back of Elspeth's hair. She gasped, as did Faith and Bernadette. Cecelia came over to see, and she could clearly make out the red wine-coloured marking at the base of her mother's hairline.

No one said anything. Elspeth sat back on her haunches, looking up at Madonna. "I think you might be my mother, Madonna."

"Shit." Cecelia had slumped on the chair behind her. "Shit. That's crazy."

"Cecelia!" Elspeth admonished her daughter as she got to her feet.

"I agree with Cecelia," Faith said. "That's just crazy shit." She couldn't help but smile and shake her head. "That's too weird."

"But it could be right. It never seemed right to me that Mama had me when she was forty-six, with absolutely no one knowing beforehand."

"Forty-six. Geesh. I didn't know that could even happen," Bernadette commented.

Madonna had been sitting there, not saying a word. She looked from face to face, confused. "I don't understand."

Elspeth knelt by Madonna again, and took her hands in hers. "The dates line up, my birth, and when you left. Father Landon arranged for my parents to take me. They were elderly, isolated, and very religious and felt that I was a gift from God. I mean, they never came out and actually told me that I was adopted, they would never have done that, and no doubt, Father Landon gave them a good scare as well. When I left home and again when Ma was dying, there was enough said to make me think twice about if I was really theirs. I knew it would kill them if I pushed it, so I let it go, and never thought too much about it. But Father Landon's name is on my baptismal certificate, and I have the same birth mark as Faith and Bernadette. I don't know. I've been looking at Faith's cowlick, so much like mine."

"Mine too," Cecelia said.

Faith reached out to touch Cecelia's hair. "And it's the same colour as mine. Well, like mine used to be. It's real colour. You and my granddaughter, Trena, are going to be fast friends, I can tell."

"And Elspeth, our hair colour now is almost the same gray, with the front hair so white and the back so much darker," Bernadette observed.

"So that would make Madonna your mother, and Bernadette

and Faith, what, your aunts?" Cecelia asked. She looked around at these women, a family, a miraculous family that had suddenly appeared before her. She had always felt so alone, so isolated, a tiny branch on a lonely tree, and she could feel connections growing around her. She felt a jolt of recognition that this may have been something she was searching for as she held hands with Bridget and Diane, a feeling of belonging to something bigger.

"And sisters," Faith said. "Aunts and sisters."

"Jerome will be pleased, won't he?" Bernadette said, laughing. "Oh, my God. We'll be all over the Internet."

"Maybe we just won't tell him," Elspeth commented.

"Maybe we just won't tell anyone," Madonna said. They all looked at her.

"We won't, Madonna. We won't. We could do the DNA thing, I guess, if we wanted to be sure. But we won't say anything, not unless you want us to," Elspeth promised.

Madonna nodded. "At least for a while. Let me get used to it. Holy Mary, Mother of God, blessed be thy name, and blessed be the fruit of thy womb ... Blessed be the fruit of my womb. Elspeth." She reached out for her daughter's hand for the first time.

"You have said you were rooted in your faith, Madonna. Has this shaken it? Have you lost your faith?" Elspeth asked, trembling with emotion, the frail hand nestled like a fragile egg in her hand.

"I have to keep my roots in my faith, Elspeth. They are so deep there and they have given me a fruitful life, but now, I have roots of a different kind, and now, miraculously, I have branches too. God has been kind to let me find you all before I died. I was his vessel, and I carried you, who carried you." Madonna reached out to Cecelia with her other hand. "And you found me. It's a miracle if I ever saw one."

* * * * *

Walking out of the Convent that evening, with the sun setting and all five of them going back to Elspeth's for a late supper that Andrew was cooking, it felt strangely familiar already.

Cecelia pulled her mother aside before she got in the car. "I'm not going to Brazil. I've decided."

Relieved, Elspeth asked, "Why? Because of Madonna's abuse?"

"No. It's because of something she said this afternoon, about how she had been pliable. That word struck me. I don't think I want to be changed, formed, smoothed into a shape of something that I don't want. I think I better take some time to figure out who I am before I give that up, like Madonna was forced to do."

"That's good to hear. Life is too short to give it up."

"And they wanted money. All the money I had in my bank account as a donation."

"What!" Elspeth's voice rose in alarm.

"I know. I know. It's not a good feeling, but it all made sense when they were talking about it. I think my old Scotch blood kicked in. I knew Dad would have a fit too, giving away all my savings." She smiled and held her mother's arm for a moment. "I have seen today too that there's a lot more I need to learn from you. I don't want to be Madonna trying to picture her mother's face from an old photo."

Elspeth's sense of relief almost brought her to tears again, but she didn't want to seem overly emotional about it. She had to stay cool. "You've been pretty gung-ho about it all. I'm surprised with the shift."

"I'm young. I can change my mind, but I'm still not going to university." Cecelia's voice sounded defensive again.

"Yes, yes, for sure. Nothing is written in stone." Retreat, retreat was hammering through Elspeth's brain. "You know what you saved yourself from, right?" she said, while smiling at her daughter.

Cecelia looked confused. "A cult?"

"No," Elspeth laughed, plunging down to her knees and pulling at her daughter's hand. Suddenly, she started singing, drawing the other women's attention. "'Cecelia, you'd be breakin' our hearts, you'd be breakin' our confidence daily … Oh, Cecelia, I'm down on my knees, I'm beggin' you please to stay home …'"

"Mom!" Cecelia was so embarrassed. She pulled her mother to her feet. She looked over at the other three women, a smile from ear to ear on each of their faces. Suddenly she felt incredibly lucky to have been part of the day, a part of a story so much bigger than her, and she couldn't help but smile in return.

"Ah, it would have been so much better with your dad accompanying me. He'll be so sad he missed it." Elspeth smiled over at Madonna. "We all have so much to learn, don't we? About how to live our lives? And each one of us will have a different path to the end."

"Enough! I'm going to walk home, enjoy the sunshine. Give you more room in the car," Cecelia said. She waved at the women and walked over the hill towards the church. The bulk of the church seemed sturdy and strong, and the barn swallows were beginning their evening slalom display in the sky. She sat down in the green grass and laid back and watched how the spire pierced the sky. She tried to melt into the ground, imagining that her heartbeat became a part of the earth, and she wondered if she had made the right decision. She watched the clouds above, and the rays of the setting sun streamed through, golden, purple, red colours coming down to the world from the sky. She felt Madonna's clenched hand on her wrist, and her pulse started racing. Madonna, her friend, a mother, grandmother, a nun. She had been given so much by reaching out and helping her, and maybe, just maybe, she could find ways to build a better world in small ways, much closer to home than Brazil. She pictured her own life as a vessel and right now, she felt fine not knowing how it would be filled.

Glossary – Gaelic Translations

Dé – What?

Ìos – Jesus

Gu h-onarch – Honestly.

M'eudail – My dear.

Anndra, tha mi trom! Thuirt i gu bheil i airson a bhith na cail-leachan-dubha!" – Andrew, I'm serious. She wants to be a nun!

Dhia fhéin – God himself.

Na gabh dragh – Don't panic.

nighean – girl

Thig sìos an staidhre – Come downstairs!

Feumaidh sinn bruidhinn riut – We need to talk to you!

Dean suidhe, caileag – Sit down, girl.

Dòmhnall – Donald

Siuthad – Go on.

mo ghràidh – my dear

Gun a-màireach – until tomorrow

Mór ás fhein – Full of himself

Tha e math d' fhaicinn. – It's lovely to see you.

Dùin do bheul agus pòg thu. – Shut up and kiss me.

Bu mhath leam a'bhith comhla riut. – I'd like to date you.

Nì sinn ar dìcheall, a ghràidh. – Let's give it a try, my darling.

Nach fhaigheadh iad geir air á seo? – Wouldn't they get fat on this?

An robh turas-adhair math agaibh? – Good flight?

Mo bhean mhiorbhaileach! Bha mi gad ionndrainn! – My marvellous wife! I missed you!

a Dhia Dhia! – Holy shit!

Tha, mo nighean – Yes, my girl

gu cinnteach – You're a comfort to me.

Acknowledgements

I'd like to start by thanking Dr. Jim St. Clair whose stories continue to inspire me and so many others. I am so thankful that he is here with his powerful voice, his thoughtful questions about the past, and his appreciation for the present. I'd also like to thank my aunts, Sister Loretta MacLennan (Congregation of Notre Dame) and Sister Theresa MacLennan (Order of Good Shepherd) for being such interesting and encouraging nuns. I was lucky to have them as a resource for this novel and they left me with a sense of wonder at their dedication to their faith. My aunt Benjamina MacIsaac, who told hours of family stories as we drove to visit her brother, my uncle Father Lawrence MacLennan, on his deathbed, was a resource as well for this book. I always felt that Father Lawrence was like a movie star when he visited, so kind and interesting and well-travelled.

This novel came out almost fully formed, but evolved slightly over time. My daughter Rebecca's input and conversations helped to flesh out Cecelia. My other early readers, Arlene Ragan, who helped guide me through some of the research snags, and Iris Campbell MacLean, have my heartfelt appreciation for reading the manuscript. The Shean Writers Group, who gave me feedback on some segments of the novel and helped me reflect on the characters and plot developments, brought me to a deeper understanding of my motivations in writing it through their insights and discussions. Thank you all!

Thanks to Pottersfield Press: Lesley Choyce for taking on the novel, Julia Swan for her questions and editing prowess, and Peggy Amirault, who oversaw the finished product. A big thanks goes out to Maria Cosme, who took on the challenge of drawing a soft, spiritual cover for the book.

I'd like to thank all the readers of my first novel, *Never Speak of This Again*. Without your positive feedback, the support from my community, and your continuing interest in my writing, I may never have tried to write a second one.

Some of this story floats way back in time to *Midday Matinees* from my childhood when I first watched the movie *A Song of Bernadette*, so I want to thank CBC. Now, more than ever, I think we all need some spirituality that ties us to what we feel is important and I would like to thank my children, Colin, Ally, Rebecca, and Jacob, who have found things that inspire them and give them a true sense of identity. My husband, Ed, who keeps me grounded in our journey to live a simple life, but also in our dedication to have some fun along the way, is my spiritual rock.

About the Author

Brenda MacLennan-Dunphy was born and raised in Cape Breton Island, Nova Scotia, and except for her various adventures world-wide, she has kept her roots firmly planted in her home ground in Inverness County. She has been married for thirty years to Ed Dunphy, who, like Brenda, is a teacher. Together they raised four children who are now carving their own path through life.

She began writing later in life when she wrote a fictionalized account of her grandparents' story which became the beloved musical *John Archie and Nellie*, produced at Strathspey Performing Arts Centre in Mabou twice in 2012 and again in 2016. Her second play, *The Weddin' Dance*, was produced there in May and July of 2013, and her third play, *Displacement*, was put on in April and November of 2014. In 2017, her play *The Rèiteach* was staged as a Readers Theatre performance in February in West Bay Community Hall.

Never Speak of This Again, Brenda's first novel, which delves deeper into John Archie and Nellie's story, was published in 2018 by Pottersfield Press. Brenda is currently working on another novel and towards putting on a full production of *The Rèiteach* in 2021, if Covid 19 restrictions allow for such theatrical celebrations.

Also by Brenda MacLennan-Dunphy

Fiction

Never Speak of This Again

It is 1917 and Nellie, 17 years old and pregnant, has returned to Cape Breton from Boston. She encounters rejection and humiliation. A passing stranger, headed to the World War I front, offers her some gifts that could help her survive, and allow him to run away from his own past. *Never Speak of This Again* takes the reader from eastern Canada to western Canada, to Boston, to Europe, and back again. In the messy existence of life, heroes can be victims and villains, and Nellie hopes there is always a chance for redemption, but she wonders how far she can risk society's scorn for her own personal happiness.

Plays

The Rèiteach (Produced as a Readers Theatre, West Bay, 2017)

Displacement (Produced at Strathspey Performing Arts Centre, July and November 2014)

The Weddin' Dance (Produced at Strathspey Performing Arts Centre, May and July 2013)

John Archie and Nellie (Produced at Strathspey Performing Arts Centre, April 2016, April and July 2012)